ALPHA
LINDA O. JOHNSTON

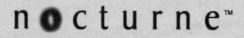
Silhouette Books

nocturne™

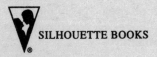 **SILHOUETTE BOOKS**

ISBN-13: 978-0-373-61803-3
ISBN-10:   0-373-61803-4

Recycling programs
for this product may
not exist in your area.

ALPHA WOLF

www.silhouettenocturne.com

Printed in U.S.A.

Dear Reader,

I am an admitted animal aficionado. That's why I've always wondered "what if" about werewolves. What if people really had the ability to change into animals, and vice versa? What if they decided not to make such a gift into a horror story, but to use it for good?

That was the origin of *Alpha Wolf*. It's the story of a lady veterinarian (my own childhood dream) who meets a hunky military man who challenges everything she has believed about science and anatomy—and love.

I hope you enjoy it! Please come visit me at my Web site www.LindaOJohnston.com. Oh, and I just happen to blog about pets at www.KillerHobbies.blogspot.com. See you there!

Linda O. Johnston

Many thanks to my delightful editor,
Allison Lyons—and may she enjoy editing
many more Silhouette Nocturnes!

Lots of love to Dr. Donald Zangwill, my stepfather,
and to Carol Boll, who's there for him.

And, as always, with love to my husband, Fred.

"You sure you'll be okay here alone tonight?"

"Are you offering to stay?" Her body ignited with the idea of this man staying the night.

"Do you want me to?" Drew countered.

"No." The word erupted from what was left of her good sense.

"Fine." But he didn't leave. Instead, he looked down at her. His amber eyes seemed to stare through her, to her soul. Setting it on fire.

Setting her on fire.

Or was that a factor of the searching heat of his lips as he bent and touched them to hers? The kiss was hard and hot and suggestive.

She ached for his touch elsewhere. Everywhere.

Except…he suddenly pulled back.

His expression had become cool. Distant. "Good night, Dr. Harding. Sleep well."

And then he was gone.

Books by Linda O. Johnston

Silhouette Nocturne

Alpha Wolf #56

LINDA O. JOHNSTON

first made her appearance in print in *Ellery Queen's Mystery Magazine* and went on to win the Robert L. Fish Memorial Award for Best First Mystery Short Story of the Year. Now, several published short stories and novels later, Linda is recognized for her outstanding work in the romance genre.

A practicing attorney, Linda juggles her busy schedule between mornings of writing briefs, contracts and other legalese, and afternoons of creating memorable tales of the paranormal, time travel, mystery, and contemporary and romantic suspense. Armed with an undergraduate degree in journalism with an advertising emphasis from Pennsylvania State University, Linda began her versatile writing career running a small newspaper, then working in advertising and public relations and later obtaining her J.D. degree from Duquesne University School of Law in Pittsburgh.

Linda belongs to Sisters in Crime and is actively involved with Romance Writers of America, participating in the Los Angeles, Orange County and Western Pennsylvania chapters. She lives near Universal Studios, Hollywood, with her husband, two sons and two Cavalier King Charles spaniels.

Chapter 1

Crack!

Dr. Melanie Harding's hands jerked. Seated at her scuffed wooden desk, she nearly dropped the financial statement she'd been studying—the first month's figures for her new veterinary practice.

Had that been a gunshot?

From down the hall, dogs started barking—one shrill and high, the others gruff and deep. The outside noise had clearly disturbed some of the patients kept overnight for observation. It hadn't been her imagination.

Not that she'd really thought so.

She glanced across her compact office toward the far window. The sound had come from that direction.

She couldn't see much outside from here. The moonlight, although bright, didn't do much to illuminate the yard or, beyond it, the thick woods bordering the town of Mary Glen.

Sure, this wasn't Beverly Hills, where Melanie had come from, but it was still a civilized area, despite its somewhat remote location on Maryland's Eastern Shore. People didn't just go around hunting here at night—did they? Too dangerous to people, let alone any defenseless animals that might be their prey.

Melanie stood, shoving her fists into the pockets of the white lab coat she still wore, resisting the urge to race out and yell at whoever was shooting. Not that she was likely to see who it was. And if the fool was still there, any movement she might make could turn her into a target.

Besides, maybe it wasn't a hunter.

Maybe it was something else. Something more sinister—like what had happened to her predecessor vet.

Despite her uneasiness, she felt compelled to glance out there. See if she could figure out what was going on.

Without being foolish, though. It was late, after ten o'clock, and except for her hospitalized patients she was alone here. She crossed to the open office door and flicked the switch on the beige wall beside it, turning off the overhead light. That way, she wouldn't be back-lighted as she stood by the window.

She edged toward the glass, stood cautiously sideways behind its frame, and looked out.

The area behind her clinic was fenced in, a place where dogs could be let out for exercise and evacuation. The surface was concrete—not as comfortable on tender paws as grass, but easier to keep clean.

The enclosure was empty now, illuminated by a gorgeous full moon that hung high in the black sky, its light obscuring any stars that might otherwise be visible.

Beyond the yard was the dense amalgamation of poplars, oaks, dogwoods and other trees that composed the local woodlands—beautiful in daylight, especially now, in springtime, as some of them blossomed…but darkly ominous at night. Melanie could make out the swaying of branches in the light breeze—like arms waving her away—but little else in that direction.

She stood still for a minute, scanning all she could see, but everything looked fine back there. Normal.

Peaceful. As if there had never been any gunshot.

Even the dogs down the hall had stopped barking.

Sighing, Melanie shook her head. Her long, deep brown hair was caught up in a clip at the nape of her neck, as it always was when she worked. It had been a long, tiring day. But enjoyable. She'd stayed later than usual to check over a litter of puppies that were born today at their home—sweet, tiny Yorkies that their owner had brought in with the mama dog for reassurance that all was well. Melanie had sent them back home with smiles and instructions.

Only then had she been able to get to the paperwork. She hadn't intended to remain this late. And now she had been interrupted.

She wouldn't convince herself that the sound hadn't occurred, but she was unlikely to learn its source. Maybe it had been a car backfiring—did they still do that? It wasn't necessarily as menacing as she had first imagined. No need to call the police and have them think she was some nervous newcomer, a city girl who imagined scary urban-type incidents here, in this pleasant country area.

Leaving the window, she grabbed her purse from a desk drawer and headed down the hall.

A soft light glowed in the infirmary. She stepped inside, and glanced from cage to cage to check on the occupants. The air smelled familiarly of antiseptic and the aroma of healing dogs.

"Hi, Rudy," she crooned to the Jack Russell terrier she had been treating for a leg injury he'd gotten on a mad dash through a neighbor's yard. "Was that you I heard barking? How are you feeling?" The small, wiry terrier stood on three legs, holding his left front paw up piteously as he wriggled for attention. A soft, flexible recovery collar was fitted over his head to prevent him from chewing at his injury. Melanie opened the front of his cage and extracted the active pup, hugging him tightly as she checked to ensure his dressing was intact.

Putting him back with more soothing words, she looked in on her other patients: a shepherd mix named Wrangler who'd had surgery for a hernia, a Great Dane named Diva from whom Melanie had extracted two tumors that fortunately looked benign—although a lab report would confirm it—and Sherman, a medium-sized dog of unknown heritage who was being boarded for a few days while his owners were out of town. She spoke cheerfully to each and gave them pats and hugs, not wanting anyone to feel slighted.

"Time for me to go home," she finally said, hanging her lab jacket on a hook near the door. "See you all in the morning."

She kept the light on low as she headed down the hall to the clinic's entrance. The reception area's mini-blinds were closed as usual at this late hour. She checked her purse to ensure she had the keys, then slowly opened the door. Not that she really expected to be shot at, but she still felt a little nervous after the earlier disruption.

The veterinary clinic was at the end of Choptank Lane, the last of several streets perpendicular to Mary Glen Road, the town's main thoroughfare. Melanie's house was next door. The two buildings were the only ones on this block, although there were a couple of antique shops on the next one, closer to the town's business district. Usually, the isolation was comforting to Melanie.

Not tonight.

She made sure the clinic's door was locked behind her and stood listening for a moment. In the light from the moon and streetlamps, her gaze darted around the quiet dead-end street.

Darn, that noise had spooked her.

Assuring herself that everything seemed fine, she started down the sidewalk toward her house, her footsteps nearly silent in her athletic shoes. The spring air felt brisk on her face.

But…was someone watching her? No, that had to be her imagination, sparked by nervousness. Still, she picked up her pace.

And stopped when she heard a soft sound behind her, like a dog's whimper.

Nervous or not, she turned back, hunting for the sound's source. An animal in trouble?

She spotted a furry heap in the opposite gutter, in

shadows, not far from where the next block began. She hadn't noticed the animal at first while concentrating on the direction toward her home.

She hurried toward it as she heard the whimper again. She dropped on her knees beside the barely moving dog.

"What's wrong, fella?" she asked soothingly. The answer was obvious, thanks to the trail of dark, oozing liquid leading up to animal. Blood. As if he had dragged himself here and collapsed.

The dog lifted its head slightly. He lay on his side, panting.

"You poor thing. Hold on." Despite the faintness of the light, she scanned the dog with professional eyes.

The loud noise… Had someone shot this dog? This grayish dog that dared to resemble a wolf.

Damn the legends around here! And damn the people who'd come seeking creatures that didn't exist except in their own perverted imaginations.

Could she lift him? She was strong, but this poor creature would be a deadweight.

"I'll be right back," she promised. She extracted keys from her purse as she ran back to the clinic. She fumbled as she opened the door, then sped down the hall to the storeroom where she kept large bags of food for pets with special needs.

She grabbed a metal cart used to transfer sacks from outside delivery points to the storage area and shoved it ahead of her. It rattled and creaked as she hurried back down the hall. The dogs in the infirmary renewed their clamorous barking.

Melanie hurried across the street and maneuvered the injured animal onto the cart's large lower shelf. Speed was important, but she didn't want to hurt the poor thing any more than necessary. She carefully pushed the cart around her driveway, rather than over the curb, up the walkway and over the stoop into the clinic.

She hustled the cart toward the operating room.

Once there, she had difficulty lifting the hurt dog onto the table but somehow managed it, even handling him gingerly, knowing that injured canines were apt to bite. She quickly sedated the creature, but not before it looked at her—trustingly, she thought—with unusual amber eyes.

"You'll be okay," she promised, hoping it was so.

Soon, the dog was asleep. He had no collar, no identification. No matter. She would help him, even if he had no owner to pay her fees.

Melanie wished this were daytime, when her technicians were available to help prepare the animal for surgery. But at this hour, in this emergency situation, she was on her own.

With an antiseptic wash, she cleansed the area where she thought the injury to be. Yes, there it was—just behind his left shoulder. She used an electric razor to shave the bloody gray-black fur from around the skin to reveal a hole. A bullet hole. And no exit wound.

Quickly, carefully, she performed the required surgery. Not that she had ever removed a bullet before. But she had operated extensively on injured animals.

When she was finished, she sutured the incision and maneuvered the dog onto the sterile bedding she had placed in a stand-alone wire crate with an open top, preparing to watch him until he awakened.

She shook her head. "Lunatic," she said aloud accusingly, as if the guilty party could hear her. "Credulous, cruel fool."

Mary Glen was full of tourists these days, those enamored with local legends.

Werewolf legends.

Using tweezers, Melanie held up the piece of metal she had removed from her patient.

She had no doubt what it was: a silver bullet.

He still watched from the woods, wishing he could draw closer, stare inside the lighted building. See what was happening inside.

But being seen, especially now, was a bad idea.

Had he acted in time? He had done his best, under extreme circumstances. Was it good enough?

This was a time he could do no more. And now he would have to wait.

Only in the morning would he learn if he had been successful.

If his friend would live.

Melanie stirred in her chair.

Chair? She must have fallen asleep somehow in the operating room. Slept sitting up, in the vinyl-upholstered metal seat she had dragged in so she could rest while observing her patient. No wonder she felt so stiff.

She opened her eyes. They felt gritty until they landed on the crate on the floor between the operating table and her. And then they widened easily as she smiled.

The faint light of dawn, creeping in the window across the room, illuminated the dog she had treated last night. He was sitting up on the bleached, sterile towels she had put inside the metal crate for his comfort. As with nearly all animals she operated on, she had attached a large post-surgical recovery collar around his neck, framing his face, so he could not chew on his sutures. If he left the wound alone, she would remove it.

He watched her with bright amber eyes. Intelligent eyes. He seemed to thank her.

She gave a quick shake of her head. No way was she going to buy into the absurd legends around here. The dog might be smart—heck, she'd guess him to be a mix between a malamute and a German shepherd, both bright breeds. He was moderate sized. His multi-hued coat was mostly gray tipped in black, but was all white in some areas, others all black. He had a long, strong muzzle and erect ears. Did he resemble a wolf? Sure. But he wasn't one.

And even if he was a conglomeration of the smartest breeds of dogs, that didn't give him human intelligence—like a werewolf would supposedly have.

"Good morning, guy," she said to him. He immediately stood in the cage-like enclosure, his long, fluffy tail wagging. "How do you feel?" She didn't expect an answer, but she knelt on the clean, sunshine-yellow linoleum floor and examined the bandaged area near his left shoulder. Good thing the gun used to shoot him apparently hadn't been very powerful. Although he'd lost a lot of blood, not much damage had been done. The bullet had barely nicked his scapula without ricocheting, then lodged there.

Not enough to kill a strong, healthy dog, thank

heavens. Was even a minor wound with a silver bullet supposed to be enough to slaughter a werewolf?

Maybe she'd need to read up on the lore, to maximize her effectiveness as a vet around here. Only so she'd be prepared for situations like this, of course.

In the meantime, she had to make a phone call. Probably should have made it last night.

"No such thing as werewolves, are there, boy?" she said, giving her patient a gentle hug without putting pressure on his wound. "But I wish you were able to talk, or at least communicate your name and where you came from. You appear well taken care of—not starving, and though you look a little straggly now, I'd guess someone brushes your coat pretty often."

He made a small whining noise, as if trying to hold up his end of the conversation. Melanie grinned as she stood. "Even if I don't believe in werewolves, I sure do a lot of anthropomorphizing." The dog's head was cocked as if he tried to understand her. "Anthropomorphizing? That's ascribing human characteristics to animals. Like now. Understand?" The dog barked, and Melanie laughed. "Maybe you do understand." She glanced at her watch. "Know what? It's nearly six-thirty. Some of my staff will arrive soon, which is a good thing. Patients, too, and that's not so good when I haven't slept much. But I'll manage. Just need a cup of coffee to get me going."

Her patient stood up and wriggled in the crate.

"You're surely not suggesting you need coffee. Water, though—I'll get you some. And you seem to be doing well enough to try a little food, too. I'll have one of the techs bring you some as soon as they arrive—it'll help them get some antibiotics and painkiller down you. They can take the collar off for a while and see if you lick."

She left the operating room and went down the hall to look in on the patients in the infirmary. They all stood at eager attention at her arrival. "Good morning," she said. "You all look chipper." She made sure they each had water available and got a plastic bowlful for her surgery patient.

Her next stop was her office, where she called the Mary Glen Police Department. "Chief Ellenbogen, please. This is Dr. Melanie Harding."

It took nearly five minutes before the chief got on the line. Her fingers thrumming in irritation on her desk, Melanie alternated between listening to public interest announcements blaring in her ear and speaking with underlings who apologized when she said she had something important to tell the chief. No, it wasn't an emergency—now. She considered hanging up.

But this was important. Or at least it might be.

Eventually… "Ellenbogen here."

"Chief, this is—"

"Yes, I was told the vet was waiting. How ya doing, Melanie?"

She had met the chief when he had brought in his own pet, a sweet, aging bloodhound named Jasper that supported the adage that people adopted dogs that resembled them. Chief Ellenbogen was as wrinkled and laid back as his pet. "I'm okay, Chief, but I found a dog late last night outside the clinic who'd been shot with a silver bullet. He's going to be okay, but since I was told that my predecessor vet here, Dr. Worley, and his wife were killed that way, I thought you'd want to know."

"I'll be right there, Melanie. I want to see that dog." He paused, then said, "Er…have you checked on him this morning?"

It was all Melanie could do to keep from chuckling. "If what you're asking is whether he's still a dog, or if he morphed into a human in daylight, the answer is '*arf.*'"

The chief cleared his throat. "Just jokin'." But he sounded more embarrassed than humorous. "See you in a few."

Melanie's head was shaking as she hung up. Werewolves. People here obviously believed in them, as ridiculous as it sounded. Even, apparently, the chief of police.

Well, she'd kind of known that before she bought this practice from Lt. Patrick Worley, son of Dr. Martin Worley, who'd been shot and killed by a silver bullet only a few months ago. His wife was killed the same way, a year earlier. The shooter—or shooters—hadn't been caught. And Melanie hadn't known before how widespread the legend was of werewolves—and how widely accepted.

Ridiculous. No doubt about that. But she promised herself yet again to take a crash course in werewolf lore, so she would be better prepared to deal with this silliness.

No. More than silliness, she reminded herself as she headed for her office door. Viciousness. A man was killed because of it—even though she'd heard no rumors that anyone considered her predecessor vet, Dr. Worley, a werewolf. But the silver bullet bit—that had to be a result of the legend.

And now she'd saved the life of a dog that someone may have mistaken for a shapeshifting human.

At least she was fairly certain that the legends said that werewolves turned back into people as the moon disappeared into daylight. No way would anyone be able to mistake her patient again for a shapeshifter.

Time to go check on him again, before her staff started arriving in a few minutes. She headed back down the hall to the surgery room, thrust open the door—and stopped.

Just inside, staring at her, was a man. He was tall, dressed in jeans and a gray sweatshirt stretched taut over substantial muscles, his black hair flecked with brilliant silver.

And he regarded her with intelligent, grateful amber eyes.

Chapter 2

Melanie barely stifled a gasp. Where was her patient? Surely, he hadn't turned into this man. The Mary Glen werewolf legends were utter fiction, the creation of superstitious minds…weren't they?

But if the dog she had treated had become human, this man had some of the features she would anticipate…

"Dr. Harding?" The man's voice was deep, throaty. All sexy. All masculine.

Human masculine.

"Yes?" she said, hating the slight tremor in her voice. "Who are you?" Good. Her voice was stronger now. "What are you doing here?" She had to see for herself. She sidled uneasily away from the doorway, where this large, compelling man commandeered every inch of her vision, preventing her from viewing the rest of the room.

She needed to see the crate in which her patient had slept last night. Make sure it wasn't empty. It *couldn't* be empty.

"I'm Major Drew Connell. I want to thank you for saving my dog, Grunge."

"Grunge?" As Melanie said the name, she finally reached a position where the man wasn't blocking her view. There was the wire crate, still on the floor between the chair she had dragged in and the tall metal table where she operated. The furry dog with the recovery collar was still in it, sitting up, tail wagging furiously.

"Yeah, Grunge."

"Interesting name." Melanie felt almost giddy with relief. The dog was still there. Of course. How silly of her to have entertained any doubts, even for a second. Not that she'd *really* doubted.

But *Grunge?* The dog looked anything but grungy to her, at least since she had cleaned the blood off him.

"Interesting dog. You should see him after a workout. He really throws himself into it." Major Connell knelt and put his arms around Grunge, obviously careful not to push the collar into an uncomfortable position, an oddly touching scene—the large, powerful-looking man and the injured dog. He backed off to ruffle the fur on Grunge's head, then gently turned the dog so he could see the bandaged area. "What happened? How was he hurt? I was engaged in a training exercise on the base late last night, so I wasn't aware till just a short while ago that he was missing."

Melanie didn't answer his question right away. She

had too many of her own. It was one thing to keep her imagination in check. It was another to take this man's appearance at face value. "Then how did you know to look for him here?"

"I couldn't find him anywhere else, so I used process of elimination and decided to check out the closest vet. And here he was." He gave the dog another rough pat, then stood again.

Did his answer make sense? Maybe. The nearest military base wasn't next door, but there weren't other veterinary clinics or animal shelters any nearer than this hospital.

"He's your dog?" Melanie demanded. She had to look way up to meet the officer's eyes. Damn, but the man was good-looking: straight, dark brows over those amber eyes, a slender nose with slightly flared nostrils, a sensuous, full mouth. All that and a hint of dark beard beneath his closely shaved skin.

"Yes and no. He belongs to the U.S. Army, but we're assigned to work with one another. He's a highly trained military dog. We use him, and others like him on the base, to help sniff out bombs and other weaponry, to attack on command, and—well, some of his work is classified."

"Yeah, if you told me you'd have to kill me. I get it." Melanie kept her tone light, but she stared at the officer. "By 'base,' I assume you mean Ft. Lukman, right?"

"Sure, our nearest and dearest facility."

"Well, military or not, Grunge should be wearing a collar with an ID tag."

"No argument there. My partner's a bit of an escape artist, though. He slipped out of his collar and decided to take a walk on his own. I'll try harder to keep that from happening again."

"Don't just try. Succeed. And you train dogs? Is an army veterinarian stationed there?" Melanie's ears had perked up at the mention of more animals on the base. Ft. Lukman was about five miles from Mary Glen. The soldiers posted there frequented local businesses for goods and services not available at the base's reputedly small BX. They would have excellent access to all medical needs. But would their animals?

"Not stationed there, but one visits every few weeks to check up on our dogs and facilities. Dr. Worley used to be available in emergencies. His son, Lt. Patrick Worley, is stationed at the base. I expect you've met him."

"Yes, I bought this clinic from him."

"I figured."

"And the answer is yes, I'll definitely be available in emergencies to help your animals. That's what I do."

"I'll remember that."

His smile was killer. Friendly. Assessing. Suggestive...of what? Hot endless nights? Mind-blowing sex?

What an imagination she was developing around here!

Forget that smile. She wouldn't let herself get lost in it.

If he'd been an invited guest, or even the owner of a patient, she wouldn't have kept him standing here like this. She'd have invited him to sit down—on that ugly, uncomfortable chair she'd slept in last night? She glanced toward where it sat near the metal shelves in which her surgical instruments, anesthetics and medicines were locked. No, that would have felt too...

intimate. She would have invited him into her office, where she could speak professionally.

But she hadn't invited him here at all, though she was glad to know that her patient had someone who cared about him. And presumably Uncle Sam would pay for his care.

But still… She asked the major coolly, "By the way, how did you get in here this morning?"

"The front door was unlocked. I didn't see anyone, so I called out but I guess you didn't hear me. Grunge did, and he barked, so I knew where to come."

"I didn't hear you or him," Melanie said. Could she believe any of this? Well, she had been on the phone with Chief Ellenbogen. Maybe she had missed Grunge's barking.

But wouldn't the other dogs have barked, too? Plus, she had been nervous. Still was. Last night, she had been attuned to listening, after hearing the gunshot. And she was damn well certain she hadn't left the front door unlocked. She had checked *all* the doors…hadn't she?

Well, Chief Ellenbogen was on his way. Some of her staff was due any minute. She wouldn't be alone with this man much longer. And despite how he had somehow gotten in, she didn't think he meant her harm. While the police chief was here, she'd look at the doors and windows to see if he'd broken in. *Where* he'd broken in.

But this large, friendly-seeming military officer was drop-dead gorgeous. So sexy that her body was reacting to him even as they held a totally innocent, superficial conversation.

And that, as much as anything else, made her mistrust everything he said. She'd learned her lesson once and well.

She would never make that mistake again.

This was a mistake, Drew thought. Verbal sparring with this lovely lady vet might be damned fun, but it was much too dangerous.

He wasn't fooling her. Not entirely, at least.

He inhaled slowly, discreetly, not for the first time, as he savored the rich yet soft floral scent of her.

The more he was with her, the more he thought of touching that smooth skin. Kissing her luscious, frowning mouth until she lost her perfect, and maddening, self-control.

But it was time to get down to business. The business of ensuring that his partner was well cared for. At the same time, maybe he could get Dr. Melanie Harding off her current train of thought—like, what the hell was this guy really doing here?

"Tell me how you found Grunge," he said. "And I want to hear the extent of his injuries. He doesn't look too bad. Can I assume he's okay?"

She had the prettiest blue eyes—startlingly sexy, maybe because they were so unusual. They were as bright as the hyacinths that the newest recruits were assigned to tend this time of year around the lab building at the base. The fragrance of the spiky flowers was almost overwhelming at times—at least to those with a sensitive sense of smell.

This woman's intriguing aroma was much lighter. She had full lips that glowed pink even though she wore no lipstick. A nose that was perhaps a little too long and narrow. Cheekbones that underscored those eyes.

But it was those eyes that defined her face. Expressive. Intelligent. Emphasized by narrow, arched brows a little darker than her sable-brown hair.

Projecting her obviously deep suspicions of everything he said.

And allowing him, now and then, to believe she was just a little turned on by him, too. Challenging him to stoke fires hidden deep inside.

Now, though, those eyes were bright yet cool, which caused him a pang of disappointment. "I'll answer those questions one at a time." She lifted her hands and began to tick answers off on fingers that were long and elegant, tipped in short nails appropriate for a woman who handled animals gently. "How did I find Grunge? I was heading for my home next door late last night and heard him whine." He winced as she described the trail of blood that led to his dog—a trail he was much too familiar with. "He'd been shot—with a silver bullet, of all things. I take it you know of the stupid werewolf legends around here."

"Sure do." He forced himself to laugh and shake his head disparagingly. Oh, yes. He knew about the legends. Which was one reason exercises were always kept on or right around the base—to prevent situations like the one that occurred last night. But Grunge didn't know about them or understand their implications. He had slipped out through a gate that had somehow been left open. So, therefore, had Drew.

"Anyway," Melanie said, "Grunge will be fine, as long as there's no infection. I want to keep him here till sometime later today, so I can be sure of his medications and keep an eye on him." The look she regaled Drew with now was challenging, as if she expected him to give her a hard time about leaving Grunge.

He didn't. "Fine," he said. "Just let me know when I can come and get him, and I will. I expect you'll tell me then about continued meds and follow-ups and all." As if he wouldn't know on his own…but, then, he was a medical doctor, not a vet—notwithstanding the highly classified experiments he was conducting at the base. And in any event, he would need to have details to ensure that he cared for Grunge properly.

"That's right," Melanie said.

Drew looked expectantly toward the door an instant before the knock sounded. He had heard signs of life in the reception area for the last five minutes or so, but the vet didn't seem to notice. The sounds hadn't been loud, so she might not have heard.

She glanced at him in puzzlement before turning toward the half open door. "Good morning, Carla," she said to the young woman standing there.

"Good morning," Carla repeated. "Hi, Drew," she said in the flirtatiously melodic tone she always used with him and some of the other guys. Not that they ever encouraged her. At least *he* didn't. "What are you doing here?"

"Long story," Melanie Harding said abruptly before he could reply. "He's just leaving, though."

"Okay. I just got here, and I wanted you to know that Chief—"

"Hi, Dr. Harding," said a gruff, older man's voice from behind the receptionist. A too-familiar voice. It belonged to the local police chief, Angus Ellenbogen. "Good morning, Major Connell. And what brings you here?"

"A lot of people seem to want to know that," he replied mildly. "My partner, Grunge, was injured last night, and Dr. Harding was kind enough to save him."

"Really?" Carla squealed.

Ellenbogen squeezed into the room around her and edged her out, closing the door behind him. "Yeah. Seems he was shot with a silver bullet, right Dr. Harding?"

Angus Ellenbogen wore the standard gray local police uniform but his short-sleeved shirt was decorated with an assortment of bars and medals, as if he'd been a well-decorated military general. His hair was as light as his uniform. His wrinkled face gave him color, though—round and ruddy. His eyes were deep-set and worldly wise, as if he'd seen it all right here, in Mary Glen.

Drew suspected that maybe he had.

"I have the bullet in a plastic bag for you," Melanie said. She had bent to stroke Grunge's back. The dog looked ready to leap out of the crate, with all the new people around to check out. Melanie flipped the top of the cage closed and latched it.

Grunge didn't look at all happy about that, and Drew knelt down as Melanie rose. He reached in to rub his dog's uninjured side with his fingertips.

"Good deal," Ellenbogen said.

The surgery room, with its operating table in the center and cabinets along the walls, was definitely over-crowded. "Can I move Grunge somewhere else?" Drew asked. The dog needed R&R—rest and recuperation—not excitement.

"I'll have him taken to the infirmary and put into an

enclosure there," Melanie said, "as soon as the rest of the staff arrives." She went over to one of the cabinets and picked up a plastic bag from a shelf. It appeared to contain something small and shiny.

The bullet.

"You should tell your junior officer Patrick about this," Ellenbogen said.

"I will," Drew assured him. He turned to Melanie. "Lt. Patrick Worley reports to me. His dad—"

"I'm well aware that his parents were killed at different times by someone shooting silver bullets," Melanie said, her blue eyes stony now. "Patrick had only recently lost his father when we negotiated for me to buy this veterinary practice. I'm sure he's still grieving, and that he wants answers."

She darted a glance toward the chief of police, who didn't look happy about it. Drew liked the little dig Melanie had gotten in. And that wasn't all he liked about the feisty vet. Hell, no.

And that was starting to worry him.

"I only wish I'd seen who fired the shot," Melanie continued, "or something else that could help identify what lunatic is out there shooting like this. Someone who believes the Mary Glen werewolf legend, undoubtedly."

"Undoubtedly," Drew agreed. If only everyone around here was as skeptical as she was, life would be a lot easier for him. But even so, the questions this sexy vet was asking could be damned hard for him to deal with.

"So Patrick reports to you?" Melanie said, regarding Drew with apparent interest in his answer. "What do you do at the base, Major?"

"Classified," he said with a shrug.

"Secret stuff," Ellenbogen said at the same time, his tone indicating his displeasure. "Maybe if they came clean about it, there wouldn't be so many rumors. One of these days—"

A cell phone rang. The chief reached down to a case attached to his utility belt and extracted his phone. "Ellenbogen," he said. His wizened face grew even more pinched. "Yeah? Where?" He listened for another few seconds. "I'm on my way." But instead of dashing out the door, he turned to Melanie. "That dog—any indication of blood on him last night?"

Melanie looked puzzled. Drew, on the other hand, felt a sense of dread. He was afraid he knew what was coming. And however it had happened, it could only harm him and the work he was doing.

"There was a lot of blood on him," the vet said. "He'd been shot."

"No, no, I mean around his mouth. Like he bit someone."

"No! None at all. He was the one who was injured. I didn't see any indication he'd hurt anyone or anything else."

"Maybe not. But I want a full report about the dogs you keep on your damned military base, Major. If there's any sign they chewed on anything they shouldn't have, I'm going to insist on sending a crime scene team there, security or no security, to take some samples. Got it?" The chief's face was even redder than usual, and his stare clearly dared Drew to disagree.

"I'll do a preliminary investigation, Chief. Believe me." That part was true. "And if there's anything to report, I'll tell you." *That* part wasn't.

"Yeah, as if I trust you."

"Sorry you feel that way," Drew retorted. He understood why the chief of police had an attitude that wasn't exactly favorable about what went on at Ft. Lukman.

If he only knew the truth…But that would never happen.

"What's going on, Chief Ellenbogen?" Melanie asked. "Did something else happen besides Grunge getting shot?"

"Yeah. Something else happened. One of our tourists was mauled, and it apparently looks like she was chewed by a damned big dog—or maybe a werewolf," he added with a snort as he rushed out the door.

Chapter 3

Melanie followed the chief to the clinic's front door. She watched him drive away in his marked car in a huge hurry, lights flashing.

"What's going on?" Carla asked, peering outside through the open slats of the mini blinds on the nearby window.

"Nothing good, I'm afraid." Melanie glanced around the small but cheerful reception area, glad that for once there were no other people with their pets waiting to be seen by her. The six metal and red plastic chairs at one side of the compact reception desk were empty. All the balls and other toys to amuse dogs while they were waiting still sat in the large wicker basket on the floor's indoor-outdoor carpeting.

Major Drew Connell had been right behind her. She had continually been aware of his presence. Now, he edged toward the exit, as well, his posture rigid. He didn't look happy.

Neither was she, at the idea of his leaving…

No! Better that he get out of here so she could assimilate and assess all that had happened.

"You're going to check to see if any of the other dogs at the base may have been involved in last night's…incidents?" Melanie asked him neutrally, using a euphemism of sorts. Something like the attack Angus Ellenbogen had described was unlikely to be kept secret, but Melanie didn't want to be the one to start spreading rumors.

Especially since those rumors were likely to fan the already out-of-control flames of gossip about alleged werewolves around here.

"Yeah, I said I'd do that." Drew's golden eyes were hard as he glared down at her, and she shivered. Was that a warning she saw in them? About what? To keep her mouth closed?

"That's what you told Chief Ellenbogen." Melanie knew her tone was icy. Better that than hurt at his change of attitude. "His reasons are different from mine. I was only asking because, if it turns out any of the other animals were injured, I'll be glad to treat them." She didn't like being accused even tacitly of speaking out of turn—or anything else.

She loved being a veterinarian. She was crazy about her patients. But she could do without having to deal with some of their owners.

She'd initially thought that wouldn't include Drew. She had believed they were on the same side. Both wanted Grunge to heal fast and well. Neither liked the absurdity of the werewolf rumors that may have resulted in a dog unfortunately loose at night under the full moon being shot with a damnable silver bullet.

Then there had been that amazing sexual attraction she had felt—still felt—for Drew. Not something she wanted to encourage, but the look in his eyes suggested he'd felt it, too.

"Do you know who was attacked by the werewolf?" Carla asked excitedly, stepping closer to Drew. "Were other dogs shot with silver bullets besides Grunge?" She was shorter than Melanie, and her ash blond hair was a mass of curls around an elfin face. At Melanie's sharp look she said, "I couldn't help hearing your conversation with Chief Ellenbogen." She looked so soulfully up into Drew's face that Melanie wanted to throw up. No, strangle her. She felt mortified that her employee would come on so obviously to a patient's owner.

"Of course you could have helped it," Melanie spat back. "The door was closed. And what you heard through it goes no further."

"Good luck on that one," Drew said, casting an almost amused look toward Carla. "I'll call you later, Doctor, about when I can pick up Grunge."

"Say hi to Patrick for me," Carla said with a sweet and beseeching smile. Lt. Patrick Worley? The youthful receptionist apparently had a thing for military men.

"Right," Drew said, then met Melanie's gaze. "See you this afternoon." And then he, too, left.

Melanie stared after him for a long moment, glad somehow for the connection that would bring him back to retrieve his injured dog. But what had he meant?

She turned to her clinic's receptionist, whom she had inherited, like some of the furniture she might not have chosen, with the practice. "Carla, I know you've been here longer than I have. And I want to keep you on. But if you're—"

"I know. Discretion and patient confidentiality and all that." The youthful receptionist looked abashed at last. "But, Melanie, the news is already out. It's on Nolan Smith's Mary Glen Werewolf Web site."

"There's a Mary Glen werewolf Web site?" Shaking her head, Melanie crossed the room and lowered herself into a chair. Obviously Drew was aware of it, and he also knew that Carla knew of it. That had to be what his ironic wish to Melanie—good luck keeping Carla quiet—must have meant.

"Sure." Carla joined her. Her hazel eyes were glowing with obvious excitement. "Nolan's an expert. He was two years ahead of me in high school and was a tech whiz even then. He loved researching urban legends and started a Web site about them. And his new Web site specializing in werewolves is turning Mary Glen into a mecca for everyone who's even a teeny bit interested in shapeshifters. Only a few people hung around in winter when you first moved here—who can blame them?—but now that it's spring again, the tourists are back. Our motels are getting booked up, and whatever happened last night will keep 'em that way. Nolan just hinted about it this morning, but by tomorrow he'll have a lot more details."

Oh, great. No wonder the rumors of werewolves around here were so rampant—much more than she'd understood when she first considered buying this practice and researched the area.

"That's why I was a little late this morning," Carla

continued. "I had to check out Nolan's site. There was a full moon last night, so I knew he'd put something up—and he did. Awesome! And he's holding a meeting for everyone in Mary Glen who's interested in the werewolves tomorrow night, at City Hall. I'm heading there right after work. You should come."

"I don't know," Melanie said uneasily. She didn't want anyone to think she believed in such nonsense.

"But you're the town vet now," Carla said. "You should learn all you can. Dr. Worley always used to go to the meetings and talk to everyone, calm them down and warn them not to start shooting at anything they think could be a shapeshifter, silver bullets or not. He treated quite a few animals hurt by the tourists."

"Until one of them shot him. Unless it was someone local."

"Do you really think someone from Mary Glen shot Dr. Worley?" Carla's arched eyebrows, darker than her hair, soared even higher in obvious incredulity. "No way! Everyone loved him."

Someone obviously didn't—although the shooting could have been accidental. In any event, the shooter hadn't been identified yet. Or at least not publicly, even if authorities had a lead.

"So you'll come?" Carla asked as the door opened and Keeley Janes came in with her basketful of Yorkie puppies.

"We'll see," Melanie said. It was only when she became immersed in examining the pups that she realized she hadn't asked Chief Ellenbogen to double-check the security of her doors. She still felt sure she hadn't left the front door unlocked. But that was how Drew Connell said he'd gotten in. Why would he lie about it?

And why didn't she feel more nervous about it than she did?

"It's started again, damn it, sir," Major Drew Connell said to General Greg Yarrow, the commanding officer of Ft. Lukman. He stood at attention in the general's office, holding his salute.

"You waiting for an *At ease,* Drew?" Greg said with a grin. "You got it." Because of the nature of their very special ops work here, they tended toward informality among themselves, returning to military protocol mostly when others were around. The general was dressed, like Drew, in his usual on-duty army combat uniform, consisting of pale green and beige camouflage fatigues. "Sit down and tell me about it."

Drew did as he was told. The general's office was sumptuous for a military command, especially a base as small and informal as this one, mostly because Greg subsidized it himself. The wooden desk was mahogany, and the U.S. flag behind it hung from a gleaming brass pole. Bookshelves lined the walls, some filled with standard volumes of military regulations and history, and others containing first editions of, arguably, some of the world's most imaginative fiction: Jules Verne's *20,000 Leagues Under the Sea,* Robert Louis Stevenson's *The Strange Case of Dr. Jekyll and Mr. Hyde,* Bram Stoker's *Dracula* and, of course, an original script from the movie *The Wolf Man* starring Lon Chaney, Jr.

He had another office at the Pentagon, which wasn't far from Maryland's Eastern Shore but seemed a world away. That office was standard issue and looked like everyone else's. Drew had been there often, especially before he was selected to head up the Alpha Force here at Ft. Lukman.

"I want to hear first about Grunge and what happened last night," the general said. He was in his early sixties but his short hair was still coal-black, receding considerably at his temples. His features were solemn, his face long and wrinkled from scowling as much as from advancing age.

"Despite all standard precautions, considering the timing, someone apparently left the gate open, and he got out. Made it quite a distance. I saw him get shot, sir, and couldn't do a damned thing about it. Not last night. Not with the full moon."

"I understand." The general leaned forward, clasping his work-hardened hands on the desk. "What about Captain Truro? Was he observing you, as ordered, while you were vulnerable?"

"Yes, sir. After the shot was fired, Jonas drew his own weapon and went after the source. Unfortunately, the shooter got away. In the meantime, I couldn't let Grunge stay there. He was wounded. Bleeding. I was able to drag him to where he would receive assistance."

"While in wolf form yourself?"

Drew nodded. "It was a full moon," he said again, almost angrily—not at the general, but at himself. For being helpless. "None of the medications that allow shape-shifting at will work during a full moon, on me or on any of the others. Not yet. I'm still working on that, but I've had no success, and I'm damned frustrated about—"

"I'm aware of all of that, Drew. I was just about to

comment on how difficult that must have been, dragging a being of approximately your own size and shape—how far was it?"

"Maybe a mile, sir."

"Through the woods? And I take it you got him there fast, since you obviously saved his life."

"Yes, sir. That's when Jonas caught up with me and got me back here—after I'd watched to be sure that the new vet found Grunge. No one saw anything so far from base, damn it all. None of the others even knew what happened. And if it hadn't been for me and this whole damned situation—"

"Grunge wouldn't have gotten shot? We can't know that for sure."

"Sure we can," Drew stormed. "Whoever did it was probably one of the crazies who're returning to Mary Glen in droves, now that winter's over and the snow is gone. He—or she, of course—undoubtedly wanted to bag a werewolf and shot at the first thing that looked like one."

"Or someone may have wanted it to look that way," the general contradicted. "Maybe an ordinary dog like Grunge was the intended target, and we were supposed to learn something from it."

"Like what, sir?"

"That's what we'll have to find out. That, and the other angle: the civilian who was allegedly mauled. Do any of our group know anything about that?"

"No, sir. But we'll get the answers. Soon. You can count on it."

"I do, Drew. Because if we don't, our entire, extremely critical operation is screwed."

* * *

But Drew was no closer to finding any answers a few hours later, when he headed his military-issue dark sedan to the vet's office to pick up Grunge.

He had spent a lot of the time with Capt. Jonas Truro, who had been his ostensible nursemaid last night. Each special operative in Alpha was assigned both a canine—or other pertinent animal—as a partner, and an officer or enlisted man, depending on the operative's rank, as an aide.

Which meant observer and, when needed, nursemaid and caretaker on nights with full moons.

By now, everyone on base was fully briefed on what had happened last night.

But despite what Drew had promised General Yarrow, no one had any answers, or any real clues that could lead to them. Not even Lt. Patrick Worley, who had grown up here. Whose father had been a veterinarian who had attempted to find some of the answers his unit now sought.

Who, like Drew, was a medical doctor and very much ensconced in the program.

Very ensconced. As in shapeshifter extraordinaire, too.

Drew put on his signal and made a sharp right turn.

Ft. Lukman had been aptly named for retired General Maxwell Lukman, a vocal advocate of the idea of using all resources to reach a goal—even the extraordinary and incredible. It was only about five miles by road from downtown Mary Glen but could have been a universe away. Most of those roads were two-lane and obscure, surrounded by the woodlands that made this area so ideal for the covert operations being performed at the facility. And the fact that werewolf rumors had abounded around here for years helped them maintain their cover.

Only, right now, those rumors were getting too much publicity. Too many nut cases were flocking here to check them out. Animals—and people—were getting hurt.

That had to stop.

Before leaving the base, Drew had called Melanie Harding to check on Grunge's progress. His dog was ready to go home, the vet had said. He smiled ruefully at himself now. He'd kept asking her questions—out of concern for his pet, he'd told himself. Only he realized even then that he simply wanted to hear her talk. Her husky, soft voice had ignited his desire almost as if she were there, stroking him.

And now he was going to see her in person.

He accelerated more—as much as he could on this awful road.

Soon, he was on what passed for a highway in this area—straighter, better paved, four lanes, and peppered by traffic lights. Also surrounded by woods. Actually a very appealing part of the world, was Maryland's Eastern Shore—especially for the likes of him. He had the radio on a station out of Baltimore that played mostly current rock music. Kept it on low. He had too much thinking to do to waste even this time.

His plans were already underway for investigating Grunge's shooting. The tourist's mauling, too, even though the army had no jurisdiction over a crime that didn't occur on federal property.

But that mauling was surely related to Grunge's injury. It was only logical that he would investigate

them jointly. Not even the bright, and territorial, Chief
Angus Ellenbogen could argue with that, as long as
Drew cooperated with him—or at least appeared to—
and didn't step on his toes.

He finally reached the turnoff for Mary Glen, drove
down the main street past the civic center—such as it
was—and shopping district, and turned onto Choptank
Lane, his heart starting to race as he got nearer to the
vet who had so affected him earlier.

He slowed, and stopped suddenly. The street was
lined with large vans with satellite dishes sticking out the
top.

No big surprise. The media had learned about the
lurid goings-on here last night.

Damn it.

He parked on the first block and strode angrily and
purposefully toward the veterinary clinic.

The media vultures crowded around the front door.
The farthest rows were filled with denim-clad people
with hefty cameras aimed at the door. The nearest to
the building, better dressed, thrust microphones toward the entry.

Where Dr. Melanie Harding stood.

Had she called a press conference to talk about the
Mary Glen werewolf stories, complete with her brave
rescue of a poor dog and removal of a silver bullet from
its shoulder?

Why the hell did he feel so deflated? Because he'd
been attracted to the pretty vet? Imagined she was
above snatching at her moment of fame? She wouldn't
know it was potentially at his expense. Hell, why
would she care?

When he had sneaked inside that morning, it hadn't been through the front door. He had found a more vulnerable entry in the back, through a window into a room where pet food and medical supplies were stored.

He could head there now but didn't want to attempt to spirit Grunge away surreptitiously. He needed everything to happen aboveboard. He'd sign out his partner, get the prescribed meds and instructions on how to administer them, then scram.

But now he would have to wait until the crowd dissipated.

In the meantime, he could listen to the woman make a fool out of herself on camera, patting herself on the back. Fomenting the local werewolf legend.

Squelching any desire he may have had for her.

He edged closer.

One of the reporters was talking, a female in a tight top and short skirt, eye-candy who was trying to sound flippant and sophisticated at the same time. "So you saved the life of a werewolf on your doorstep last night, Dr. Harding? Tell us all about it."

"What I'd really like to do is get back inside and help my patients, but even though I'm sure your viewers are smart enough to have understood the first time—" she rolled her eyes from the interrogator back toward the camera, which Drew took to imply that the audience was a lot brighter than the reporter "—yes, I discovered a poor dog outside the clinic last night. A very intelligent dog, to have come here, by the way, so I could help him. He'd been shot by a lowlife who apparently wanted to encourage the local werewolf legend."

"Then he was shot with a—"

"Yes, as I told the reporters who interviewed me before—but I would imagine you were primping for the camera instead of listening, right? Oh, excuse me. I didn't mean to insult you."

Which was exactly what she was doing. Drew smiled a little in admiration.

"In any event, you've got part of this right: my poor patient was shot with a silver bullet. But was he a werewolf? Well, I've started to bone up on the legends so I could be sure, and they say that werewolves change back to human form when touched by daylight. I was with my patient at dawn and he didn't metamorphose into a person. Too bad." Her smile was mocking. "I'm a scientist, you know. I didn't move to Mary Glen because it was reputed to be overrun with werewolves. A good thing, too, since I haven't run across any."

She looked indulgent. She looked exasperated. She looked completely in control.

And then her eyes met Drew's. And as soon as she saw him, even at this distance, that sensuous energy that had pulsed between them before was back. Her face flushed, and she looked away.

Heat surged through him that had nothing to do with the warmth of the spring afternoon. Damn, but Dr. Melanie Harding was one incredible—and hot—female.

"You haven't met any werewolves *yet,*" contradicted the reporter, mugging for the camera. Apparently being insulted before her audience hadn't fazed her.

"*Yet,*" Melanie agreed, her attention back on the microphone. "But as a veterinarian, I'm a scientist. I'm open to learning new things. If Mary Glen really has any werewolves, bring 'em on."

Drew snorted silently. The sexy vet might have had the drooling media leeches in the palm of her hand right now, but she didn't know what she was saying, not really.

Bring on the werewolves?

If she weren't careful, Dr. Melanie Harding just might get a whole lot more than she had bargained for.

Chapter 4

Despite the cacophony of noise from the media scum and their eager audience, Drew heard the quiet sound of familiar footsteps behind him. He turned.

"What are you doing here, Truro?" he asked even before his gaze landed on his longtime friend and colleague, Captain Jonas Truro.

"Same as you, Major." Jonas lifted his right arm and gave a mock salute. "Even though you said he'd be okay, I was still worried about the spoiled old mutt."

"Grunge isn't old," Drew countered.

"Just a spoiled mutt."

"That's a highly trained, well-cared-for army issue K-9 to you."

"Yes, sir." Jonas grinned. He was about thirty years old, nearly as tall as Drew but with a heavier build, mostly muscle. His skin was the shade of the chocolate kisses he popped in his mouth almost as often as he drank water. Drew sometimes goaded him about how he was turning into one of the sweets. In turn, Jonas always kidded him about his jealousy. Drew and chocolate didn't go well together.

Like Drew, Jonas was ostensibly on duty, but they weren't on base so neither was in uniform. Jonas wore jeans, too, but Drew's wine-colored T-shirt was plain compared with Jonas's, which proclaimed the University of Maryland around a black, gold, red and white depiction of the Maryland state flag.

"That the vet?" Jonas jerked his nearly clean-shaven head toward Melanie.

"Yeah," Drew said. She was chatting vivaciously with her receptionist, Carla, while using her body as a blockade against the media horde and the tourists who might rush the clinic to check out the supposed werewolf. She combined tact and determination, both admirable qualities.

"She seems to think the werewolf legends are really crap, doesn't she?" Jonas asked. "I've been here long enough to hear her give it to those reporters."

"Sounds that way to me, too."

"Some interesting lady, isn't she?"

"Yeah, interesting." Drew had intended to make the word sound a lot more scornful than it came out. Ignoring Jonas's smirk, he continued, "Come on. I'll introduce you."

He led the way through the dissipating crowd to the clinic's front door. As the now-ignored reporters finally turned away, the vet met Drew's eye. There was a challenge in her expression, as if she expected him to try to barge past her, too.

Instead, he stopped several feet away.

"Hi, Major," said Carla, giving him a big wink.

Drew was used to her flirtatiousness and didn't take it seriously. He nodded at her, then turned to Melanie. "Dr. Harding, this is Captain Jonas Truro. We're here for Grunge."

Jonas stepped around him. "Major Connell told me about all you did for Grunge last night, Dr. Harding. I work with him, too, and really appreciate it. And I watched you handle those media types. Great job."

"All in a day's work in werewolf country," the vet said with a rueful smile. She shook hands with Jonas— and Drew found himself envying the small contact.

Which irritated him.

"I'd never have expected so many reporters here in Mary Glen." Melanie's tone sounded both baffled and disgusted.

"Yeah, the tourists like to get word out there if any hint of shapeshifter stuff happens around here," Jonas said. "They've lots of contacts at the D.C. and Baltimore newspapers and TV and radio stations."

"So I figured." Melanie shook her head.

"How's Grunge doing now?" Drew interrupted, more abruptly than he'd intended. "You're sure it's okay to take him home?"

He ignored the annoyance and curiosity in the vet's bright blue eyes. She seemed to be scoping him out, trying to read why he'd snapped at her. Damned if he knew. But that conversation with Jonas had gone on long enough.

"He's doing well," she finally said. "And, yes, he can

leave." She led them into the building, closing the door behind Carla, who followed them. She locked it.

The place smelled like a hospital—clean and medicinal—even with the overlay of multiple animal scents.

"It's after six o'clock, at least," Melanie said. "No more appointments today, right, Carla?"

The receptionist nodded. "Right. I checked the voicemail at my phone extension just in case, but no one's called, so our next appointment's tomorrow morning at nine."

"Good. This way, gentlemen. Oh, that's right, Major Connell. You know the way." Melanie shot him a look full of irony, then turned and preceded them down the hall. Her hips swayed gently, causing her white lab coat to swing in an enticing manner. They passed a guy wearing a turquoise medical top. "All the dogs okay, Brendan?" Melanie asked.

"Sure are, Doc. I'm outta here now, okay?"

"As long as you've fed everyone and made sure their crates are clean."

"Always." The young man grinned and hurried past them.

Melanie's dark hair, clipped at the nape of her neck, flicked around as she stopped and looked back at Drew and Jonas. "You'll need to keep Grunge on antibiotics for the next ten days. I'll give you pills for him to be taken with food. A painkiller, too, if he needs it, poor dog. I'm sure silver bullets are just as painful as lead or whatever they're made from these days."

"Join me for dinner and you can tell me more about how you saved him," Drew said. "And your suggestions for his continued care."

He had decided that this vet could be a useful resource. But only if he could learn what she knew.

They'd had access to her predecessor, of course, but Dr. Worley had known the truth about what was going on. Although he had always passed along anything he heard, he had lived here all his life. No one would have attempted to update him with anything supposedly new, sway his opinion.

Could be very different with Dr. Melanie Harding, fresh to the area. What had she heard about the alleged Mary Glen shapeshifters? This wasn't likely to be the new vet's only encounter with the legends, maybe not even the first. And his unit's gathering of knowledge, even of rumors, could make the difference between life and death.

More important, she might hear something about whoever shot Grunge. And how the tourist was attacked. Drew wanted answers to both—fast.

"Well, I don't—" she began.

"I'll take Grunge back to the base," Jonas said.

"Good," Drew said. "Let's see Jonas off with Grunge, and then we'll eat."

Why had she agreed to this? Or at least not given Drew an unequivocal no?

They stood outside the Mary Glen Diner. "Would you like to eat out here, on the sidewalk?" he asked.

Although half a dozen tables sat there, only a couple were occupied. It was still early enough in spring that the air was brisk. She had traded her lab jacket for a navy cardigan, but Melanie shivered anyway at the idea of staying outside.

Or maybe it was the idea of staying longer in Drew

Connell's company that made her tremble—in suppressed irritation at his continued arrogance. Yet there was something about him that chiseled away at her decision to swear off men. And it wasn't his sparkling personality.

"Let's go inside," she said, as much to take control of the situation as anything.

They were met at the door by Angie Fishbach, who owned the diner. She was a short, slightly chubby woman with laugh lines crinkling the edges of her small eyes. Only she wasn't smiling now. And deep lines were gouged into her forehead by her frown.

She wore thick-soled athletic shoes that made her yellow uniform-like shirtwaist look even dowdier. "Two?" she grumbled, then turned her back, leading them down the aisle between the rows of booths.

Odd. Angie had always been cordial to Melanie before.

The diner was one of only a couple eating establishments in town that weren't a pizza parlor or fast food joint. Melanie dined here now and then, mostly at breakfast before the clinic opened. Alone, with her copy of the *Baltimore Sun,* delivered each morning to her door.

Angie often stopped at her table and chatted, unless the place was too crowded or the staff too thin.

This evening, competing aromas of grilling meat and baking pastries also filled the air. Most booths and tables were occupied, and the acoustics turned the atmosphere into a loud hum of conversation. Melanie recognized a lot of people, some from prior visits here and many who brought their pets to the clinic.

Angie showed them to a booth near the windows. "Here." She slammed the laminated menus down on the stone-look Formica table. "Crystal will be with you soon."

Melanie shot a glance toward Drew. He slid into the booth and opened the menu, without seeming to notice Angie's abruptness. Maybe he hadn't been here often enough to expect anything else. Melanie sat down, too.

"Hope you're hungry." He lowered the menu and looked at her. "They charbroil a mean steak here."

"I know," she said. "But not for me."

"Are you a vegetarian, Doc?"

"No," Melanie said. "I believe in the natural order of things, and of course animals devour each other to survive. We're theoretically more advanced, but as much as I love the taste of red meat it's not healthy for humans to eat a lot of it."

"Could be. But it's okay to live dangerously now and then, don't you think?"

One corner of his full lips quirked up in an almost-smile. Melanie's insides ignited. Was that last sentence intended to be a double entendre?

Well, sure, she found the guy hot. Who wouldn't? And here they were, out for dinner, on the first date she'd had since arriving in Mary Glen. The idea of sex with this man had crossed her mind more than once since she'd caught him in the clinic. In fact, it had flowed down from her brain and now sizzled in her body as if her blood had turned into lava.

It had been ages since she had thought about sex, longer still since she had indulged.

Which was, of course, the problem, she realized as

she pretended to study the menu without responding to his provocative question. Not only was she rusty at the whole dating thing, but she was also horny. She would read innuendo into the most innocent of statements.

He was simply teasing her, right? Only, he didn't seem to be the teasing type. Her deprived, conservative nature was undoubtedly obvious to this man who had to live dangerously more than the now and then he'd suggested. He was in the military, wasn't he?

The most daring thing she had done in her life was to leave everything and everyone she knew in her hometown of Los Angeles and buy the veterinary practice here.

But she'd had to make a change, a drastic one, after all she had gone through at the time. Her parents were dead, and her sister lived with her husband and kids in Seattle. There had been much more reason to leave than to stay, once she had learned what her former fiancé had been pulling.

Well, she could take care of herself. And that meant flirting. Why not? It wouldn't hurt to practice, even if she had no intention of anything more.

"You convinced me," she said to Drew. "I'll go for the small sirloin. And a salad on the side. Need to have something that's arguably good for me."

"T-bone for me," he said. "Large. If I have any left-overs, Grunge will be willing to take them on. Without the bone, in case it's the kind that'll splinter. Right, Doc?"

"Sure." Rusty or not, this was a date. She wasn't here to be super vet, lecture the guy against feeding his injured friend table scraps instead of sticking to dog food. Drew's raised eyebrows suggested he was prepared for her to give him an earful. Instead, she shrugged and smiled. The extra treat would be good for Grunge's recovery.

Their waitress, Crystal, soon came over bearing glasses of water, and a notepad to take their order. "Decided what you want?" She was an older lady with a bored expression. She had served Melanie before. They gave their orders and Crystal moseyed off.

"Where are you from, Melanie?" Drew took a sip of water, and his unusual amber eyes regarded her steadily, as if he gave a damn about her answer.

"L.A. And you?"

"A huge place like that, and you wind up in pint-sized Mary Glen? Why?"

"Why not?" she countered, slightly miffed that he had ignored her question. He'd asked, and she had responded. It was his turn. But she decided not to make an issue of it. "It's a great area," she finally said. "Lots of people with pets. And obviously a vet's services are needed. And you? Where are you from? And why are you—"

Before he could answer—assuming he would— Angie appeared at their table. "Why would you do such a thing, Melanie?" Although her voice wasn't raised, her words pelted Melanie as if hurled at her. "How could you save the life of a…a murdering creature like that? Didn't you know what he was?"

Melanie blinked as she stared up at the obviously upset woman. "Would you like to sit down, Angie?"

"No," Angie snapped. "Everyone in town knows about that supposed dog you found last night, Melanie. I heard that a bunch of reporters came to ask you about it, and you didn't even have the courtesy to tell them the truth."

Melanie swallowed the retort that sprang to her lips.

"Dr. Harding told the truth, Angie," Drew said, his voice low. "She saved my dog's life."

"Why didn't you just let that creature die?" Angie didn't look at Drew as tears flowed from her puffy eyes.

Melanie felt herself stiffen. She hadn't sought answers about who had harmed Grunge. That was Angus Ellenbogen's job. But now she had to know. "Did you shoot that poor dog, Angie? Or do you know who did?"

"Someone smart," the woman shot back. "And brave. Oh, yes, I'd have done it if I'd have been there and seen that damned wolf, believe me. I knew it was a full moon last night. Everyone talked about it. I thought about hunting, but…but…I was afraid. And now one of our tourists is suffering because I was a coward." Her last words came out in a wail.

Swallowing her anger, Melanie put a comforting arm around Angie's back as the woman began to sob.

"I don't understand," Melanie said, puzzled. What was wrong with the woman? How could she—

"You saved the life of a fiend," Angie screeched. "A shapeshifter. A werewolf, the one who must have chewed up poor Sheila Graves. And he, or a creature just like him, killed my husband."

Chapter 5

"I don't know what hurt that tourist," Drew said, his voice low as he leaned over the table, "but the way I heard it, Angie killed her own husband."

Melanie had watched a waitress she didn't know lead Angie from the table. She turned back to face her dinner companion, expecting to see a joking smile on his face. Instead, it remained somber. Serious.

And damned sexy.

How could those eyes of his be so excruciatingly intense?

He leaned back, lifting his glass of the house Merlot and taking a healthy sip. He continued to watch, as if awaiting her response. Was *she* supposed to laugh?

"I...I don't know how to react to that," Melanie said truthfully. "Care to elaborate?"

Crystal approached, carrying plates heaped with steak,

fries, and small green salads. Mostly comfort food. And right then, Melanie needed all the comfort she could get.

This was all too much. Too incredible. A sweet, severely injured dog—her patient—accused of being a wild, mythical creature. A visitor to Mary Glen attacked, purportedly by just such a non-existent beast. And now, their hostess had claimed that one of the area's legendary creatures had actually killed someone.

"T-bone?" Crystal looked from one of them to the other.

"Here," Drew said, and the waitress thumped a plate down in front of him.

When Melanie's sirloin dinner, too, was set down noisily, Crystal rounded on Melanie. "I don't know what you said to upset Angie, but I know what you did. Oh, sure, the werewolves bring in tourist money and are good for this town in some ways. But when they hurt people—well, killing them cleanly with silver bullets is too good for them. And for people who help them."

Drew suddenly stood over Crystal. His smile held no humor. "If I didn't know better, I'd think you were threatening Dr. Harding," he said. "Not a good idea, Crystal, to scare off your restaurant's guests. I think an apology is in order."

"No need." Melanie kept her tone light to try to defuse the uncomfortable situation, though she appreciated Drew's attempt to defend her. "But I'd like to eat before our dinners get cold."

"Angie's husband, Bill, was a good man," Crystal muttered and stalked away.

Melanie felt every eye in the diner focused on them.

But damn if she'd let herself feel embarrassed and slink out. She'd done nothing wrong.

As Drew remained standing, muscles clearly tense beneath his T-shirt, Melanie pasted a challenging smile on her face and shot it toward some of those who stared—until they were uncomfortable enough to turn away.

When Drew sat back down, his anger had apparently dissipated. Turned into something else, maybe. The way he studied her so intensely, his gaze hinting of wry humor and appreciation, shot little sparks through her veins, simmering her blood.

Okay, knock it off, she told herself. So what if this gorgeous, sexy guy looked at her as if she was a woman, not just a veterinarian? He was a military man. Weren't they all full of uncontrolled testosterone? She, on the other hand, was completely under control.

"You've got guts, Doc." His tone sounded approving. She liked the feeling it elicited from her. Not that she'd show it.

She shrugged a shoulder nonchalantly. "Obviously, this werewolf legend has a lot of believers around here, not just the tourists. Angie certainly takes it seriously. Crystal, too, I guess." She carved off a bite of steak and tasted it. "This is good. Maybe it's even worth all this aggravation."

"Maybe." Drew bit into a healthy chunk of his meat.

"But maybe not," Melanie continued. "Now would be an excellent time for you to elaborate on what you said before. Angie obviously blames werewolves for killing her husband. You said she did it herself. What happened?"

She glanced around. Not a single patron seemed to

be paying attention to them. If anything, they were making a studious effort to ignore them.

A good thing.

Drew took another bite. "Okay, here's what I heard. It was the night of a full moon, which was handy for the story Angie later told. She was driving, and her husband was her passenger. They'd both been drinking. Maybe they were arguing, but only she would know that. I gathered that they had a roller coaster of a relationship. The way Angie tells it, they were on a twisty road surrounded by woods when they rounded a bend. There, in the middle of the pavement, stood what looked like a wolf. She swerved to miss it, but its eyes glowed, and not just like something reflecting headlights but throwing off some kind of internal, hypnotic light."

"Is that part of the werewolf legend?" The little bit of research into the mythic creatures that Melanie had begun on the Internet hadn't disclosed that detail.

"Not that I've ever heard of. Although I don't claim to know all the nonsensical parts of werewolf tales. Anyway, she claims the thing stood up on two legs and launched itself at her car, and was strong enough to shove it toward the trees. There was a crash. She survived. Her husband didn't."

Melanie twisted her fork in her salad. "That's why you said she killed her own husband. So maybe her werewolf story is a rationalization, to keep her from feeling guilty."

"Assuming she even believes it herself. Could be that they were fighting and she crashed the car on purpose to get rid of the guy. Or not," Drew added as Melanie glared at him.

"One way or another, the poor woman was driving, and she lost her husband. If it was an accident because she thought she saw something, or even if it was due to an angry impulse, she's probably still grieving."

He nodded. "I've never heard anyone mention the wolf, or, more likely, a dog, that she might have hit on the road that night. Maybe it had a grieving family, too."

Melanie's fork stalled halfway to her mouth. That sounded like something she would say. "Guess you're really an animal lover, too," she said.

Angie again appeared in the diner. She walked toward them in the crowded room. Melanie's appetite wavered once more. She'd had enough confrontations that day.

Angie stopped at their table, a sad, sheepish expression on her round face. "Sorry, Doc," she said. "I know you were just doing your job when you saved that animal. But when I hear certain things… Well, I shouldn't have gone off like that. I hope you won't hold it against me. Tell you what. Dessert's on the house tonight, for both of you. We have some great peach pie. Okay?"

Before Melanie could respond, she saw Angie stiffen and look over her shoulder. Melanie turned.

A tall, thin man had walked into the diner. Melanie saw nearly everyone turn to look at him.

"Who's that?" she asked.

"Nolan Smith," Angie said. "He's been on vigil at the hospital with that injured tourist." She rushed toward the man.

"I've heard of him." Melanie remembered Carla mentioning him. He was the one who maintained Web sites on urban legends…and the Mary Glen werewolves.

Before she could tell Drew, Smith called out, "Hey, everyone." The room had started to hush when he appeared, and his voice projected easily over the few continued conversations. "Good news. I've just come from Sheila Graves's hospital room. Looks like she'll be okay."

It was past 7:00 p.m. by the time they left the diner. Since it was early spring, the illumination outside, along the sidewalk of Mary Glen Road, came from street-lights. The rest came from the moon, which, despite its healthy glow, was no longer full.

Melanie was glad. No one should imagine seeing a werewolf tonight, thank heavens. Less chance of another poor dog getting shot when not even the credulous could believe werewolves were on the prowl.

"Nope, no supposed werewolves for you to heal this evening," Drew said.

Startled, Melanie turned to him. Surely, he hadn't read her thoughts.

He laughed, a low, deep and somehow seductive sound. "I saw you staring at the moon. Not much of a jump to imagine you had shapeshifting creatures on your mind."

"I guess not." She forced a smile. Okay, so her musings were predictable. Even so, with all the talk of things supposedly supernatural around here, she was feeling spooked.

Not to mention turned on by this strangely compelling man.

Shivering slightly in the cool evening air, Melanie picked up her pace. She needed to get back to her clinic and check on her overnight charges.

She couldn't ignore Drew's presence as he kept up with her. If he was chilly in just his muscle-hugging T-shirt and jeans, he didn't show it.

"So…where are you parked?" she asked.

"Near your place."

Okay. They were heading the same direction. No need to inflate this friendly dinner into something it wasn't.

Still, it had been a pleasant evening. Mostly. But also uncomfortable at times, and not just because of the werewolf lunacy. Partly—largely—because of Drew.

The guy made her think—constantly—of passionate nights. She, who had sworn off men. Who'd had no trouble at all swearing off sex, too.

Till now. She was fully aware of his tall, stimulating presence. Only, she had no intention of following through, even if Drew had similar ideas.

Although if she were so inclined, she suspected that hard, muscular body of his would be worth falling off the wagon for once or twice.

The silence between them grew, broken only by an occasional car driving by, and the whisper of a breeze disturbing the trees along the street and behind the buildings. Not a lot of traffic in little Mary Glen, not even along the main street.

The stores they passed were dark. Shadows ruled, despite the moonlight and artificial street lamps.

Presumably, the nuts around here wouldn't shoot at something they chose to perceive as a werewolf tonight.

Still, she'd been reminded that she had saved the creature that the credulous believed to be a shapeshifter.

Was she in danger of being stopped—permanently— from doing it again?

Maybe it was a good thing to have a military man walk her home. Even if his presence did churn her insides into steamy liquid.

"So what do you do on the base, Major?" she asked to break the silence.

He walked close enough that she thought she felt his body heat radiating in the cool air of the spring evening—even though they weren't touching, and he wasn't dressed warmly enough. Her imagination, of course. Her *over-libidinous* imagination.

"Classified stuff, mostly related to the units training K-9s at the base," he said.

That didn't tell her much. And classified stuff? Of course. He had a professional reason to keep secrets. And he obviously excelled at it.

Maybe that was a good thing. She despised secretive men…as her fiancé had been. He'd owned the veterinary clinic where she worked. Gave her lots of experience running the place.

And, while supposedly working on a hush-hush veterinary research project for a local university, took the lady professor in charge of the project as his lover.

That should keep her from wanting to see more of closed-mouthed Drew.

Instead, she focused on what was really important to her. "So how many K-9s are there on the base?"

"A dozen or so."

"Without a resident vet?"

"Their handlers are trained in animal first aid. And despite what happened to Grunge, the dogs rarely get ill or hurt."

"So they're taken care of better than the people?"

"Absolutely." But he'd spoken a little too quickly. Was he holding something back?

Something about the animals' welfare?

"Why don't you let me schedule a check-up for each animal on the base?" she asked. "A baseline, so to speak, in case there's a problem in the future."

"They're checked out by military vets before being put into service and have official veterinary visits now and then," he said. "But I appreciate your offer. May take you up on it, but first I'll have to clear it with my commanding officer. I'll let you know."

Don't call us, we'll call you. That was the underlying message, Melanie was sure. She suspected that Drew wouldn't allow a little thing like military protocol stop something he really wanted. He'd figure out a way around it.

Which meant he was humoring her. "Fine." Squaring her shoulders, she increased her pace, and he kept up.

They soon turned the corner onto Choptank Lane and passed the antique stores nearest the main street. Of course they were dark at this hour.

Melanie slowed. Looked around uneasily. This was near where she had found Grunge last night.

Was he shot right here? And was his assailant still around?

Her state of mind lightened considerably when they arrived safely at her clinic. She pulled her key from her purse. "I have a few dogs to check on. No need to wait."

But she somehow hoped he wouldn't rush off—not when she still felt a little nervous.

"I'll come in. Make sure everything's okay."

"Not necessary." But she didn't stop him. Not with the relief she felt.

The idea of remaining in his company a little longer didn't hurt, either.

"Your irritating some of the locals and tourists for being nice to Grunge last night might not be good for your health," he said, accompanying her inside.

"I figured." Melanie nearly exploded with frustration. "Why on earth do so many people around here believe in such absurd stuff? Werewolves. Shapeshifters. The value of silver bullets."

"Keeps them from getting bored, I'd imagine." In the light from the fixtures beside the clinic doors, Melanie could see his shadowed smile.

"That stuff seems pretty boring to me," she grumbled.

"Really? I thought you enjoyed it."

"What!"

Holding the door open for her, he grinned, sending awareness skittering up her spine and down to her most intimate areas. Again.

She couldn't help smiling back.

He followed her inside. Nothing seemed out of order. Thank heavens.

The dogs in her infirmary greeted her eagerly. She gave them small treats after allowing them out in the dog run to deal with nature's call. Did they remember Drew being there with Grunge? They all greeted him eagerly, tails wagging, heads down as if they recognized him as a military man, used to giving orders. An officer, and therefore alpha in attitude.

Despite herself, Melanie appreciated that Drew stayed with her. And when she was done at the clinic, he accompanied her next door, to her home.

Again, he held a door open. An officer and a gentleman. So what if she felt sexually attracted to him? There was nothing personal in what he was doing. He was just…well, being gentlemanly.

She watched as he checked out her house. Everything looked fine.

She walked him to the front door.

"Thanks again for helping Grunge." He looked down at her. She shivered slightly at the expression in his eyes. Their heat seemed to char her.

She wasn't surprised when he pulled her into his arms. His body was as hard against hers as she had anticipated. All of it—especially where his hardness signified he was turned on, too.

She wasn't the only one thinking about sex.

And that was both gratifying and a little scary.

When he lowered his mouth to hers, she participated willingly, concentrating on that kiss. His lips. The suggestive strokes of his tongue.

He tasted of steak—of course. And more, although she couldn't define it. Something wild. And exotic, somehow. And much too addictive.

His hands roamed up her back, and every place he touched seemed to come alive with sensation. He made a low, rumbling noise in his throat that only made her shudder with the added aural stimulation.

She, too, stroked him—his back only, and what she

could reach of his shoulders, and the taut, ropy muscles of his arms. As he had done, she moaned softly. Wanted more.

But she had just met this strangely seductive, secretive man. He had appeared in her clinic with no doors opened to him.

Slowly, as if withdrawing from a powerful magnetic force, she pulled away.

"Thanks again for dinner, Drew," she said, out of breath and fighting the urge to kiss him again.

How could a mere first kiss be so erotic?

"Any time," Drew said, his voice hoarse. "Goodnight, Melanie." He looked down at her one more time, and the intensity of his gaze ignited additional flames everywhere inside her.

And then he walked into the darkness, toward the street, where his car was parked.

She stood watching him until she heard a car engine start. She closed the door.

Only then did she castigate herself for that kiss. It had been wonderful.

It had been meaningless. It had to be meaningless.

Time to return to the routine of being home alone at night.

She checked her locks, then went into her garage to retrieve her mail from the box beneath its slot. Bills, a couple of veterinary magazines. Nothing much.

She went into the living room to turn on the TV news and saw the blinking light on her telephone answering machine. She pushed the button to retrieve the message.

And froze, as a voice, obviously mechanically altered,

said, "Werewolves exist. Other shapeshifters exist.
Believe it, Dr. Harding. And if you help them, you will
not exist. Remember the vet you replaced, Dr. Worley.
Dead Dr. Worley." There was a click, and no more.

Chapter 6

"**I**'m ready to try it," Patrick Worley said.

"I figured, Lieutenant," Drew said dryly. "You're always first to volunteer when we come up with a new formulation. But this time I'll play guinea pig."

"You just like the alcohol in that elixir of yours."

"Of ours, now," Drew countered. "All of us."

It was Sunday morning, nearly eleven hundred hours, and they were in the clean room. It was part of the lab tucked below the building in a corner of the base that housed kennels for the K-9s used as decoys for what really went on at Ft. Lukman.

Drew considered the location ironic. Dogs weren't exactly known for their sanitary habits, but these pups helped to obfuscate the most sanitary conditions imaginable from the few military personnel and civilians employed on the base who didn't know its real purpose.

"Even so, you have all the fun," Patrick grumbled.

Drew turned from the table where they had been sealing some of the newest vials of liquid for later use and faced his friend and military subordinate. Like him, Patrick was dressed in white hooded coveralls, face mask and vinyl gloves. Drew knew they looked like characters in a horror film—yet another irony, considering who and what they both were.

"We can always share the honor," Drew said. "And the initial bellyache if this new version of my good old family recipe doesn't do what we planned. And the potentially really nasty consequences in that case. Swallowing an antidote. Puking our guts out. Pain. And—"

"You win." Patrick raised his white-gloved hands and rolled his pale brown eyes—nearly the only part of his body that was visible. "I'll just turn on the lab's manufactured moonlight to get the formula to do its thing, and watch, this time."

"Next time, the pleasure is all yours."

As Patrick laughed, Jonas Truro's voice blared over the room's automatic intercom, "Drew, the guard at the main gate called. You have a visitor. A very persistent visitor without military ID who insists on seeing how Grunge is."

Drew froze. "One of those loonies wanting to visit the reported werewolf?"

"She doesn't look any loonier to me today than she did the other day when she treated our buddy with the wagging tail. I dropped by the entrance to see her myself."

Drew's shoulders relaxed, but not the rest of him. No question now of who it was, but he didn't want to get into a verbal sparring match with the lovely, and persistent, Dr. Melanie Harding.

A physical skirmish, like that kiss, was another matter. But unwise. Really unwise.

"I wonder who that could be." Humor still resounded in Patrick's voice. "Hey, invite her in. I haven't seen Dr. Harding since I sold her my dad's clinic. She struck me as being pretty conscientious when it came to treating animals. Wouldn't hurt for Grunge to have a follow-up exam today. Or even for Duke to get checked. My dog's been acting a little irritable—though that could be because our resident cat's been teasing him. But other animals around here could use a little TLC, too, Major. Like me, after I change. What about you?"

"Stow it, Lieutenant," Drew growled. "But you're right about Grunge. And Jonas is right about the woman's perseverance. I'll let her make sure her patient's healing fine, then send her on her way."

If it hadn't been for Grunge and the other defenseless animals reportedly sequestered at Ft. Lukman, Melanie would have turned around on the spot and driven as fast as possible back to her clinic. After, of course, making an obscene gesture toward Major Drew Connell and his military base.

Who cared whether Drew could have seen her immature behavior?

She did.

But so many things had happened in the last several days that were out of her control. And way outside the realm of tangible, comprehensible reality.

She had even been threatened. Although she had immediately called Chief Ellenbogen and played the message over the phone, he hadn't held out much hope of finding out who the caller was.

At least he had come to her home early yesterday morning to take information for a report. For whatever good that would do. He'd called later to tell her he'd gotten the phone company to check the source—but the call had apparently come from a limited-use cell phone bought somewhere in Washington, D.C. Untraceable.

Melanie might not be able to control much, but she *could* make sure that the animals at the army base were safe and healthy. She didn't intend to leave until she did.

And seeing Drew in his military surroundings, with lots of people around? Safer, much safer to her state of mind, than seeing him alone.

"Well?" she called out her window to the young fellow in a blue uniform. He sat inside the guard kiosk where visitors apparently had to show some official ID she didn't have in order to enter. "Have you reached Major Connell yet?"

"I'll let you know as soon as I hear if the major can see you, ma'am."

"That's 'Doctor Ma'am' to you, soldier," she said in a semblance of the tone she heard military types use in movies.

The serious-looking African-American almost cracked a smile. "Oh, I'm not a soldier. The government hired my private security company to help out here and free more soldiers to serve overseas."

"Really?" Melanie said. "Interesting. So, Mr. Private Security, let me pass."

But he still didn't let her drive any farther. At least this was Sunday afternoon. She didn't have regular office hours, although she was always available for emergencies. Not that she wanted to waste her time sitting here. But at least she had the ability to be pushy, if necessary.

The fort was more remote than Mary Glen. At least the road through the woods to get here, though twisty, was well maintained. She had tried checking on Google Earth to see the layout and size of the military facility, but all that showed was a lot of woods just like the area surrounding it. Only part of a roof here and there was visible through the trees. Even driving by, chain-link fencing was apparent only intermittently between the large oaks, sycamores and other mature trees that obscured it from the road.

She couldn't see much of the base, but the parts of buildings in her view, among the trees, were long and low, none any higher than a couple of stories, every one in pale stucco. Seemed very military, except for the forest ambiance.

She heard a noise inside the kiosk, and the security guard spoke low, as if over a radio. He looked at her and continued talking. And then he stood.

"Major Connell's on his way."

"Thanks." She only had to wait a few minutes longer until she saw a black SUV drive up the road inside the gate and park. Drew got out, and so did Grunge, who was on a leash and still wearing the recovery collar she'd sent him home with. They walked past the kiosk toward her.

Drew was dressed in a military camouflage outfit in green and brown shades that were probably too light to render him invisible if he walked in the woods inside and outside the facility. He was tall and military-straight, his stride even and resolute in his boots. The silver in his short, dark hair seemed even more prominent in the sunlight.

Grunge walked to heel, keeping pace with his companion with only a slight limp and no other indication of pain. A good thing.

Drew's expression was stern, unwelcoming. Not a good thing.

Even so, Melanie's skin seemed to hum, as if electrified, at the sight of him. If he'd been in a crowd of similarly clad soldiers, she'd have recognized him immediately by his bearing. His magnetism. His eyes.

Since they were coming to see her, she assumed she wouldn't be permitted onto the base to visit the other animals there to make sure they were healthy and well cared for. That was part of the reason she had come, not just to check on Grunge. And certainly not using the animals as an excuse to see Drew again.

There was a paved parking area beside the entrance, and she pulled her beige minivan that sometimes doubled as an animal ambulance into an empty space. By the time she opened her door to get out, the officer and dog were beside her. She ignored Drew, kneeling to hug Grunge. "Hi, boy," she crooned. He didn't flinch as she carefully probed the white bandage, making sure it hadn't come loose and that there had been no seepage indicating infection or bleeding. "You feeling okay?"

Grunge's tail wagged, and he pranced in place.

"Looking good," she told him, then rose. *Looking good,* she thought again as she said, "Hello, Drew. It appears my patient is healing."

"I'd have been in touch if Grunge showed any sign

of distress." He sounded cool, and his frown suggested she had insulted him. Well, tough.

"I figured, but I wanted to check on him."

"You didn't need to come here, Melanie. I planned to bring him back to your clinic in a day or two for a checkup."

"That's okay. It wasn't any trouble."

But seeing Drew again…well, that did feel troubling. She hadn't slept much over the last few nights. She had felt uneasy, being in a remote location with a lunatic shooter on the loose.

And that phone message had run through her mind over and over.

So had their kiss…

"Besides," she said firmly, "while I'm here I'd like to check on his K-9 buddies."

"Sorry." He didn't sound at all regretful. "Everyone who comes onto the base has to have a military ID or security clearance. But you can be sure that if any of our K-9s require medical attention, we'll bring them to you. Your treatment of Grunge was greatly appreciated, but you know that."

He sounded so formal. So remote. So…untouchable.

Melanie's intention of checking on the base's animals clearly didn't matter to Drew. *She* didn't matter. So why the heck had he kissed her?

She glared straight into those unsettling eyes that were now virtually expressionless. She wanted to evoke some emotion from them. From *him*.

"Not everyone appreciates it," she blurted angrily. "Like Angie Fishbach. And the person who shot Grunge in the first place. And the person who left me a threat-

ening message on my phone the other night—although
that could have been the shooter. Not that I'd ever allow
an animal to suffer, but if I'd known that by removing
that bullet from Grunge I'd be subjected to all this, I'd
have driven him—"

"What threatening message, Melanie?" Drew's voice
was ominously quiet. But she had finally succeeded in
getting a reaction. His face was not expressionless now.
Instead, its angles grew more pronounced around a
scowl that made her shiver.

"It's not—" she began.

"What threatening message?" he repeated, his tone
brooking no resistance. "And why didn't you call me?"

She told him now. "And I did call Chief Ellenbogen,
of course. He's still looking into it."

"As if that'll do any good. Has he figured out who
hurt that tourist or Grunge? Does he have enough cops
to protect you? Does he—"

"There's a community meeting tonight that Nolan
Smith called to talk about the werewolf legends,"
Melanie said. "I'm planning to go. Maybe the police
will have an answer by then and announce it. Or at least
give suggestions about how ordinary citizens can
protect themselves from whoever is doing this."

But Melanie knew she wasn't simply an ordinary
citizen. By saving Grunge, she had put herself in the
category of enemy to the person who had shot him.

"Don't count on that," Drew growled, echoing her
thoughts. "And I'll see about coming to that meeting."

A while later, when Melanie pulled her van into her
driveway, she noticed that Carla's small yellow sedan was

in its spot beside the veterinary hospital next door. Melanie had asked her assistant to pop in now and then in off hours to check on patients and animals being boarded, and had found Carla to be diligent about that, even on Sundays.

But Carla's wasn't the only vehicle in the five-space lot. A gray SUV sat beside it.

Uh-oh. Was an emergency awaiting? Melanie hurriedly pushed the button on the wall to shut the garage door behind her and hurried next door.

The door to the reception area was unlocked, as anticipated. She hustled inside.

"It's just not right," shouted a voice Melanie didn't recognize. She scanned the waiting room for a pet needing medical assistance, but saw none.

Instead, Carla sat on one of the chairs facing a young man. He stood immediately and approached Melanie.

"You're Dr. Harding?" He looked to be in his late twenties, had long legs stuck into loose blue jeans, and wore a bright red T-shirt that said Bite Me. His light, long hair hung in unruly waves from his head.

"Yes," Melanie said. "And you are…?"

"Mike Ripkey." His deep brown eyes bore an expression that looked to Melanie like anguish. "I came here because of the Mary Glen werewolf Web site. So did Sheila Graves. We were curious, that's all."

Sheila Graves. That was the woman who had been injured the other night—and some believed she had been attacked by a werewolf.

"I understand curiosity, Mr. Ripkey. It's a very human trait, and we all—"

"Don't try to humor me, Doc. I need some answers. I've spent the last couple of days with Sheila, and fortunately she'll be all right—assuming she doesn't turn into a werewolf during the next full moon. But people all around town were talking about a dog you treated that some brave person shot with a silver bullet. And then in the morning he changed into a man. Dr. Harding, it's just not right for you to have saved the life of the werewolf who attacked Sheila, and my group plans to do something about it."

Chapter 7

"You know how rumors start, don't you, Mr. Ripkey?" Melanie took a seat on one of the reception area chairs.

"Call me Mike," he said. "Sure, I understand rumors. That's all Nolan has on his Web site, along with shadowy photos and stuff like that. But Sheila's injuries were real. She was bitten—the doctors said so. And she's in pain. Since no one's produced the animal that hurt her, she'll have to have rabies treatments, though we all know she wasn't attacked by an ordinary rabid wolf. Plus, someone will have to watch her during the next full moon, just in case...well, you know." His earnest tone was reflected in his expression, and Melanie wanted to shake him. Wake him up. Make him see reality.

She had no doubts that Sheila was hurt. Even

attacked by some wild animal, if that's what the hospital physicians determined from her injuries. Maybe it was a rabid dog, although Melanie hadn't run across any rabies cases in the month she had been there. Maybe the tourist was as credulous and kooky as Mike Ripkey, and had sneaked up on some creature in the woods, startling it so it attacked in self-defense.

Maybe it was something else altogether. But a werewolf? Oh, right. This was Mary Glen.

"Anyway, this dog you treated," Mike continued. "Supposedly one of the animals from Ft. Lukman. That was what I heard, and what the news reported. But in the morning, he'd changed back into human form, right?"

"Wrong," Melanie said firmly. "The news reported that, too. His owner, an officer from the base, guessed he was here and came to make sure he was all right."

And somehow sneaked into her clinic, Melanie thought. She might still be perturbed about it, but irritating behavior didn't turn a man into a legendary monster.

"I saw them together, too, Mike," Carla piped in. She had stood up to help Brendan, one of the technicians, who carried a couple of bags of cat litter.

Bless her, Melanie thought. Maybe between them, they could defuse any rumors Mike Ripkey might spread by intentionally misinterpreting what he found out here.

Mike looked at Carla, apparently assessing Melanie's elfin assistant. She certainly looked trustworthy—didn't she?

"Don't you both get it?" he contradicted, shaking his head.

"Shapeshifters are supernatural creatures. They can do things to people and you'd never even know it. Maybe this one hypnotized you or messed with your minds in some other way so you still thought you saw the wolf when you saw it in human form."

"Really?" Brendan, in his early twenties and as thin as an underfed Great Dane, gawked at them. During the week, he worked at the clinic most afternoons, and on weekends, like today, he popped in each day to check on the animals and organize supplies.

"Anyway," Mike continued, "I don't know if you've heard, but there's going to be a meeting tonight at Mary Glen's City Hall. Nolan Smith called it, but the mayor will be there, too, and Chief Ellenbogen. Sheila won't be, since she's still recuperating. Nolan is going to talk to us about the local werewolf legends through the ages and see how the stories may fit with this attack on Sheila. And if there's enough evidence, we'll demand that the officials do something. Arrest whoever that officer was that you claim was the beast's owner, keep him in custody until the next full moon and see what happens. That's when everyone will know that the Mary Glen werewolves are real."

"I don't like this, Major."

"Neither do I, Greg," Drew said over his cell phone to Ft. Lukman's C.O., General Greg Yarrow. He was driving toward Mary Glen, Grunge alongside him in his army issue vehicle. "But Dr. Harding sounded really distressed on our behalf." *On* my *behalf,* Drew thought. The way she told it, he was about to be arrested and held forever in some civilian facility.

Or maybe not forever. Only until the next full moon. He would change then, since he would have no control over it. And they'd kill him then, with a silver bullet directly to the heart, without even learning what control he *did* have.

He appreciated Melanie's warning, especially after their uneasy confrontation that afternoon when he'd had to shelve his own uncomfortable impulses and treat her like the unwelcome civilian she was at the base.

Nevertheless, she had called him. Told him that Grunge and he would be primary topics of discussion at the town meeting that night, and that it might be a good idea for them to make an appearance. Either that, or leave the area altogether.

She made it clear she would be there, which gave Drew pause. He had seen a lot of Dr. Harding over the last couple of days. Maybe too much. She was curious. And she aroused all-too-human animal urges in him that had nothing to do with his wolfish side.

After tonight he could have one of his men bring Grunge to her for his next post-op checkup. And she was unlikely to show up at the base again after the way she was treated that day. Something he couldn't help regretting.

In any event, no more need, after this evening, to see the vet again. A good thing, considering how his body kept reacting to her.

It was nearly eighteen hundred thirty hours, still daylight. He had just reached downtown. Every parking space along the street was occupied. The lot beside the picturesque, aging City Hall had no available spaces, either.

He drove toward the far end of town. Almost instinc-
tively, he turned right onto Choptank Lane. Not many
people parked there, so he found a space immediately.

"Come on, Grunge." He snapped the leash onto the
dog's leather collar behind the soft plastic collar. Poor
animal hated the recovery gadget. But in this, at least,
Drew would follow vet's orders.

Late afternoon in Mary Glen was a time of interesting scents. Tonight, exhaust fumes from recently parked
vehicles mingled with the cool, green humidity of trees
swaying in the evening breeze. The woodlands nearby
proffered the odors of small animals—mostly rodents—
beginning to stir for nightly foraging. Grunge, in his uncomfortable surgery collar, managed to keep his nose
in the air, sniffing one way, then another.

They were nearly alone as they passed closed retail
businesses. No last-minute shoppers, no pedestrians
lingering on the sidewalks. Was everyone already at
the meeting?

Drew tugged gently on Grunge's leash and they
strode up the steps into Mary Glen's City Hall. The
building was only three quarters of a century old but had
the look of an older structure, emulating those in the
nation's capital not far away. It was domed and marbled,
pale in color, and its huge, high-ceilinged entry was
adorned with sturdy columns.

That entry's smooth stone floor, also marble, was
almost empty, except for a few souls spilling out the wide
doorways, craning their necks so they could see inside.

Recognizing a couple as reporters who had confronted Melanie the other day, Drew halted and
motioned for Grunge to do the same. Fortunately, his

rubber-soled black shoes made little sound on the floor, but Grunge's nails created rhythmic clicks that might catch the attention of the vultures, even over the roar of the crowd inside. Turning, they left the foyer.

At the side of the building, Drew peered into some windows. The meeting room was a large auditorium. Sounds emanating from cracks under closed doors around the back told Drew which way to go. The first door was locked. The second knob turned in his hand. He opened the door and slipped inside with Grunge. They stayed against the wall in the shadows, but from there Drew could see and hear what was going on, inhale the variety of smells emanating from the room's occupants.

Several people stood on the stage behind a podium.

"Of course there's no need to panic," the mayor was saying.

Mayor Ed Sherwin was in his mid-sixties, with a large gut and ruddy face. He had once visited the base as General Yarrow's guest, carefully shepherded around so he never saw anything he shouldn't.

"I understand everyone's concern," Mayor Sherwin continued, "but, well, it's one thing to hear lectures about things that go bump in the night, enjoy being scared and all, but to believe that it's real and going on around here—"

"Of course it's real!" shouted Nolan Smith. Drew knew who he was, though he had never spoken with the guy. He posted shadowy photos on his Web site and claimed they were werewolves. But those shadows were caused by optical illusions in wind swept woods.

Real werewolves looked nothing like them.

Smith was a tall man. His Web site picture showed a paunch above his large silver belt buckle with the likeness of a wolf. From the back, Drew saw he wore the same wide belt tonight.

Before the mayor could respond, Drew saw someone else scramble onto the stage and to the podium—a young man he hadn't seen recently, dressed in jeans and a blue denim jacket. "Since this isn't a formal town meeting, can I speak now?" He glanced toward the mayor but didn't wait for an answer. "Hi, I'm Mike Ripkey, President of the ShapeShifter Tracers—the SSTs. We're a national organization dedicated to locating beings like werewolves, making sure the local citizenry is informed about them, and protecting people from them whenever possible."

Great, Drew thought. The current head of the group of nuts who periodically invaded the area. He waited to see how this guy would be received.

Apparently with open arms, since no one booted him off the podium.

"I held a vigil the last couple of nights in the hospital with poor Sheila Graves," he intoned sadly, "after she was attacked by a Mary Glen werewolf. I'm sure you've all heard the creature was shot with a silver bullet. I want to applaud whoever did that, even if you're too afraid to come forward. But your nice but misguided town veterinarian saved its life. Now she won't even acknowledge that the thing she saved was a shapeshifter."

"Let's get real," shouted Melanie. In moments, she, too, was at the podium. She wore a gray suit and tailored red blouse, and looked entirely the professional that she was.

And, even so, as sexy as hell.

"For anyone who doesn't know me, I'm that 'nice but misguided vet,'" she said into the microphone. "A couple of nights ago, I saved the life of a dog. A *dog*." Her tone was emphatic. "Mr. Ripkey will tell you I'm a weak-minded dork who was hypnotized in daylight by the animal's human counterpart, so I imagined I saw both him and the dog I treated at the same time. That's not so." She turned to Mike Ripkey. "I'm really sorry about your friend and how she was injured. But there was no indication that the dog I saved attacked anyone or anything. I'd suggest you cooperate with the local police in finding out what really happened. And also help figure out who shot that poor animal. If one dog can get shot, so can others. Or people. Like the vet before me, Dr. Worley, and his wife. Maybe if you cooperate in finding out who shot the dog the other night, their murders can also be solved."

A smattering of applause resounded from the audience, punctuated by boos. Lights blazed toward the podium from the media jackals' equipment. Like Melanie's unplanned press conference, this was being recorded for the American public and posterity. Which meant that the loonies seeking publicity for their cause, like that Ripkey nut, would be encouraged to continue their histrionics.

"Dr. Harding." Nolan Smith spoke stiffly into the microphone. He sold advertising on his Web site, so he would appreciate the hype. "You're new around here. You come from Los Angeles, where crimes go unsolved all the time. People there don't always have their minds open to what's really happening around them. Or who's behind all those crimes. But we care about what happens in Mary Glen. Citizens here have experienced things caused by those local shapeshifters."

"Did someone believe Dr. Worley was a shapeshifter? Or his wife? They were both shot with silver bullets. But I've never heard that they were claimed to harm anyone or anything." Melanie, sounding disgusted, obviously wasn't playing to the cameras.

"Well, no. We're watchful of such things, and we've no reason to believe any of the Worleys—including their son, Patrick—were werewolves. No, we think that Dr. and Mrs. Worley were killed by shapeshifters."

Melanie shook her head slowly, as if in incredulity. "Then why would some supernatural creature that could only, theoretically, be harmed by ammunition like silver bullets, use it against someone else?"

"A ruse to disguise their real killer, of course," Nolan said patiently. "Undoubtedly a shapeshifter. Now poor Sheila has been mauled. I, for one, really want to see that supposed dog you saved. And the supposed person he turned into. And—"

"Excellent idea," Drew called out, stopping Melanie from talking. Judging by her furious expression, she was probably about to tell Nolan Smith what a fruitcake he was.

Not that Drew could fault that. Even so, he strode up to the podium with Grunge at his side.

Melanie's eyes narrowed. "Glad you're here, Major," she said aloud. More softly, she added, "But I probably shouldn't have told you to show up. There are more of these SSTs and their fans than...other people." Drew read that as meaning *sane* people. "And those horrible tabloid types are here, too. I'm not sure there's enough security to protect you. And Grunge." Raising her voice again, she said, "Of course, the sensible thing is to demonstrate the truth to these…folks." *Fools,* was the word she wanted to say, judging by how she rolled those lovely blue eyes.

"Thanks for your concern, Dr. Harding," Drew said into the microphone. "But I wanted to make it clear to the people of Mary Glen what happened the other night." He noticed some recent arrivals slip into a corner at the rear of the auditorium. With a slight nod in that direction, he turned toward Melanie and shielded the microphone so it wouldn't pick up what he said. "And in the unlikely event I can't handle it myself, the U.S. Army's capable of protecting Grunge and me. Some of the guys from Ft. Lukman just arrived." Back into the microphone, he said, "Now, tell us: is this the dog you treated?"

Melanie looked down at the canine in question. Then she knelt, despite wearing a skirt. "Hi, Grunge." She motioned to both Nolan Smith and Mike Ripkey. "Come here, you two. I'll lift his bandage so you can see his wound."

When they stooped obediently beside her, she peeled back the tape from the shaved area of Grunge's skin. The poor dog looked uneasy, not that he'd bite.

Drew had observed the wound before. Had seen that the area looked clean and uninfected, the sutures skillfully done.

"See that?" Melanie said loudly enough for the microphone to pick it up. She pointed toward the injury. "This dog was hurt. If I had to testify under oath, I'd say I removed a bullet. Those sutures are my handiwork. This is the animal I treated."

She maneuvered the bandages back into place, then stood and approached Drew.

Her sable-brown hair was loose this evening instead of fastened behind her head. Her scent was the same he had noticed before—light and floral—and reminded him of the kiss they had shared…before he turned her away from the base. He had to keep in mind that she was defending Grunge, not him.

"Okay, Major Connell. Take off your shirt."

"What?"

"We need to show these people you're not hiding a similar wound. That you're not the being I removed the bullet from."

"Right." He grinned and unbuttoned his shirt.

And saw, with some satisfaction, that she tried, unsuccessfully, to look disinterested as he removed it.

In a minute, he revealed he had no wounds on his body. Nor scars.

"Okay, Major Connell. You're the *person*—" she stressed the word "—I saw in the morning with Grunge. My assistant, Carla Banyan, was there, too. Gee, it looks like these folks are wrong, and you weren't the animal I treated. Oh, unless, of course, you just hypnotized—how many people are here? A hundred? A hundred fifty? Oh, and the cameras those media types are using, too, unless they're picking up something we don't see in person."

She turned back toward the two screwball werewolf aficionados, Smith and Ripkey.

"Okay, guys. Explain how this dog and this man are one and the same creature."

Chapter 8

"It was all so absurd!" Melanie exclaimed, though she kept her tone muted as she stood with Drew and Grunge near the stage. The crowd had started dispersing. Even with the hum of conversations, she did not want to be overheard.

Mayor Sherwin had left the microphone after trying to shift the topic to a spring flower show planned for Mary Glen Park. The audience became restless, and he gave up.

If he'd talked about a werewolf demonstration, Melanie felt sure everyone would have remained seated and enrapt.

No one had moved an iota when Nolan Smith and Mike Ripkey attempted to meet her challenge and explain how a man without a scratch on him was the human version of the dog who'd been shot—and who just happened to be present at the same time.

After starting to listen to the ridiculous theories and rationalizations, she had shaken her head and headed down the stage's narrow stairway. Drew and Grunge had followed. That was where they still stood, Grunge lying on the floor by their feet.

Drew had put his black shirt back on and buttoned it. He still looked breathtakingly handsome, even dressed, but she had really appreciated the view when he had bared his chest and back to demonstrate his lack of injury.

But why hadn't he spoken up as loudly as she had?

"I mean really," she continued, as if she needed to convince him. "Shapeshifting? Ridiculous. And impossible. I know you're not a veterinarian, but the scientific and medical areas I studied, like anatomy, cell and molecular biology, physiology, and even neuroscience—none would allow for a complete, rapid and reversible metamorphosis like that. Can you even picture what a dog changing into a person would look like—or vice versa?"

"Not a pretty sight," Drew agreed, looking down at her with his unusual eyes. She realized now that their amber color helped to keep his expression neutral at times, like now—not revealing an iota of what he was thinking.

Which made him seem even more of a challenge. The guy could be the epitome of secretiveness, thanks to that damned classified military base of his. It was the kind of challenge she didn't need. Not again. No matter how much the guy intrigued her and got her hormones percolating.

"Hey, Major," said a voice from behind Melanie, and she turned. Captain Jonas Truro stood there. The guy who had come to her clinic to take Grunge home was dressed in jeans and a black leather jacket. "So why didn't you slit your skin open to look like you and Grunge had the same wounds? That would really have given these people a thrill."

Behind him stood two other men. One was Lieutenant Patrick Worley.

The other man stood in a stiff military stance.

"Tell you what, Truro," Drew said dryly. "I'll gladly slice you once or twice so you can claim you're Grunge's alter ego."

Jonas lifted his hands in a backing-off gesture. "Not me, Major. I faint at the sight of blood, especially mine."

"I can vouch for that," said the other man. He was broad at the shoulders and neck, and dressed in jeans and a gray sweatshirt. "I've been on training ops with the captain when he's skinned an elbow. I'm Lieutenant Seth Ambers, Dr. Harding." His dark hair was just long enough that she could detect its waviness. "I heard about all you did for Grunge. Everyone at the fort has, and we're all grateful."

"Yeah, and you did a great job with these crazies," Jonas said, lowering his voice, then paused as more people slipped by. "We owe you," he finished.

"We owe her dinner," Patrick said.

"That's just your way of saying you're hungry," Drew said. "But if you all want to grab something while we're in town, let's do it. You, too, Melanie. Hey, we'll go back to the diner."

"Last night just whetted your appetite?" Melanie didn't attempt to disguise the irony in her voice. "Angie Fishbach was in the crowd here this evening. Did you see her? She might not be thrilled about your coming to her restaurant again after proving not only to her but to everyone else that you weren't the werewolf that supposedly killed her husband."

"All the more reason to go there," Drew said. "It might be interesting to hear reactions to tonight's meeting. Maybe someone will drop a clue about who shot Grunge." He bent to touch his dog's head, causing Grunge to look up and wag his tail. "Then there was your vivid demonstration. I'd like to see if anyone's bent out of shape about it."

As he rose, his gaze caught Melanie's and she suppressed a shiver of uneasiness.

She understood his subtext. And appreciated his concern...kind of.

She had been threatened. Would someone now be angry enough to carry through? If so, she doubted that person would be dumb enough to vocalize, in public, the anger that might result from tonight's meeting.

But just in case, it made sense to eavesdrop on the town's reaction—with a bunch of military men at her side.

"I'll take first watch out here with Grunge," Seth said. "Who's with me? Wish I'd brought my own dog, Spike."

They had reached the sidewalk seating area outside the diner. The group hadn't been the only troop heading the two blocks from City Hall, so the going had been slow. And they'd received more than one heated stare, which none of the guys bothered to acknowledge.

But Drew stuck close to Melanie, especially when she shook her head or rolled her eyes at some of those model citizens. Yeah, he found her guts admirable. And hot. But right now, inciting more antagonism wasn't in anyone's best interests.

Drew hadn't thanked the guys yet for showing up at that potential disaster of a town meeting, but he appreciated it. Of course they hadn't done it solely for him or Grunge. Alpha's entire mission could be blown by what was going on now in Mary Glen, so they all needed to stay alert. Gather intelligence. Watch each other's backs.

And above all, maintain the confidentiality of who they really were and what really went on at Ft. Lukman.

"I'm hanging out here with my buds," Jonas said to Seth. His leather jacket was unzipped and he wore a Baltimore Ravens cap over his shaved head.

"You'll be glad those gas heaters out here are turned on." Melanie tugged at the front of her gray suit jacket. "It's getting cold. I thought it was spring."

"You're from Los Angeles," Drew said wryly. His long-sleeved shirt allowed cool air to pass through to his skin, but he wasn't particularly uncomfortable. "Try eating out here in March instead of April."

"You ever done it, Major?" Patrick asked. "Grabbed a bite outside in winter?" He, too, was dressed in nothing but a shirt and slacks. But like Drew, he didn't seem to notice the chill. "My folks and I used to eat out here while there was still snow on the ground."

His folks. Both from around here. Both gone.

Both slain with silver bullets right through the heart, in separate unsolved murders. Which helped explain his determination to assist Drew and learn who had shot Grunge.

"Well, I'm going in, gentlemen," Melanie said. "Anyone joining me?"

Following her inside, Drew inhaled the diner's distinct aroma of well-cooked food. He recognized a lot of people who'd been at City Hall, for the restaurant was packed. Even so, they didn't have to wait long. Angie Fishbach personally showed them to an empty booth.

"Enjoy your meal," she said curtly. "Oh, and if you think that little game you played before will change anyone's mind, Dr. Harding, you're wrong. You just had the wrong guy take off his shirt." She turned her glare on Drew, then Patrick. "You want to strip for us, too, Patrick? You know what was said about your mom and dad."

Patrick had been sliding into the booth, but he stopped. His glare was a blowtorch of fury. "You ready to tell me who shot them, Angie? You're one of the most outspoken believers around here in shapeshifters, and you don't even bother to hide your hate. You've got to know a lot more than you're saying. Maybe you even shot my folks yourself."

"You'd better leave, Patrick," Angie spat. "This is my place. I won't be accused here of killing anybody—even if they deserved it."

Drew did not try to quash the angry conversation. He, too, figured Angie knew more than she had ever told the authorities. Could be, if they got her even angrier this evening, she would spill something helpful.

Melanie, who had slid into her seat, glared at Angie. "I just don't get any of this," she retorted, anger flashing in her brilliant blue eyes. "Would you please send someone sane over to take our order?"

Drew could have kissed her—and the thought stirred a primal reaction from his body. She'd no idea how helpful her angry response might be to him and his men, but her apparent characteristic forthrightness acted as an aphrodisiac.

But she didn't—couldn't—know just what she was actually in the middle of. Explaining wasn't an option. Listening was. And then, if necessary, he'd perform damage control.

"Sane?" Angie shouted. "One of you accuses me of being a killer, and now you're claiming I'm crazy?"

"What else can I think?" Melanie demanded. "First you accused me not only of being a liar, but of protecting werewolves, of all things. *Werewolves!* When I bought my veterinary practice I'd heard of the legends but thought they were just fairy tales that people around here liked to tell. I had no idea so many of you were credulous enough to take such silliness seriously. I don't suppose you know, do you, who shot Grunge? Or who's been making threats… Never mind. I'm not going to accuse you or anyone else." Although Drew figured she just had, or had at least implied that she believed Angie was involved. And no one had mentioned the threatening phone call Melanie had received, but he was sure that's what she was referring to. "But I'm not going to run away, either. And I won't waste my breath by demanding that you apologize—or you, Patrick—but let's drop this ludicrous subject and pretend we're all friends. I want my dinner."

"Sounds like a plan," Drew said mildly. He appreciated what she'd said, even if she hadn't gotten her facts anywhere close to being correct. And he certainly had enjoyed hearing her talk while Angie's expression grew increasingly angry. At least Patrick knew better than to pursue this any further. Drew had warned the obviously furious lieutenant with a commanding officer's glare. Of course, if it were proven to be true that the owner of the diner had something to do with his parents' deaths—well, Patrick would be entitled to help ensure she paid for it. And if Melanie's insinuations were correct, and Angie was involved with the current goings-on, she'd have to answer for them, too. "You want some beer to start with?"

"Yes," Melanie said with no hesitation.

"Great. Make sure the guys outside with Grunge get what they want to drink, too, Angie. And eat. It's on me. Let's make our meal tonight memorable." He'd intended that they all enjoy it—while learning what they could by listening to surrounding conversations. His men knew that.

But what he didn't know was how memorable it would become.

Considering the incomprehensibly odd way the evening had started—the even weirder way the past few days had been—Melanie had a wonderful time at dinner, once she had calmed down. She joined her two male companions in enjoying another steak, with Crystal as their server again.

Melanie had gotten to know Patrick Worley a few months earlier as they'd discussed his sale of the clinic. He seemed a Renaissance man, with knowledge about many subjects, including veterinary medicine, Maryland's Eastern Shore, the U.S. Army and, of course, local legends.

He was cute, too. His hair was light and cropped, his face long, and he had a cleft in his chin. During their negotiation, he sometimes had his own military K-9, Duke, with him—a large shepherd-wolfhound mix. But him, a werewolf? After what had happened to his parents, Melanie hadn't been surprised at Angie's oblique accusation earlier, but she'd shaken her head at the absurdity of it.

Melanie's mind inevitably slipped to her suspicion: Angie's accusations might be a poor attempt to mask her own involvement in some recent events. The threatening phone call had been from a man, but Angie could know who it was. And she might even have shot Grunge herself.

That evening, Patrick took the lead in their conversation, focusing on training of K-9s—or at least what he said wasn't classified. She found it fascinating.

Drew listened more than he spoke—and not just to the conversation at their table. His interest in what was going on around them should have been a turnoff. But it was just the opposite. Somehow, she appreciated his quiet watchfulness, maybe because she understood it. Even if they weren't talking about that dumb werewolf legend now, maybe others were. And some of the most outspoken aficionados from the town meeting sat nearby.

Maybe he would hear something about Grunge. Or her.

She wondered, not for the first time, exactly how old Drew was. The silvery strands in his otherwise dark hair made him appear older. Distinguished. Yet his facial features were well defined without deep crevasses or wrinkles. She guessed him to be around her age—early thirties—but wasn't sure.

Well, heck, she could always ask him.

Melanie was taken aback when, as they finished their meal, some other patrons rose from their tables and approached. One was her assistant, Carla, sashaying toward them beside Nolan Smith, curls bobbing as she looked up adoringly into the man's face. She'd been sitting with people Melanie mostly didn't know, but they'd been among the first to cheer when Mike Ripkey and Nolan took the microphone. A couple of technicians from the clinic also sat with the group: Brendan and Astrid. Carla and the rest did their jobs well and seemed to care for the animals. But were they on the werewolf loonies' side?

"I know you believe we're the nuts around here, Dr. Harding," said Nolan Smith, his smile baring white and uneven teeth. His small, dark-rimmed glasses had a prescription strong enough to make his blue eyes appear fuzzy.

Carla clutched his hand…and looked often at Patrick Worley, as if making sure he saw whom she was with.

Interesting dynamics, Melanie thought. Or they would be, if everything around here wasn't so offbeat.

"Please try to keep an open mind," Nolan continued. "Things aren't always what they seem." He stole a glance toward Patrick. "I don't want to point any fingers, of course, but, well, despite what I said to the crowd earlier…"

From over his shoulder, Mike Ripkey, self-proclaimed head of the ShapeShifter Tracers, called gleefully, "I'll point fingers. I'm always so excited to be in the presence of someone who's probably a hereditary shapeshifter, like Lt. Worley. I know how you lost your parents. A shame, of course. But—"

"Excuse me." Crystal muscled through the crowd.

"Here's your check." She slammed it on the table. Melanie noticed that Angie stood, arms folded, near the kitchen door, and suspected she had sent Crystal over to keep the peace.

When the group didn't dissipate, Drew started to rise. Although there was no overt menace in his expression, she saw his fingers tighten into fists, the muscles in his arms tauten. He drew his wallet from his pants pocket and pulled out his credit card, waving Melanie's away when she offered her own.

And still the crowd surrounded them. Uneasy, Melanie sought an escape route but found none...until Chief Angus Ellenbogen serendipitously entered the restaurant. As he headed toward their table, people made way. "Okay, folks. Time to finish eating and clear out. All of you." His glare at the milling throng seemed to cause them to back off.

"Thanks, Angus," Melanie said.

"Yeah, well, I'd just as soon not have a riot on my hands tonight. But rumor's been spreading that you've called all these lunatics, lunatics. That right?"

Melanie managed a smile.

"She did a damned fine job of it," Drew told the chief. "But I was just about to call a military escort for her."

"I thought I had a military escort," Melanie contradicted.

"Could be."

By the time they headed outside, the crowd had obeyed Angus's orders and dispersed. "You want me to have some of my guys go home with you, check out your clinic tonight, Dr. Harding?" Angus asked.

"I'll make sure she gets home safely," Drew said from behind her.

What about what *she* wanted? "Thanks," she said to Angus. "But I'll take the major up on his offer."

She felt even more appreciative when the others from the base, including Grunge, walked her back to her clinic and inside, to ensure there were no unwanted visitors. Then they walked her home. When everything checked out, Seth, Jonas and Patrick said goodnight and led Grunge away.

"You sure you'll be okay here alone tonight?" Drew asked as they stood inside, near her closed front door.

"Are you offering to stay?" She poured irony into her tone even as her body ignited with the idea of this man staying the night. What if he said yes? Would she agree?

That could only lead to trouble.

"Do you want me to?" he countered.

"No." The word erupted from what was left of her good sense.

"Fine." But he didn't leave. Instead, he looked down at her. His amber eyes seemed to stare through her, to her soul. Setting it on fire.

Setting her on fire.

Or was that a factor of the searching heat of his lips as he bent and touched them to hers? The penetration of his tongue into her mouth as she returned his kiss, hard and hot and suggestive in its slow thrusts and parries. One of his firm hands cupping her breast, he moved a thumb back and forth against her nipple until she nearly cried out with wanting more.

Did she want more? Did she even want this? She couldn't think. Reason had been replaced by the ache for his touch elsewhere. Everywhere.

Except…he suddenly pulled back.

His expression had gone cool. Distant. "Goodnight, Dr. Harding," he said. "Sleep well."

And then he was gone.

Locking the door after him, Melanie felt anger mix with frustration. And confusion. What had caused his abrupt change of mood?

She stifled the urge to open the door again, just so she could slam it and symbolically banish Major Drew Connell from her evening. From her life.

She'd treat his injured dog, if needed. Of course.

But after that, she vowed never to see him again.

Chapter 9

Drew's head hurt. Plus, it spun as if he had chugged an entire bottle of vodka. Rotgut.

Not a good way to be driving. Especially on twisting country roads, in the dark. Accidents happened here. Fatal ones, and not just the one that had killed Angie's husband. A local died only a year ago, soon after Drew had arrived in the area.

Things would be pretty damned bad now, if he didn't make it back to the base soon.

He leaned forward to watch the pavement shimmer and bounce as his SUV swerved slowly from side to side.

Too bad he wasn't simply drunk on sharing that explosive kiss with Melanie. He wished he could have continued. Allowed things to progress. Let his body rule his mind. It argued with him all the time to do that anyway.

Good thing Melanie didn't know who he really was

yet. What he was. He'd never have engaged in a battle of lips with her. Battle of wits? Whatever.

She'd have doubted her own sanity. And he'd have backed off. Way fast. Wouldn't trust her. He didn't trust any regular, normal woman. If there was such a thing. They didn't keep secrets. They wanted to profit from secrets.

As a tree walked into his path, he slammed on his brakes. Oh, yeah. Something was definitely wrong.

Not only was he dizzy, his bladder felt suddenly and extremely full. And every noise around him was amplified from its usual loudness into a sharp, keening blade that sliced at the inside of his skull.

He scowled at the tree. It stayed where it was as he pulled around it. Drove slowly off.

And within another five minutes saw the welcoming entry to Ft. Lukman.

He pulled up to the guardhouse. Dropped his wallet on the floor as he fumbled for his ID. Good thing the guard recognized his car. And him. Drew's vision was too blurred to make out who was on duty that night. "Go on in, Major."

Fortunately, his place was not far from the entrance. He saw the officers' quarters building loom to his right. In duplicate. He carefully drove into the parking lot and found a spot—two spots?—and pulled his SUV in.

And sat there, holding his head, for…how long? Not even the first time he had gone through the transformation had he been in such agony. And that hadn't been any picnic.

When next aware of what he was doing, he fumbled with his key in the lock to his digs—a nice-sized apartment allotted to officers of his rank. Where had the key come from? Probably his pocket. Had he changed, then come back? He studied his hands. No indication they had been anything but human tonight. No telltale strands of hair. No curving, like paws, to be straightened.

So what was going on?

Usually, he did a quick check of the lab on returning to base, no matter what time it was. Tonight, he'd never make it. He'd call one of the other guys to do an ad hoc inspection. Might be a good thing anyway, get another set of eyes and ears, another nose, to ensure all was well.

He fumbled his way inside his apartment and closed the door. "Grunge?" he called. Jonas and the others, when they brought his dog back to the base, always let him into his quarters. They had the key, just for that reason.

But Grunge didn't come out to see him.

"Grunge?" Drew called again. The rottenness of how he felt hadn't changed, but now he was also worried.

Before he could start his search, though, he headed for the bathroom. He needed to relieve himself. Badly.

In a minute, he stumbled back into the hall. It was empty, well lit, as always at night. All doors were closed. Someone had cooked with garlic that day. The others like Drew would rag on that person in the morning. He should have known better.

Drew tried to walk a straight line, but rammed his shoulder against the wall. Went on, then heard the door behind that wall open behind him. "Major? Drew?" The voice was familiar, but Drew was unsure whose it was. "Are you okay?"

"Hell if I know. Need to see Jonas. Seth. Patrick. Find Grunge."

The shadowy, duplicated figure with him resembled one of the female officers, Lt. Nella Reyes. She was in Alpha, too. Sleek and smart, she was all feminine. Feline. And when she changed, she became a lynx.

Her sand-toned hair was mussed now, and she wore a white robe tied about her waist. Must have been sleeping.

Drew should be sleeping, if he could close his eyes with all the pain.

But first…Grunge.

"We'll find him, Drew," Nella said. "Get back inside, Sunshine." She was talking to the large golden cat that appeared beside her. Or was that *her?*

Drew felt her arm go around his back, and when he nearly stumbled she helped to support him.

Jonas's quarters were down this long hall and around a corner. Usually seemed close. Tonight it felt like a twenty-mile marathon.

Drew made it. Leaned on the wall as Nella knocked. Waited. "I don't think anyone's—" She stopped, listening.

Drew's senses were as acute as always, despite whatever had happened to him. Maybe more so. He heard a whimper. Nella reached into the pocket of her robe and pulled out a cell phone.

"Security? This is Major Reyes. I'm in the officers' quarters, near Unit 19. Send someone *now.*"

Turned out they'd all been drugged—Jonas, Patrick and Seth, too. Not Grunge, at least, Drew thought as he dragged himself into the shower of his quarters a few hours later and turned the water on hot and fast so it spewed loudly out of his custom showerhead. He stood on the bland beige tile, trying unsuccessfully to wash away the night's turmoil.

Grunge had been with Jonas, and had been temporarily placed into the base kennel with the other K-9s when the medics showed up. So was Duke, Patrick's dog.

Now, Grunge was back with Drew, pacing and whining through the apartment, as if he understood that something bad had happened that night.

Good dog, Drew thought as the water pelted his back. He lathered up a wash cloth and rubbed the rough terry-cloth hard against his bare skin. Too bad he wasn't going to change that night into his alternate form. If he did, he'd be able to communicate on some enhanced canine level with Grunge. Assure him things were all right now.

Nella had gotten the four of them transported to the base hospital. That's what they called their medical facility, the size of a two-bit infirmary but equipped with some of the most high-tech equipment there was. Had to be, with all that went on at the lab building way off in one forested corner of Ft. Lukman. That was where Drew brewed his concoctions, a combination of ancient herbal potions developed by his family over centuries, mixed with complex modern medications utilizing the breadth of sophisticated twenty-first century pharmaceutical knowledge.

In the early morning hours that day, the four of them had puked their guts out, thanks to the combo of antidotes to the substances, which Nella, a doctor like Drew and Patrick, determined from the blood tests, were most likely to blame for the symptoms all evinced: dizziness.

Blurred vision. Dehydration. And pain—a whole bundle of it, right where it hurt worst, their heads.

Fortunately, whatever they'd ingested wasn't lethal. The suspected substance was an overdose of a diuretic combined with something else yet to be determined. Emptying their bodies of fluids so fast could lead to the dehydration symptoms they all exhibited. They'd observe whether there were ongoing effects.

Drew sure as hell hoped not.

He finished his shower and turned off the water. He had already rinsed his mouth but would do it again before hitting the sack, to get rid of the rest of the sour taste. He hoped.

Also fortunately, none of the townsfolk they'd been around that night had apparently suffered similarly. One of the base's enlisted men had been designated to check with the nearest civilian hospitals and urgent care facilities, but there'd been no admissions of anyone with the same kinds of symptoms.

And Drew had been coherent enough to instruct the private to call Dr. Melanie Harding, make sure she was unharmed, and, if she was okay, make up a story behind the inquiry to be sure she didn't dash to the base. Ask if she was available to treat a veterinary emergency that night.

According to the private, she had sounded as if she had been awakened, but she was clear-headed and had asked cogent questions. And was angry to have been awakened when told her services would not, after all, be needed.

Drew grabbed a large white bath towel off the nearby rack and rubbed himself down. Grunge wandered back into the room and looked at him, then whined.

"I'm okay now, boy," Drew said. "Thanks for checking." Their communication wasn't like conversation even when Drew was in wolf form, but it was better than this. Now, he had to use educated guesses about what was on the canine's mind.

A short while later, Drew settled into his bed with its stiff mattress and sheets that smelled like citrus laundry detergent. Grunge leapt up beside him and settled in, whining once more.

Despite how exhausted he was, Drew didn't fall asleep immediately. His mind raced.

The night's events had raised a lot of questions. What was the source of whatever he and the others had ingested? *Who* was the source?

And why?

Why had no one else, apparently, also been drugged?

How could Drew find answers without enlisting Angus Ellenbogen's assistance? If this had something to do with the covert activities on the base, no way should outside authorities be involved.

Besides, Ellenbogen had been at the diner. That made him a suspect.

Angie Fishbach seemed most likely to have poisoned them. She was overt in her dislike of werewolves, and they had belittled her concerns. Only, if it were she, and that was the reason, why hadn't she harmed Melanie, too? The lovely veterinarian had been the one to demonstrate how the injured Grunge was not Drew's alter ego, and she had correctly sworn that Drew was the man she had seen when she first looked in on Grunge the next morning.

Who else? One of the fruitcakes who'd been at the

town hall meeting and then at the diner? That would include the local Nolan Smith, and his buddy Mike Ripkey.

And Carla Banyan had been hanging out with them, a groupie to this oddball bunch of supposed werewolf seekers. But why would she poison anyone at all, let alone the guys from the base?

Unless… She obviously had a thing for Patrick, and he wisely wasn't buying. Could this be a ploy for attention?

Then why drug all of them?

Drew had also recognized a couple of technicians he had seen at Melanie's clinic. And—

He realized his eyes had closed despite the way his head spun. He wouldn't solve this tonight. And his body was way too exhausted to do anything but sleep right now.

His last thought, before drifting off, was of that kiss he'd shared with Melanie the night before, and all it had done to this now aching body.

She, too, was at the diner. Could she be a suspect?

She was a human being, wasn't she? As enticing as she was, she had been humiliated because of claims of what Grunge was. And what he, Drew, allegedly wasn't.

He knew how civilian women, faced with this kind of inexplicable situation, tried to turn it into something they could understand.

Could use. No matter at whose expense.

Damn. Maybe he had been used again, despite all his intentions to stay far from any woman who wasn't part of his real life.

The last—and only—time that had happened, the woman he'd thought he loved had been shocked to hear what Drew was…at first. And then she'd determined to profit from his secrets.

Until he had convinced her he had only been testing her love with his outrageous supposed confession of shapeshifting. And she had failed.

Fortunately, she had never seen him change. Angry, she had disappeared from his life quickly, without selling to the media the story that he had withdrawn and ridiculed.

Thinking about her, Drew pounded a fist into his top pillow, startling Grunge, who whined yet again.

He would find out, tomorrow, what was going on around here.

He knew part of it nearly right away, when he entered his lab in the morning.

Chapter 10

Drew managed to wake early the next morning thanks to Grunge, who took a quick romp outside.

Still groggy and uncomfortable, Drew showered once more in an attempt to clear his fuzzy mind. He needed to use his brain again. Get it working on problems with his latest formulation—enhancing his, and his fellow shapeshifters', sensory abilities to beyond feral levels, even while in human form.

While he was at it, he'd hopefully alleviate the worries creeping around the corners of that same troubled organ, thanks to last night's events.

He fed Grunge, then got damp again as, wearing his standard camouflage army combat uniform, he tromped through a spring shower. The lab building was on the far side of the base. Few other soldiers were out that early on a Sunday morning. Only a couple of cars sloshed by on the streets as he walked on wet sidewalks and beneath the dripping, overhanging tree branches. He reached his destination quickly.

First, he checked on the K-9s on the upper floors. All the mutts looked fine, already cared for that morning by their handlers. Drew headed downstairs.

Unsurprisingly, he was first to enter the lab that morning.

The others were probably smart enough to be sleeping off the residual effects of what they had ingested. Maybe they wouldn't come here at all today, since it was Sunday.

Drew's sense of the importance of his project—not just for himself and others like him, but for the country—drove him. Kept him at it nearly every day. Maybe 24/7, if he counted the time his mind focused on the issues, attempting to solve them.

As always, he checked to ensure that the clean room was locked and remained uncontaminated. It was. Then he looked at the pre-mixed medicines he had stowed in the small refrigerator beneath one of the main lab's metal counters, to ensure they, too, were secure.

No problem there, either. Time to get to work.

He sat at his small desk in the corner and prepared to boot up the computer…except that it was already on, in sleep mode. As he touched a key, it sprang to life. The wallpaper on the screen was a bland U.S. Army standard. Nothing classified showed. But the machine had been tampered with. Drew was sure he had shut the computer down properly the day before, as always.

Damn! Had whoever had drugged them done it to cause a distraction so he—or she—could get into the lab and hack into the computer?

He entered his password—a complicated one, case sensitive and filled with random letters and numbers—and quickly checked the files. Only those he'd been using appeared on the menu of those accessed recently. But that didn't mean someone else hadn't opened them. Or knew the way to stop other files from appearing on the list.

Drew ran a security scan. No viruses or bombs, real or e-version, showed up.

In fact, everything appeared fine. But he and the others had been drugged. And someone had been here. To assume the two were unrelated coincidences would be naïve and foolish.

Drew was neither.

He picked up the secure telephone on the desk and pushed in a number. "General? We have a problem."

There weren't many appointments scheduled for early that Monday morning. Melanie's first patient, a pit bull mix brought in for shots, had just left. No one else was in the waiting room except Carla, at the reception desk. And Astrid, one of the technicians, was in the back.

This was the opportunity Melanie had hoped for.

Before stalking out to confront her assistant, she pulled a pen from a pocket of her white lab coat and finished the notes on the patient's chart. This gave her the opportunity to think through what to say.

No need for this to be a confrontation, just a fact-finding mission. One that would also provide a little oblique criticism that she hoped Carla would heed.

Besides, she reminded herself, part of her irritability this morning was because of the interruption to her sleep caused by that dumb phone call last night. Who on earth would get her adrenaline churning by claiming to have a veterinary emergency, only to end it by implying it had been a practical joke?

Was this another punishment for her having allegedly saved the life of a werewolf? At least, if phone calls were as bad as it got, she could deal with it.

Of course she appreciated the backup Drew and his fellow officers had given her last night. She had certainly appreciated their company, both at the town meeting and afterward.

Most especially afterward. And most especially Drew. She really had to get her head on straight about the sexy major, though. Okay, so she was attracted to him. But she was too smart to let a kiss or two make her believe there was anything but sexual awareness between them.

A *lot* of sexual awareness… So why had he left so abruptly? Was there something wrong with her?

Enough. Melanie finished her musings along with her notes and returned the file to the slot on the examining room door. Time to talk to Carla.

She kept her pace calm as she entered her reception area.

"Carla?" she said, then realized her tone mirrored her thoughts—still prickly. She cleared her throat as her assistant raised her head, looking up with hazel eyes that appeared wary. "Carla, I appreciate that you kept me informed about the people who come here chasing the werewolf legends. I know you're friends with at least one of them. That's fine, of course. Your business. But—"

"But you don't like it." Carla's small mouth curled

into a pout. Her gauzy pink top made her elfin appearance seem even more ethereal. "I understand, especially since some are mad at you. I don't think Grunge was a shapeshifter, of course. I took care of him while he was here. But the timing and all, for him to be loose and then shot like that. The SSTs are such believers, and they're so much fun to be with."

Melanie swallowed her sigh, and her urge to subject Carla to an inquisition. Like, if they believed in nonsense, *lived* it, how much fun could they be?

Instead, she said, "Well, at least this month's full moon is over with. Won't they all leave now?" she asked hopefully.

"Well, no. See, there are different versions of shapeshifter legends. In some traditional ones, like in those old *Wolf Man* movies, changing only happens during the full moon, but around here some people think the Mary Glen werewolves can shapeshift at any time."

"Oh?" Too bad. And even more ridiculous. Did the SSTs and other nutcases just make up a new thread of legend when they wanted things to follow their wishes?

"Nolan explains it on his Web site," Carla said eagerly. "Here, I'll show you."

Rolling her eyes, Melanie nevertheless entered the cubicle at one side of the reception room. Carla had her own phone extension to field calls and make appointments, and a computer to keep track of those appointments and hold records of patient bills and payments. She was organized and efficient. Her work area was, as always, clutter-free, although a cup of coffee was perched precariously on a pile of file folders.

By the time Melanie maneuvered her way behind

Carla, the Web site was on the screen. The homepage showed a woodsy scene in the rain—and in the misty distance was a form of an animal that could have been a wolf. It could also have been a dog, or a coyote, or even a large cat.

As Melanie watched, Carla clicked on a link that took her to another page with more text than pictures. "Want to sit down and read this?" Carla asked. "Nolan has researched the shapeshifter legends forever, and has information about lots of versions and where they come from. He's quite fair and unbiased, although I know he buys into the Mary Glen version more than anything."

"Which means that shapeshifters can be anywhere, anytime?" Melanie attempted not to sound as if she mocked Carla. Or Nolan, for that matter.

"Could be," Carla said. "Honestly? I don't know what to believe. But around here, with all the sightings there've been, I have to think there's some truth to the stories." Her decisive nod caused her curls to bounce. "Besides, some believers have died in strange accidents, like Angie Fishbach's husband, and some others who've hunted werewolves. One guy, Charley Drake, had a car accident, too, last year. And others, like—"

"I gathered, from the way you hung around Nolan last night," Melanie said, "that you might believe anything he told you." She didn't really want a rundown of all accidental deaths in Carla's recollection. Like Angie, people around here might accept losses better if they had someone—or something—to blame for them.

"Oh, Melanie," Carla responded in an exasperated tone. "I thought you understood. Not that I want word to get out about how I feel, but the thing is, I like Nolan a lot, and his ideas about shapeshifters are awesome. But I'd dump him in a second for Patrick Worley. I'm hoping to get his attention by pretending not to give a damn about him. He's gorgeous. And if anyone knows about shapeshifters, it's got to be him, since his mom and dad probably were werewolves."

"Then wouldn't he be one, too?" Talk about absurd. As Carla opened her mouth to reply, Melanie continued, "Come on, Carla. You worked with Dr. Worley. Did he give you any reason to think he was a werewolf?" Melanie didn't try to keep the scorn from her voice. But Carla had spent a lot of time with her predecessor vet. Did he actually give Carla—or anyone else, for that matter—reason to think he was a shapeshifter?

As ridiculous as it seemed, the answer to that had to be yes, at least with respect to *someone*. Dr. Worley had been killed by a silver bullet. And so had his wife.

"Well…not really." Carla looked down at her hands on the computer keyboard. Her fingers were slender, her nails tipped with pink polish. "But he never had an absolute attitude against them, either. He always told me to keep an open mind, that animals had more intelligence than people gave them credit for, and that sometimes people had to make a leap of faith for reasons besides religion. I suspect that he believed, even though he never really owned up to it."

Melanie couldn't fault the man's values—or at least his advice. Animals were special, sometimes more than people realized.

But sometimes leaps of faith hurled people over cliffs from which there was no turning back.

"So," Melanie said, "has Patrick Worley ever given you any reason to think he changes into a monster under the full moon?"

"Well, no, but I'm not sure I've ever seen him during one. He's always one of the guys who hangs out at the base to protect the K-9s on those nights."

"Okay, then, does he ever act aware of you as someone other than his dad's former assistant?"

"I think so." Carla smiled tremulously at Melanie. "At least I hope so. I'm going to keep trying to get his attention anyway. And if you could put in a good word for me when you talk to him next, or to Drew Connell, I'd appreciate it."

The outside door opened, and a man walked in carrying a sad-looking shepherd mix. "Can you help, Doc? He saw a cat and jumped off a wall after it. I think he broke a leg."

"Bring him right this way," Melanie said. "Carla, please call Astrid up here to help."

As she started checking the dog's injuries, her mind added one postscript to her conversation with Carla. Not *when* she talked to Drew next, but *if.*

Truth was, he had others caring for Grunge who could bring the injured dog back for a final checkup.

And the idea that there was really no reason for them to speak again made her feel even more depressed than the appearance of her new patient with the possibly broken bone.

Chapter 11

"I heard that some of you got carried away drinking last night, Major. You're sure that's not what gave you the idea someone broke into the lab?"

General Greg Yarrow, speaking in a low voice, stood stiffly in the lab's office area. His scowl carved deep wrinkles into his high forehead.

Drew remained standing near the desk, though his body, still reacting from whatever he had ingested last night and the effects of purging it, ached to sit down. "I'm not sure where you got your erroneous info, Greg," he said, "but Patrick, Jonas and Seth came into Mary Glen as my backup, not drinking buddies."

The other three were also in the lab, although out of earshot of this conversation. Also in uniform, they were carefully checking out the other areas. So far, they'd found no evidence of the identity of the intruder, or how he or she had broken in.

Drew described the town meeting. "After I demonstrated that Grunge isn't my alter ego, we all ate at the diner. Apparently we were drugged."

"That's what I figured." The general's narrow shoulders relaxed and he took a seat in one of the uncomfortable chairs facing the lab's desk. "The information, such as it was, was called in anonymously over a secure phone line that we couldn't trace back to the source."

Drew's skin prickled uneasily. "I assume you used all available resources."

Greg nodded. His long face appeared even more drawn than usual. "Best we could figure, it was a cell or computer line bounced off a satellite a time or two."

Drew shook his head slowly, even as his mind raced. "Seems odd, doesn't it, that someone with that kind of toy at his disposal…I assume the caller was male?"

"We think so, though the voice sounded electronically altered."

"Big surprise. Anyway," Drew continued, "why would someone with access to major electronics systems bother to call about a few military slobs who allegedly got drunk one night—unless, of course, that someone was the one who drugged them, and a side benefit was to discredit them with their commanding officer."

"My thoughts exactly." Standing, Greg crossed his arms. "So consider yourselves discredited, at least as far as anyone outside this room goes."

"Then you obviously won't believe that the computer has been touched at all."

"That's right." Greg pivoted to observe the rest of the

room. The lab looked fine, and most of it, apparently, was untouched. The gleaming metal wall cabinets inset with unbreakable glass were locked, as always. The metal counters were pristine, and so was the white, specially constructed floor that extended into the adjoining clean room which, fortunately, remained sealed. All drawers were closed, as was the door to the small, built-in refrigerator.

"That also means I won't spend a lot of the unit's resources finding out who broke in," Greg continued. "And that part, unfortunately, will have to be genuine, since unlike my state of mind it can be proven."

"I figured." Drew stood. "That's why I'm planning to use my own best resources tonight to help in the investigation."

"Not solely your own anymore." Greg's dark eyebrows rose wryly.

"I owe a lot to you and Alpha for all the support," Drew admitted. "The ability to formulate and test enhancements to my old family recipes is something we'd only dreamed about as I was growing up. And the additional backup is great. I appreciate it all. Sharing with this group is the least I can do."

"The military benefits, too. Or it will, once this unit is good to go." Greg took a step around the desk. He wasn't scowling now. Instead, his taut expression seemed filled with concern. "Assuming it ever is, after this. Just be careful tonight, Drew. I know things around here are never what I once would have called normal, before being put in charge of Alpha, but something's going on. Something bad. And dangerous."

"Yes, sir. Which is exactly the reason I've got to figure out who pulled those stunts last night, and why."

The change tonight had hurt his already aching body. But now, it was recon time. Time to put his enhanced senses to work.

He approached the areas that had been violated by last night's intruder.

And howled.

"What's wrong?" *asked Jonas, his backup. His handler who, as always, smelled of chocolate. That stuff would make Drew ill if he ate any, even if he hadn't changed. Chocolate and canines didn't go together.*

At the moment, he could not explain to Jonas what had set him off. But the intruder had clearly known what to do to mask any residual identifying scent. There was something slight, something vaguely familiar, but it was overwhelmed by harsh odors that took his breath away. And worse.

Perhaps, in his other form, he could have given them names.

Now, all he could do was to follow them without inhaling. Without allowing them to injure one of his most valuable assets—his incomparable sense of smell.

The ugly and painful scent trail was easy to follow, through the laboratory. Into the hallway. Up a stairway that should have been locked. Out through a window on the floor where his four-pawed fellows were housed. Among the thick growth of sheltering trees, and into a parking lot.

Where it stopped.

Had the intruder driven onto, and off of, the base?

Did the interloper have a suitable ID to get through the entry in the usual way? Or had some additional subterfuge been involved?

And was the end of the trail also the end of any possibility of his identifying who it was?

Not if he could help it.

"Now you take good care of our girl," Melanie said to Shirley Wells, owner of Diva, the Great Dane. They stood near the door in the cheerful waiting room, while Melanie discussed the friendly beige dog's favorable prognosis and future treatment. Diva, like so many of Melanie's surgical patients, wore a recovery collar, and she tried to scratch it off while sitting on the floor. Melanie had removed two tumors from Diva and, fortunately, the lab in Baltimore to which she'd sent them for biopsy analysis had found them benign.

It was late in the day, and no other patients were scheduled—which never precluded emergencies, of course. But for the moment, none of the waiting room's chairs was occupied.

Shirley, maybe mid-forties, seemed much too tiny to have a dog as large as the fortunately well-behaved Diva. "Thank you so much, Dr. Harding. I'm so relieved. Diva's like my baby—my big baby—and if anything happened to her…" Her voice caught.

"Let's hope she keeps doing this well," Melanie said. "Wait, though. I'll send you home with antibiotics, and a painkiller in case she needs it." Melanie had directed one of the technicians to the storeroom for the medications. Diva, who'd stopped scratching, sat on the floor panting, and Melanie patted the top of her smooth head, then rubbed behind her pointed ears. "You be a good girl, now," she told the dog, who licked her hand with a large, rough tongue. Melanie laughed.

"She will." Shirley knelt to hug her dog. She looked up at Melanie. "You know, Dr. Harding, even though we'd gotten a great referral to you, I had second thoughts about bringing Diva here. Over the past few days, people around here have said things about your veterinary practice that got me concerned. But you've been great with Diva, and that's all that matters."

The smile on Melanie's face froze. "Really?" she said lightly. "Who's been saying what?"

"I don't want to get anyone in trouble," Shirley said nervously, standing again. "And it just sounded like you've been busy arguing with people about what's real around here and what's not, instead of treating animals like you should. Not that I believe it, of course." She raised her hands as if erasing what she had said.

Are you one of those nutcases who believes in those nonsensical shapeshifter stories? The words sprang to Melanie's lips, but she didn't say them. Instead, she jammed her fists into her lab jacket pockets and managed to say, "Well, thanks for your support."

Fortunately, Astrid entered the waiting room. Melanie's technician was nineteen, with wavy brown hair worn in a ponytail. Her lab coat was aqua, with a dog and cat embroidered in white on the breast pocket. "Here, Dr. Harding." She handed Melanie two plastic pill bottles. Melanie studied them to make sure they contained the pills she had ordered and that the instruction labels she'd had Astrid generate were correct.

Melanie handed the bottles to Shirley. "I'll want to

see Diva again in a week to remove her sutures and check her progress."

After further thanks and goodbyes, Shirley and Diva left. Melanie, who'd forced herself to smile, let herself deflate.

"Something wrong, Dr. Harding?" Astrid's small, concerned voice nearly made Melanie's eyes water. She looked at her young assistant. Astrid had smooth, chubby cheeks and a slightly snub nose beneath small but alert brown eyes.

"I'm just a little tired, thanks, Astrid. If you're done checking our supply inventory, it's fine for you to leave."

"Great. Oh, and Dr. Harding, I just want you to know I think you're doing a fantastic job. And even though I know it's not a good thing for you to take sides, lots of people here in Mary Glen really aren't happy about the dumb werewolf legends, even if the tourists are good for our town economy."

"You don't believe in them?"

Astrid shook her head so vehemently that her ponytail lashed back and forth. "Not my family, either, and they've lived just outside town since my grandparents moved here. We knew the Worleys, too, and thought it awful that both Dr. and Mrs. Worley got killed that way. We're just glad that Patrick's around and hasn't been hurt."

"Me, too," Melanie said.

As Astrid exited, Melanie thought again about eating dinner with the military contingent yesterday. Patrick had been there.

And Drew.

She hadn't heard from him today, but why should she? Just because she thought about him a lot. And the way he kissed her. And backed off.

"Hey, Doc." Carla slipped behind her desk from somewhere inside the clinic. "I've checked the patients in the infirmary. Everyone's doing great. Okay for me to leave now?"

"Sure."

"I've got a hot date, though you won't want to know the details."

"You're right," Melanie said dryly.

"Here's a hint." She unbuttoned the yellow cotton blouse she wore over her jeans to reveal a white T-shirt beneath. It said "SSTs. We'll find the answers or flip." The picture on it showed a cartoon dog sitting on his haunches—with the head of a man baring fangs.

"Carla, please." Melanie couldn't help raising her voice. "If you want to continue working here, you can't keep encouraging that nonsense."

"I'm seeing Nolan on my own time." Carla's face screwed into a pout. "It's exciting, you know, even if it goes way beyond reality." She grabbed her purse from a drawer and tossed its strap carelessly over her shoulder. "And I'm planning to make sure Patrick hears about it."

"You think you'll get any positive attention from Patrick this way?" Melanie demanded.

"Guess I'll find out." Carla breezed out the door, leaving Melanie alone in the clinic.

And, suddenly, lonely.

At least she wasn't the only one not caught up in the weirdness around here. Maybe she should get to know Astrid and her family better.

But for the moment, she felt as if the sane were out-numbered in Mary Glen. And outside it—well, the military sorts from Ft. Lukman certainly had no love for the shapeshifter loonies.

And that group wouldn't allow her through their front entry.

Melanie sighed. Then she began her routine of locking doors and shutting off lights, until she reached her own small office.

She decided that loneliness could be used to her advantage. She had more paperwork to catch up on, an endless task. And then there were the articles online that she had intended to read.

Except, as she sat at her desk, she thought about Grunge. How was he doing? He was, after all, her patient. And doctors can always call about how their patients are progressing, can't they?

She pulled up Grunge's information that Carla had entered onto the computer. It included a general telephone number for Drew. Melanie pressed his number into the mobile handset she lifted from its cradle on her desk. It rang three times before a click indicated it had been answered. The voice was Drew's—his voicemail greeting.

Melanie took in the deep, masculine tone as she equivocated about whether to leave a message. At the sound of the tone, she nearly hung up but figured her number would show anyway, in missed calls.

"Drew, this is Melanie," she said briskly. "Just checking on Grunge again. Call me." She hung up, telling herself not to hold her breath.

It was likely to be a long time before she heard from Drew again.

* * *

Crack!

Melanie's hands jerked on the keyboard. "Oh, come on, you fools," she shouted aloud. Was this going to be another night like when she had found, and treated, Grunge?

Another night when at least one of those werewolf loonies was out shooting at anything that moved, in the hope of bagging something supernatural? Déjà vu, all over again?

She stood at her small desk, clenching her fists and listening, trying to manage her fright. No more sounds from outside, although she couldn't tell for certain, since the few dogs still in her infirmary were barking, validating that she hadn't imagined the sound. Surely, there wouldn't be another injured animal out there, left to possibly die in the gutter. But she couldn't take that chance.

Of course, the other night, when she had gone outside to look around, she had been more naïve—and better respected. Now, she might have some…well, if not enemies, at least people who realized she wasn't exactly on their side.

And a person who had threatened her. Well, okay, maybe she did have an enemy, even if she didn't know who it was.

Was the gunshot intended to lure her outside so the person who had called her could cause her harm? Shoot *her?*

Okay, what she should do was call Angus Ellenbogen.

Melanie immediately lifted the phone and called 911, knowing she would be connected to the Mary Glen Police Department.

"A gunshot?" said the dispatcher. "Has anyone been hurt?"

"I don't know," Melanie said. "I'm nervous about going outside to check."

"Good, ma'am. Stay inside. We'll send a car to take a look."

"Thank you," Melanie said.

No more than five minutes later, a Mary Glen PD car drove up. The two uniformed officers questioned her, then again urged her to stay inside while they looked around.

She watched them through the clinic's front window, then lost them as they went into the woods, illuminated partway by their squad car's headlights. They returned soon. "Didn't see anything, Dr. Harding," said the older and heavier of them. "But you be careful. If you hear anything else, or see anyone, call 911 again. We'll drive by here as often as we can tonight."

"Thanks," Melanie said. Then, feeling nervous, she got them to accompany her next door, to her home.

She was too keyed up to get ready for bed right away, so she settled in front of the TV, turning on the news.

Only, she heard sounds from somewhere outside. Not another shot. No, this was more of a scratching noise. And it sounded as if it came from behind her house.

She thought of calling 911 again. What if the person who had left the threatening phone message was here to harm her?

She tiptoed through her kitchen, to the back door, and stood there, listening, ready to grab a carving knife, if necessary, from one of the drawers near the stove.

She heard the scratching again. Shivering, she held her breath.

And then heard a whine. It sounded like an animal in pain.

Very slowly, very carefully, she cracked open the door.

And wasn't very surprised to find another large, wolflike dog that resembled Grunge lying on her back stoop. But it wasn't Grunge. This dog was even bigger, and had more of a resemblance to a sharp-muzzled, gray-and-black-coated wolf. Its injury was bloodier. The animal was conscious and obviously in pain.

Second verse, too similar to the first. Still keeping uneasy watch for movement, for someone who might shoot again, Melanie hurried next door to the clinic, retrieved the wheeled trolley from her storeroom and maneuvered this dog onto it and inside her clinic.

Again, she anesthetized the animal and operated. This time, the bullet had passed through, so she could only suppose it had been silver. This injury was nearer to the heart but hadn't done much damage.

When she had finished the surgery, Melanie was exhausted, but she kept watch over her patient while he slept, intending to call the police as soon as the anesthetic wore off and she could say with more certainty that the dog would survive.

Only, sitting in the same uncomfortable chair from the waiting room, Melanie dozed off in the operating room…again.

This time, she was awakened by a noise from the dog. She must have been dreaming, since the whimper sounded more like a human moan.

Except, when she opened her eyes, she gasped, then screamed at what she saw.

Chapter 12

As with Grunge, Melanie had left this dog in an open-topped metal crate lined with clean towels for comfort. The animal had knocked it over. Now it crouched on the floor half-facing Melanie. Its lips were drawn back in a snarl. Somehow the face had become less furry and resembled a human with teeth bared in a grimace of pain.

Melanie shook her head, trying to clear it. Her fists clenched, digging her nails into the soft flesh of her palms. Assuring her, much too horribly, that she was awake.

But no way could she be seeing what she thought she was.

She had used surgical tape to attach a bandage over the area where she'd operated, but it now hung partially off. The skin beneath was also hairless. Of course she had shaved fur away to better disinfect and treat the area, but that trimmed area had somehow grown to a much larger patch of bare flesh.

In fact, even as she watched, the fur on this creature seemed to be sucked back inside its skin until it was nearly smooth. But that wasn't all. The very limbs of the dog were changing—growing fuller. Thicker. Longer.

"What…what are you?" Melanie's voice quivered as much as the rest of her. She feared she knew the answer only too well. Feared? Hell, everything about this situation was terrifying.

Her question might be better phrased, "*Who* are you?" And that answer she also knew, as the facial features continued to contort, then smooth into a familiar shape and size.

The whimpering moan she had heard earlier continued softly, as if in inexpressible agony. Low skitterings of canine nails on the floor turned to thumps as those limbs she saw appearing thrashed and hit the surface on which they ultimately rested. The aroma of antiseptic didn't change, but the faint scent of dog was somehow replaced by a hint of human sweat.

Terrified yet fascinated, Melanie was unsure whether her body was burning up or icy cold. She shuddered, trying hard to swallow her screams, feeling tears of fright and disbelief well in her eyes.

The legends. The ridiculous, incredible, absurd legends—they were true!

Melanie had no concept of how long she watched this extraordinary process. Seconds? Hours? When it was complete, Major Drew Connell lay prone on her surgery room floor. Naked. Under other circumstances, she might have stared at his smooth, muscular body in admiration. Even sexual attraction.

But just then, all she could do was gape at the taut muscles of his back and firm buttocks, his excellently formed legs, even as she panted like a wounded dog herself, trying to catch her breath. She couldn't even imagine what her pulse rate must be, but felt her heart thumping hard and fast inside her chest.

He started to move, then collapsed back onto the floor. "Melanie." Her name was whispered through lips that only a short while ago could not have formed a human word.

"Wh-what are you?" she managed to demand shakily.

"Guess." How could he have a sense of humor now, or imagine that she did? "Help. Please."

Oh, lord. He was probably in pain. She had operated on the dog, cleaned and sutured the wound and given him antibiotics and painkillers appropriate for the canine patient he had been. But she was a veterinarian, not a medical doctor. And whoever—whatever—Drew was, he was clearly, at this moment, a human being who had suffered the same injury as the dog had.

"Drew," she said as matter-of-factly as she was able, "I'm not equipped to handle an injury like this to a person. I'll call 911."

"No!" The word came out sharply, and he managed to turn his head and glare with amber eyes that hadn't changed much from when he was in canine form.

In canine form! Oh, heavens. As frightened as she felt, on some level she was accepting this situation as if it were normal, describing it in her mind almost dispassionately, as though she was one of the people she had—was it only minutes ago?—considered lunatics. She had to be in shock.

"I'm a medical doctor, Melanie." His voice was weak but clear. "I'll tell you what to do to help me through this until I'm stabilized enough for you to call Patrick or Jonas to come and take me back to the base."

"A medical doctor? Why didn't you tell me?" And how absurd was that question? She was suddenly extremely perturbed that he had kept secret that he was a human physician. But that had to be some kind of internal rationalization, to keep her from focusing on that other little secret. Little? Hell, it was gigantic. He genuinely was a creature she had, until now, considered a piece of utter fiction.

Well, whatever he was, he was obviously a living being. She cared for all living creatures. It was her job. Her calling. She could at least attempt to make him more comfortable.

"You're probably too heavy for me to lift," she said, trying not to stammer. "Can you get up? I don't have a bed or even a couch here that will fit you. Maybe if we get you next door…"

"I need to lie where I am right now."

She couldn't leave him on the cold floor any longer. She removed the towels from the crate and spread them on the floor, then got additional towels from shelves along the room's outer wall. Quickly, she created a bed of sorts for him. "Here," she said. "Let's get you onto this."

He managed to pull himself up, and with her help he rolled onto the towels. Now he was on his back, and she again thought of what a gorgeous specimen of male—

human male—he was. Muscles? Oh, yes. His chest, with a scattering of dark hair up the center and down his abdomen, was as well-formed as a bodybuilder's. His arms, too. And his most private parts—all human male's, and all sexually enticing, even in repose. But the two wounds in his shoulder—the entry and exit wounds—looked raw, painful and bloody.

"Drew, you really need to have that shoulder looked at." She grabbed yet another towel off a shelf and, kneeling, covered his hips. She stood near his feet with her arms crossed, carefully watching his face so she wouldn't seem to be staring—much—at what she had concealed. Apparently he noticed anyway, since the area appeared to grow beneath the terrycloth covering. He was injured. This wasn't the time for sexual awareness.

But it was there anyway.

"I'll have it looked at later," he breathed, obviously hurting, which brought her attention fully back to reality. "Patrick's a doctor, too. Right now, here's what I'd like you to do. Please." He described how to clean the wounds and tape them closed, what veterinary medicines to use and in what doses they would work optimally for people. "I've studied such things as part of the work I'm doing at the base," he told her.

And other matters relating to his health and well-being in both incarnations, she figured. How did that all work? She was full of questions. Number one, was she sane? Numbers two to infinity…but this wasn't the time to ask. One thing she couldn't help inquiring about. "Do you know who shot you? Did you see anyone?"

He shook his head slowly, and the movement seemed

to cause him pain. "No, damn it. It was dark. I was off the base, looking for..." His voice trailed off. "Never mind. But I'm aware of my surroundings when I'm...changed. My senses are enhanced, and I was watching for... I thought myself a whole lot more observant that I obviously was."

"Why won't you tell me what you were looking for?"

He didn't respond, which annoyed the heck out of her.

"Look, if you want me to help you—"

"There are things I can't talk about," he said. "National security."

How convenient. "Okay, then tell me this," she said. "What do you really do at the base, Major? And don't just tell me it's classified. Or 'national security.'"

His dark, silvering hair was mussed, and there were lines of pain around his eyes, but he smiled slightly. "You don't give up, do you, Melanie? Look, help me out here, and in exchange, I'll tell you everything I can."

Feeling insulted, Melanie shot back, "I'd never withhold help to get information."

"You're not in the military," he responded wryly. "Okay. The two aren't tied together. But please do as I ask. I'll forever be in your debt. Oh, and one more thing. As you help me get into shape for transporting to the base, see if you can come up with a way to keep the werewolf groupies and media from assuming I was a dog you treated last night that changed this morning into a person."

"But you *were* the dog I treated last night." Melanie was amazed that she could laugh, even a little.

"Yes, but let's keep that our little secret, shall we?"

And this time, when Melanie considered what she thought about men and their awful little secrets, she nearly choked.

A painful while later, Drew sat in the chair where Melanie had spent the night. His lap was draped strategically with a towel. He couldn't help watching Melanie's every move as she did as he requested, carefully wiping away the blood, then cleaning and taping his wound closed as skillfully as if she treated humans every day. The antibiotics she had on hand were not ideal, but what he needed would be available at the base.

For now, he had requested that she do a temporary patch job to keep him from bleeding more until he could get genuine human medical stitches. That was exactly what she was doing. And doing an excellent job of it.

If only he felt stronger. At least he hadn't fainted from the pain…yet.

What was Melanie really thinking, though, after seeing what she had? She acted almost accepting. Scared, yes. Even angry. Humorous. But accepting. How could she?

Well, logically, she couldn't discount what she had seen with her own eyes. And now that she knew, what would she do with that information?

The look of concentration on her lovely face as she worked gave him an urge to reach out and smooth away the frown that marred her high forehead. While he was at it, he wanted to run his fingers through her long, brown hair. She obviously hadn't intended to accomplish any further medical treatments this night—rather, this morning—so her hair was loose around her shoulders instead of fastened in her usual clip behind her head. As always, her scent was a soft combination of lavender and rose and something more exotic. Jasmine, perhaps.

And her fingers—long and slender and adept at accomplishing the medical attention he needed. He had seen her avoid staring at his bare body earlier, and, despite how badly he ached, he'd been well aware of how he had responded physically.

A bad idea, of course—even if he hadn't been shot. But no worries. Now that she knew what he was, she'd have no interest in mindless, hot sex with him. As long as she didn't intend to profit from her knowledge…

"Ouch!" he gasped as she did one final pinch to pull the edges of his torn skin together. That hurt, damn it! Not that his change had been any more of a piece of cake than usual. In fact, it had been a lot worse, since he was injured. He always anticipated the normal stretching and tearing sensation and had learned to simply slip through them. But his wounds had added another agonizing dimension. And the underlying pain hadn't eased. This additional tug had been extra agony.

"Sorry," Melanie said. "I…you're not going to nip at me, are you? That's what my patients do if I hurt them during treatment."

He turned to glower at her and found her attempting an evil, yet wobbly, grin.

"You did that on purpose," he growled, even as he stifled an urge to grab the back of her sexy, long neck and bring her closer for a kiss.

"Not really." She seemed to sober quickly. "I don't enjoy hurting any creature…er, patient. Anyone."

"I figured." He couldn't quite look away from her sad blue eyes. Not at first. But he remained in pain even after the initial shock of this last inadvertent assault ebbed, and he didn't want her to know how much. "All right," he finally said. "You've done a great job patching me. Now, can I borrow a phone? I need a ride back to my place."

"I'll drive you—to a hospital in Baltimore. Here's what I've come up with to keep your secret from the media."

Surprise shot through him. She had apparently taken his request seriously. He'd have imagined she would gladly turn him over to the media or anyone else just to get him away from her, whatever he was.

Especially if she could profit from it—like the last woman he'd cared for had tried.

Instead, Melanie had apparently given his dilemma genuine consideration. And her idea made sense. He nodded as she explained that, if anyone asked, she had found him—a wounded *man*—as she was walking home late last night. He had been coming to her place to make sure she was all right, since she had received a threatening phone call a day or so ago. And with all the craziness around here, she figured he'd been shot by one of the werewolf-chasing nuts.

As a result, after she had determined that his wounds weren't life-threatening, she did some first aid, then drove him to a place where he could receive appropriate medical treatment. Around here, someone would undoubtedly claim he was a werewolf shot in animal form, who then changed back into a human. In a more sophisticated area, that kind of nonsense would never be in question. Meantime, on their way to Baltimore, she would call Chief Ellenbogen to report this latest crime—at least as bad as the mauled tourist.

"Sounds like a hell of a good approach," he told her, feeling pleased and amazed that she was apparently willing to lie to protect him, no matter what she thought of him. "Only one change I can think of."

"What's that?" she asked, her determined expression turning wary, as if she expected him to poke holes in her plan.

"We'll have one of the guys from the base meet us on the way. I'll need some clothes when I show up at the hospital."

He enjoyed watching the flush steal up her neck and face at the latter comment. "Probably," she agreed. "At least pants. I'm not sure we can rip a shirt and smear it with your blood in a way that would prove what we're claiming happened. You wouldn't necessarily have dripped blood on the ground, and I've bandages I can show that have your human blood on them—it's different when you're in your other form?" He nodded, impressed by how her mind grasped details so quickly and thoroughly. "But maybe you simply weren't wearing a shirt when you were shot."

"And my shirt was off because…?"

"Because—well, let's change the story. You were already in my house, and we were…well, engaging in some sexual conduct. You heard a noise and went outside half-dressed. That's when you were shot."

"That'd work." And the idea of them engaging in sexual conduct…well, he must be feeling a little better, since the idea made him glad the towel bunched in his lap enough to conceal his growing interest. "But…why are you helping me, Melanie, after seeing what you did?" He wasn't sure he wanted to hear her answer.

A beat. And then… "Because you were shot. Grunge was shot. And the Worleys, and who knows who else? Unless, do…people…like you deserve it? Do you harm others, the way the legends say?"

"No!" Drew replied sharply, then inhaled as another wave of pain shot through him. When he could talk again, he said, "Look, I'll call Jonas Truro and make arrangements for us to meet with my clothes. And on our drive to the hospital, I'll tell you what I can."

None of this was really happening, of course, Melanie thought a short while later as she drove her minivan along the twisting highway north, toward the Francis Scott Key Bridge linking the Eastern Shore to the mainland. Shock? Hell, she had to be delirious. Hallucinating.

Except, beside her in the passenger seat, rode Drew Connell.

He was silent a lot of the time, although now and then she heard a sharply indrawn breath as he fought the pain of his wounds. The only light came from her headlights on the road, so she could only see a shadowy outline of his body. His human male body.

The body that had belonged to a wolfen-appearing dog when she had taken it inside her clinic.

And then had looked so gorgeous, naked, after she had watched him change from a dog to this man. No! That hadn't happened. It couldn't be real.

"Drew?" She didn't like the shrillness that had crept

back into her voice. "It's time. Talk to me. Maybe that will help keep your mind off your pain." *And make me wake up to reality again.*

"Worth a try." He spoke through gritted teeth. "So, what do you want to know? Why am I a freak of nature? Why is the legend so prevalent in Mary Glen? What do I do at the base—at least as much as I can reveal without violating its top secrecy?" The more he spoke, the less his tone sounded forced and in pain.

"That's right," she said curtly. She clutched the steering wheel even harder, watching the road carefully. Otherwise, she might run off the narrow pavement in the darkness and kill both of them.

Or could he even die at all, let alone in an accident?

"That was supposed to be multiple choice." This time Drew's voice expressed both humor and a touch of exasperation. "Which do you really want to know?"

"All of them. What would you want to know, if you were in my situation? First, though, tell me everything about…shapeshifters. Werewolves. Apparently they do exist. Why? How? And how is their presence usually kept so secret?"

Melanie braked as a reflection of her headlights glowed briefly in the eyes of a small creature at the side of the road. Another shapeshifter? Only if people morphed into raccoons as well as larger creatures.

Drew apparently sensed what she was thinking again, since he said, "Don't run over Cousin Rocky." She must have flinched, since he laughed. "Just kidding—this time. If that animal was a kindred spirit, I'm not aware of it. Besides, the only shape-shifters of my acquaintance change into wolves and large cats like lynxes and tigers, a couple of raptors, not smaller creatures. And truth be told, Melanie, I don't think I can explain everything you're asking even if I wanted to."

She aimed a brief but irritated glare at him. "Go ahead. Change the way you did, right in front of me, and then say you can't explain it. Or are you going to claim now that I was hallucinating?"

"The point is that I don't know everything, even though I've made it part of my life's work to learn it. I'll probably never find out where we come from. My current hypothesis, which is shared by most of us who've researched the area, is that we evolved in our own way just like non-shifting humans did. My family has had werewolves in it for generations, but no one has an answer about how it all began. There are all sorts of fictional works that revolve around shapeshifting as magic, or the result of being bitten by another shapeshifter, or even willing oneself into a transition. That's all hype."

"So what's true?" Melanie asked, driving even more slowly, in case more animals jumped into her path. She hadn't stopped shaking for hours, it seemed, although her trembling was less intense now. Even so, she wondered if she should be driving. But what choice did she have? He certainly couldn't.

She hazarded a glance toward Drew. He had leaned back in his seat, and his eyes drooped closed. Great. Was he going to fall asleep on her, or pretend to, so he'd have an excuse not to talk after all?

"What's true," he eventually said, "is that shapeshifting runs in families. It's hereditary. I've studied research done by my ancestors and others who went into medical fields to learn all we could about our situation. There is a shapeshifting gene, and it's dominant."

"So every time people—er, whatever—like you have children, they, too, are shapeshifters?"

"Yes. Same usually goes in mixed marriages, so to speak."

Melanie's foot twitched on the gas pedal, but she lifted it off quickly to avoid going any faster. "You mean, your kind mates—is that the right term?—with others who aren't like you?"

"More often than not," he said.

"Why would any person in his or her right mind…or are these situations where the truth isn't revealed, or at least not till it's too late?"

He didn't respond for many long seconds, and Melanie glanced at him again. His posture was now stiff. No way was he falling asleep. And when he spoke, he might as well have been growling like a real wolf. "Oh, the truth is revealed, all right. And sometimes, that's a huge mistake."

She must have hit a nerve. Had Drew been in a relationship with a normal person and been dumped when she learned what he really was? If so, Melanie couldn't help sympathizing with the woman. But she definitely could understand why, whoever that woman was, she had been attracted to Drew in the first place. In his human form. The way he was now….

"All right, so you don't know how *it* started," she said. "Explain *it*. I mean, the legends say werewolves change at night, under a full moon. Of course I didn't see you on the night of the full moon, just the morning after. Did you change then? And how did you change last night, when the moon wasn't full?"

"This is where we get close to some questions I can't answer, because the information is classified."

"Yeah, I bet the fact that you're a werewolf is classified, too. Assuming that anyone else… Hey, are there other shapeshifters at Ft. Lukman? Is that your wolf pack? Is Patrick Worley one? Were his parents werewolves? That would explain their being killed by silver bullets. But you *are* one. Why didn't you die? Oh, that didn't come out right. I'm glad you didn't die."

"Thanks." Despite his coolness of a moment ago, his smile reverberated in his tone.

Melanie had stopped at a stop sign that led to an entrance to a highway. Streetlights illuminated the area, and she glanced toward her passenger. Sure enough, there was a grin on his face.

"You sure ask a lot of questions," he continued.

"Your situation generated them."

"Yeah, I get that. Okay, Melanie, look. Let's get through this alibi scenario now. Once we do, I'll do something I never anticipated doing before—going through proper military channels to be able to disclose classified information to a civilian without top-secret clearance. But you're right. You deserve answers to a lot of your questions. One condition, though."

Still not driving forward, Melanie regarded Drew suspiciously. "What's that?"

"Now that you know what you know, I'm going to suggest taking you up on your offer to become the base's official veterinarian. There are other dogs like Grunge that could use additional care."

"What about the shapeshifters?"

"Would you like to help them while in animal form?

Because I think you could be of real assistance. And you might even get some of your curiosity satisfied. Interested, Dr. Harding?"

"Of course." But Melanie wondered exactly what she might be setting herself up for.

Chapter 13

"So how the hell did you get off the base without me seeing you?" Captain Jonas Truro demanded the next day, stopping the Army issue sedan at a red light on the way back to Ft. Lukman. After flicking on the left turn signal, he turned to glare. That didn't bother Drew, who knew his aide felt guilty about what had happened. Better that he react by grousing than blaming himself.

Even though he should have been more alert. Sure, Drew had been fully aware of what he had been doing when he had slipped through the back gate in the chain-link fence surrounding the base, but he'd thought his subordinate would remain close behind him. Watch his back, as always.

Like when Grunge was shot. Jonas had, as usual, been assigned to keep watch over Drew while he was in wolf form on the night of the full moon. That same gate had somehow been left ajar, and a couple of K-9s had gotten out—chaos on a night like that, when so many in the unit were in animal form.

Drew had, of course, gone after Grunge. At first, the pace had been leisurely, even over a long distance through the fragrant and fascinating woodlands. But at the sound of that gunshot, Drew had taken off at the speed of a pursuing wolf, leaving Jonas far behind. Drew was alone when he found Grunge and managed to drag him to the area of the veterinary clinic.

"I'd like to know how you lost me, too," Drew told him. "I wasn't attempting to elude you, especially after last time. You were with me when I picked up the scent in the lab. I figured you'd follow me as I tracked it into the parking lot."

"I did." Jonas's frown seemed to age his otherwise young face, pleating a forehead exaggeratedly high thanks to his nearly clean-shaven head. "And I watched you leave the parking lot. Thought you were going back inside, but then I saw you head toward the lot behind the BX. Only it wasn't you. It turned out to be one of the K-9s that had gotten loose." He scooped a chocolate kiss from where he'd put a bunch on the dashboard, unwrapped it and stuck it in his mouth.

"If you've seen one K-9 pack member, you've seen us all, right?"

"Yeah, after a night of dizziness and puking," Jonas admitted. "Next time, don't initiate a change to take advantage of all those enhanced senses of yours till I'm at my best."

"Fine, if whoever broke into the lab is nice enough next time to wait till the mood suits you."

"So how'd you get off the base this time? And why the hell did you go all the way to Mary Glen?"

"I went through the back exit, along the dirt road till it entered the highway. Didn't know you weren't behind me." Of course, he hadn't checked. He knew that someone had gone to a lot of trouble to get onto the base, then disguise his—or her—scent in a painfully odiferous manner most likely to sour a canine on following it.

Only…the trail had led to a parking space where a vehicle had been dripping oil. And that was the scent Drew had followed off the base. Along roads, both paved and not, toward Mary Glen.

Until he lost it. And was shot.

Drew settled back into the passenger seat and closed his eyes, exhausted and hurting. He wasn't used to being a passenger as much as he'd been since last night. He preferred driving. But that only worked well when he could see straight. And at the moment, while he was pumped full of painkillers and antibiotics, being a passenger beat running off the road.

He had stayed overnight at the hospital after Melanie brought him in yesterday. It was part of his cover story. Shapeshifters surely couldn't be treated the same medically as any ordinary human being. At least that would be their argument if anyone tried to assert that he'd been brought into Melanie's clinic as a wounded dog and left as a wounded person.

The truth? Fortunately, his secret was unlikely to be revealed in the hospital stay. Shapeshifters in human form were regular people, with normal blood and body parts. Difference appeared genetically, though. Research was a continuous process, refined as technology improved, and always conducted covertly. What was know so far was that the DNA of the shapeshifters appeared to contain extra, dynamic chromosomes that resembled some from the kinds of creatures they shifted into.

It was now late afternoon. Melanie had left early that morning to return to her clinic for its regular hours and give a report of the shooting to Chief Ellenbogen.

The shooting of an unarmed man by an unseen sniper.

"You doing okay?" Jonas eventually ventured.

"Well enough, all things considered." They were nearing the fort now, and Drew's mind spun with all he had to accomplish.

Like convince the C.O. to make Melanie part of their team. General Yarrow would get it, but he wouldn't like it.

Melanie had seen him change, and he'd not been able to do a damned thing to prevent it. Surprisingly, she hadn't gone mad with terror or horror. Had even accepted it—maybe.

Damned admirable woman. Too curious for her own good? Maybe. Even so…

She was the only non-shapeshifter besides Alpha team members who had ever watched him in transition. She had taken it amazingly well.

They could use her services as a veterinarian, which she had already offered.

That way, they could also keep an eye on her. Convince her to keep what she'd seen to herself—or get a feel for whether she intended to take advantage of her knowledge, tell the world.

That possibility gnawed at his gut.

Been there, done that, he thought—and put an end to it in time. At least his ex hadn't seen the real thing. He'd merely told her about it. And when she'd threatened to sell the story, he'd laughed that she had believed the "lie" he had told to test her, then dumped her like a bucket of sewer water.

"Anyhow, I'm sorry," Jonas mumbled. "I shouldn't have let you out of my sight." He pulled the car up to the entrance, and the familiar guard in the kiosk waved them in. "Good thing silver bullets aren't what those damned stories claim they are to shapeshifters. Otherwise, you'd be toast. Literally."

"Well, they still hurt like hell," Drew said mildly. "And it came awfully close to the heart—which would have been the end." He figured that was one of the many things that stoked Melanie's curiosity—how he had survived, since to her he probably really seemed the stuff of legends. He'd have to ponder just how much to tell her, assuming he was given clearance to tell her anything.

Or whether he would do it anyway.

He left Jonas returning the car to the motor pool. Fortunately, he got in to see Greg immediately. The general waved Drew into a soft leather chair facing his mahogany desk. Drew sank into it gratefully. He was tired. And sore. Still in jeans instead of his uniform.

And not particularly looking forward to this meeting.

The general stood beside the U.S. flag near his office window. He wore a formal uniform that suggested he had visited his Pentagon office earlier that day.

He had known, of course, that Drew intended to take a dose of the current generation of tonic that allowed shapeshifting when the moon was not full. Measures beyond normal investigation or recon had been urgent due to the lack of clues about who had broken into the lab.

"Okay, so you accomplished your change and followed the scent trail. Any success?"

"Yes, as far as it went." He described finding the fresh oil smell and tracing it all the way to Mary Glen. "I was jazzed, felt I was hot on the trail. But I figure now that it all was a setup."

"You mean that whoever broke into the lab intended to lure you to Mary Glen to shoot you? Seems a stretch."

"Yeah. But nothing appeared to be missing. The only indication was the computer abnormality. There had to be a reason for the break-in. And the trail wasn't hard to follow."

Greg, in his leather desk chair, folded his arms, his long face pinched and irritable. "What's your plan to figure all this out?"

Drew's turn to frown. "What plan? I need to finalize the latest form of tonic and let the others try it, too. The trail, such as it is, will be cold by then. But there's something else we need to talk about: Dr. Harding. We can enhance the cover our regular mutts provide to Alpha's mission by having a vet make scheduled visits…and at the same time we'll get a veterinary view of our situation when in animal form."

"So you've decided the vet can be trusted?" The general's tone was clipped, his expression skeptical.

"Affirmative—maybe. If nothing else, I need to ensure her discretion. She was present when I changed back to human form yesterday."

Greg glared at him. "Bad move, Drew."

"No choice in the matter, considering the condition I was in. She took good veterinary care of me when she figured I was all dog. And later, though she had to be freaked out after watching me change, she helped me work out a cover story. But I had to promise her a better explanation than I've given so far."

The general rose. "If you're asking my permission to tell her more, it's not like you've left me a choice, Major."

"Not my choice, either, Greg," Drew said stonily. Trust her? Hell, he trusted no one. But so far, Melanie hadn't pushed his mistrust button overly hard. "If we expedite her security clearance and bring her on board, we can also make it clear what the penalties are for breaching that security."

"Do what you have to." The general sounded resigned. "I want to meet her as soon as possible. And I'm relying on your opinion."

Drew exited the office, churning with ambivalence. Yeah, he'd see Dr. Melanie Harding again. Despite how attracted he felt, that might be a damned bad decision. He'd even vouched for her—sort of—with the general.

With his track record of relying on the wrong people, he could only hope he wasn't about to endanger not only himself, but all of Alpha.

"That reporter June Jenkins is still in the waiting room." Carla stood outside the examination room Melanie had just exited, arms folded and face glum. "She won't leave till you talk to her."

"Or until Chief Ellenbogen gets here," Melanie said. "He'll throw her out." She hoped. But she had been back at the clinic seeing patients for a few hours, and so far the only cops who'd been there were a couple of Angus Ellenbogen's subordinates. They'd asked numerous questions and acted as if they didn't believe even a fraction of her answers.

Shoving her fists into the pockets of her lab coat, she wondered if they'd have accepted what she said better if she'd told them the truth. This was, after all, Mary Glen. Home of wild werewolf tales.

She swallowed hard. Never—until last night—had she imagined any were true.

"Any idea when Angus is coming?" Carla sounded as dubious as Melanie felt.

"Soon, I hope." She'd been told he'd stayed in Annapolis overnight after attending a meeting for state police chiefs in Maryland's capital. That had been a good thing, since he hadn't come right away when Melanie called the station this morning to report last night's shooting. If he had arrived immediately, asking questions, pressing her about the story already circulating in Mary Glen that there'd been another dog shot rather than a person, Melanie might have a harder time covering for Drew.

Why did she even want to cover for him?

Heck, she knew exactly why. She was attracted to him—really attracted and turned on by him as a human being. And the fact that he was so different, *not* so human…well, how could she accept that?

She couldn't. And yet, what choice did she have? She had promised to help him.

Even so, under these circumstances, how could she? And would her mind ever clear of this confusion?

"Want me to call the police station again?" Carla

asked. "Tell them to send someone else to chase that reporter off?"

"I'll deal with her," Melanie said, thrusting aside, for now, how conflicted she felt. "You check on how Astrid is doing with cleaning the storeroom shelves."

"In other words, stay back here so I don't get interviewed, too?" Carla seemed to pout. "Are you afraid I'll spout some of Nolan's stuff?"

"No use taking any chances," Melanie said lightly. When Carla stomped off down the hall, Melanie headed toward the reception area. She grinned when she spotted Keeley Janes sitting there with her Yorkie. "Hi, Keeley," Melanie said, relieved to have a fun diversion. "How's our new mama doing? And the pups?"

"The babies are thriving." Keeley beamed. Matronly, with her pudginess emphasized by the tightness of her Baltimore Ravens T-shirt, she looked like a doting grandma. "But poor Missie is getting sore from their sucking. Is there anything I can rub on to make her feel better?"

As Melanie discussed possibilities for easing the puppy nursing process with her patient's owner, she stole a glance toward the far end of the reception area. A familiar woman in a bright red suit sat there, unabashedly listening. Acting like a reporter.

Melanie ignored her until she sent Keeley and Missie on their way with some healing salve to rub onto the sore mama dog. And then she approached the grinning woman, who stood and held out her hand. "Dr. Harding? I'm June Jenkins, with the *Maryland Reality Gazette*. I interviewed you before."

"I recall seeing you," Melanie admitted with a frown, "but I'm not familiar with that publication."

"The *Gazette* isn't large, but we're growing," June said. "Well-respected. We syndicate our articles, plus they're available online." She handed Melanie a card.

Melanie wondered if this reporter also did television news, since the amount of makeup she wore seemed over-the-top. She might have been attractive, if not for all that pink blush emphasizing her high cheekbones and the dark purple shadow around her eyes.

At least she was here alone.

"Not that I'm complaining, but how come you're the only one here? The other day, there were hordes of reporters bombarding me with questions and they wouldn't leave."

"You also didn't say much that they found interesting," June chided. "I talked to a couple after we got word that you treated another dog that had been shot, and they yawned. Not me. Tell me, did that *dog* turn into a person in daylight?" She had a personal digital assistant in her hand—recording this conversation, Melanie felt sure.

"I don't want to be interviewed, and certainly not recorded," Melanie asserted. "But at least get your basic facts correct. I did not treat a dog or any other animal last night. However, I did assist a man who had been shot by some imbecile who'd apparently used a silver bullet." She looked June Jenkins straight in her skeptical brown eyes. "Now, please excuse me, I have patients to treat." She turned her back.

Good thing liars' noses didn't really grow, as Pinocchio's did, or her muzzle would be as long as a...wolf's.

She swallowed her own ironic snort, happy to hear the clinic's door open behind her. Good. Was the reporter leaving?

She turned to check and saw Chief Angus Ellenbogen entering the reception area. June Jenkins strutted up and introduced herself.

"I know who you are," said the police chief. "And right now, I'll have to ask you to leave. I need to speak to Dr. Harding alone."

"I'll just wait outside, then, and—"

"This may take a while. You can return when Dr. Harding invites you."

Melanie shot him a grateful smile. "Certainly, Chief. I'll see you…oh, let's see. How about when hell forms an ice hockey team? Goodbye, Ms. Jenkins."

"I'll see you a lot sooner than that, Dr. Harding." The reporter flounced out.

It didn't take long, though, before Melanie half wished she weren't alone with the police chief. Where was Carla now that Melanie wished she'd barge in as usual?

They both sat in waiting room chairs as the chief asked questions. He seemed to doubt her answers. She'd thought he was smart enough not to believe in those— supposedly—ludicrous werewolf stories. But this afternoon, she wondered what he really thought as he went over and over the same information.

"You say you called Major Connell because you were nervous after hearing what you thought was a gunshot?"

"That's right, Angus. Your officers were very kind, the way they looked around, but they didn't see anything. After the night I treated the major's dog Grunge for a gunshot wound, I knew he would understand, so I asked him to come over…and, well…we've become kind of close…." She felt her face redden. Had she forgotten anything? She would have to claim that Drew drove up sometime between cop patrols and parked his car in her fortunately two-car garage. And later, some guys from the base drove it back.

"So, the major was here, you heard some other noise and he went outside?"

"That's right." Would the timing work? This story would presuppose the sound of two gunshots. But she was the only one who reported hearing any.

"And the two of you were having sex?"

"That's not what I said." But she had implied that the act wasn't far from their minds at the time. And the thought of having sex with Drew…well, even if it wasn't something she felt comfortable talking about, the idea sent bolts of lightning through her body.

"But you did say he wasn't fully dressed."

"Why ask, when I've already told you the answers?"

"Then you do have something going with the major?" Angus Ellenbogen might resemble his easygoing bloodhound Jasper, but his personality was all bulldog. He wasn't going to let this go in any manner that would let Melanie keep a shred of dignity.

Should she tell him the truth—and let him think her crazy, instead of sex-starved?

"I've said enough, Chief," Melanie said. "The people you sent—the investigators? They examined the room where I took Drew and gave him first aid before driving him to the hospital. They took blood samples—" from an area she'd designated where she could be sure they were the human Drew's "—and also looked around outside for any evidence of the shooter. Why don't you go talk to them? I've said all I'm going to."

They hadn't found the bullet. She had…after Drew told her just where he had been when he was shot. Tampering with evidence? Sure. But she couldn't exactly leave it where it was and allow the crime scene folks to have the blood on it tested and determined to be canine…or whatever its analysis would reveal for a shapeshifter in animal form. She had hidden it until she could clean it.

"Well, Doc, we'll see if we need more information from you. But we're through for now. I'll call on your friend the major, though. He was shot here, on my turf. The case is mine."

"Next time I talk to him, I'll tell him what you said."

Melanie was glad to see the chief go. Only then did Carla and Astrid enter the reception room. "We couldn't help overhearing you," Carla said, her hazel eyes sparkling.

"It's not really our business, Dr. Harding," Astrid said, but the young technician smiled broadly. "But…well, that Major Connell is hot. Is he as good in bed as he looks?"

"If you two want to keep your jobs," Melanie said through gritted teeth, "drop the subject. I had to talk to Chief Ellenbogen because there was a crime committed last night. I don't need to discuss this with you." Melanie shouldered past them and slammed her office door behind her.

And sagged against the wall.

Her life had suddenly become a morass of tiptoeing around subjects she would never have even thought of addressing before: her sex life.

Her belief, or lack thereof, in the stuff of legends. Shapeshifters. Real ones.

And sexy Drew Connell.

She would be a hell of a lot better off if she simply forgot what she had seen. Had she even seen it? This far removed from last night, she wondered if she'd dreamed it all. Had a nightmare, from which she had still not completely awakened.

If she truly had been having sex with Drew Connell, would she still think it had been a nightmare?

Yes, her mind shouted, even as her body tingled at the thought.

Well, one way or another, she had to get past all this. She had one more patient scheduled for that afternoon, in a quarter of an hour. Then she could go home. Better yet, go for a drive away from Mary Glen. Eat dinner by herself, maybe in Baltimore's Inner Harbor. Yes, that would be—

Her phone extension rang, and Melanie picked up the receiver. "Dr. Harding here."

"Melanie?" She recognized the deep, husky— sexy—voice immediately.

"Hello, Drew." She put more strength into her tone than she felt. This man, or whatever he was, was wreaking havoc on every aspect of her life. "How are you? Are you still at the hospital?"

And are you still in human form?

"I'm back at Ft. Lukman, and I'm calling to invite you to join me here for dinner tonight."

"Oh, I'm so sorry, but I have other plans," she lied, even as she kicked herself for rejecting the invitation. Damn it all, but she wanted to see him again.

To squeeze his arm and see if he was real?

"That's too bad," he said. "I've gotten clearance to ask you to be the base's vet. And if you're interested, I'll want to start getting your security clearance as soon as possible. Meantime, those matters you inquired about before? I have some answers for you."

"Everything?" she demanded.

"Everything."

"I'll be there at six."

Chapter 14

"My official permission to tell you everything depends on your security clearance going through," Drew said to Melanie. "That could take weeks. Maybe months."

She nearly shouted in frustration. She had come to Ft. Lukman this evening, churning with unanswered questions. Not to mention her conflicting thoughts about Drew, and what she knew she had seen, and what she'd told everyone about what had happened. And now, he was putting her off. Why would he have bothered asking her here if he...?

Then she caught the humorous glint in his sexy amber eyes. And no matter how much her insides flip-flopped, she couldn't help smiling back.

She sat facing him at a small, round table in what passed for a food court at Ft. Lukman—a cafeteria-like setting in a room barely larger than her clinic's fenced-in yard. A few other tables were occupied, mainly by men and women wearing the familiar camouflage uniform that Drew's shoulders and chest filled out so well. There was a salad bar at one end of the room, a grill in the center, and an area where prepared foods were dished out at the end. A small beverage bar sat beside the checkout line. It served decent coffee, and Melanie had a tall foam cup in front of her.

She took a sip of the dark, strong brew, keeping watch on Drew's wry expression. Two could play at his game of teasing. "Well, in the meantime, while I'm not bound by any agreement to keep things quiet, I could sell my story. I didn't have a huge bombardment of reporters around today, just one, and she seemed very persistent. A tabloid type. I'll bet she could come up with a nice sum of money if I convinced her I had something interesting to say about the Mary Glen werewolf legends."

"Don't even think about that, Melanie." Drew's tone was abruptly stony, his look menacing.

Which made her shiver inside. There was a genuinely feral side to this man. If she got him angry, might he do something to harm her?

She didn't really think so…did she? He'd said his type didn't hurt regular people, despite all the legends to the contrary. Still, given a good motive…

"I won't tell anyone anything, as long as you keep your word and answer my questions," she said airily.

"Yeah. Right." He stood, scraping his chair against the wood floor. He was tall and straight and forbidding, and she winced at how scary he had turned in just an instant. Had she pushed the wrong button? It certainly felt that way. But he'd asked for it. "Maybe this is a bad idea."

"Maybe so," she said softly.

She, too, rose, then stopped. Something about this man really attracted her, even after what she had seen. If she left now, she would have no answers. No way of seeing him again. And a story she would have to keep to herself anyway, unless she wanted to join the lunatic fringe—or be counted as one of them.

"I won't just leave, Drew. I saw what I saw. And even though I've no intention of shouting it to the world, you owe me more explanation than you've given so far. Plus, I'm concerned about the dogs on this base. If I can help them, and…well, any other animals around here, then I want to do it. Give me a chance, will you?"

"Do I have a choice?"

How had things gone so bad so quickly? Melanie reviewed what she had said…and realized her teasing could have sounded like a real threat. "Everyone has choices, Drew." She drew closer and put her hand on his sleeve. The material felt smooth, warmed by his body heat, which made her even more aware of him, and how he aroused her without even trying. "Let's start over. Why did you ask me here this evening?"

"To enlist your help. And I know I have to trust you, whether or not I like it."

She jerked her hand away, hurt as much as if he had slapped her. "True," she said coolly. "And whether or not you believe it, I won't betray that trust. Now, show me how I can help."

She brought her cup of coffee along as he led her from the small BX and out into the chill spring air. Although the sun had set, darkness was kept at bay on the base by bright lighting along the narrow streets.

The buildings, mostly nestled among thick canopies of trees, all looked alike—low and long and generic. A few had lovely spring flowers blooming in rows in the small patches of lawn in front, mostly hyacinths.

They walked along the sidewalk until Drew led her down a remote walkway to a building nearly hidden in a corner of the compound. Melanie heard barking from inside and couldn't help smiling. Finally, a hint of the familiar—dogs.

Assuming, of course, they were real canines.

They were. There were a dozen, all large and probably well trained, kept in indoor fenced pens that seemed almost luxurious for working dogs. The gates to the outdoor fenced enclosures were shut. Each pen was fitted with a doghouse with soft, clean bedding inside, and there was room in each area for the dogs to stretch their legs. They couldn't leap over the fencing to fraternize, but they could see, smell and hear each other, so none was truly alone.

Grunge wasn't among them, and Drew explained that each of the shapeshifters had a special pet who shared their quarters, as part of their cover.

"Nice setup," Melanie said. "May I check over a couple of them?"

"That's what you're here for."

"Among other things," Melanie said dryly. But she smiled as Drew opened the nearest gate for her and the occupant, a German shepherd, approached with tail wagging.

For the next hour, Melanie examined each of the dogs. All were friendly. More important, they all seemed well cared for. They weren't hungry or thirsty, and were clearly accustomed to human company. She noticed no signs of ill health.

She knew some military facilities had onsite veterinary care for dogs trained for protection, bomb- and drug-sniffing, and other K-9 specialties. A veterinary corps even existed. But no such facility was nearby. And this base apparently wasn't regular army. Melanie suspected she now knew at least some of its unorthodox reason for existing, despite having no confirmation yet from Drew.

As a result, they might be able to use a little unorthodox assistance from a non-military vet.

Each dog received an initial and parting hug from her. She ignored Drew, except to allow him to lead her from one enclosure to the next. But of course she was always aware of him. Of where he stood. His expressive, sometimes chilling, very upsetting silence.

Then there were her own mixed emotions. She was angry with how he treated her. Angry he didn't trust her, especially when he knew she held such an amazing secret about him, one she could have already disclosed to the world if that was her intent.

But through all that—or maybe because of it—she felt a strong bond with Drew. She wanted to touch him, though not the way she hugged the dogs. The man was, in some ways, a needy animal, requiring reassurance.

At the same time, his presence pulled her to him. Was it a supernatural lure, since he was more than a man? In any event, she wanted to sink into his arms. Kiss him. More.

Eventually, she'd checked on all the dogs. There was no further reason to stay here—except that he still hadn't addressed all her questions.

Outside the door to the K-9 quarters, Melanie said, "Thanks for letting me check the dogs, Drew. And of course I'll make myself available for veterinary services. But…I want to know what you really do here."

She expected him to lie. That would have been the easy way, to tell her that he simply worked with the K-9s, and the only secret was the one she had already viewed.

Instead, he said, "You've only seen the area where our cover story is played out. You don't have clearance to see the rest."

"We've already been through—"

"Let me finish. I've already put my life in your hands in more ways than one. That's why I'll start the process for your security clearance and attempt to expedite it—but for now I'll act like you already have it and suck up any consequences. I've already run the possibility by my superior officer, and he's kind of on board. I'll introduce him to you soon. For now—well, I'll show you some answers to what you're asking—what we do, and why."

He led her to a narrow door that could have opened into a closet. Instead, it led to a stairway. At the bottom of the stairs, they stepped into a well-lit hall lined with several additional closed doors. Drew led her toward one, used a key card to open it, and motioned for her to walk in.

Melanie stepped inside the huge room, stunned. All this, in the basement of a building that was, essentially, a kennel?

She had seen a lot of laboratories during her veterinary school days, and generally made a habit of visiting the labs where her patients' samples were sent to be tested. But none compared with the technological essence of this place.

Metal counters on top of equally shiny cabinets formed a labyrinth. On top were spread all kinds of equipment, most of which she couldn't begin to identify except for the familiar electron microscopes and some obvious equipment for monitoring respiration and circulation.

"Whoa," was all she could say.

"Nice, isn't it?" Drew responded.

"I'll say. But…okay, what's it really for?"

He took her elbow. Even through her blouse and suit jacket, she felt his fingers, his heat. "Let's sit down," he said.

He led her to a compact office cubicle in a corner, neat yet not as pristine as the rest of the lab. She sat on a metal chair, and he took a seat behind the desk. He stared at her for a long moment, as if again assessing her ability to keep secrets.

"You've already seen what I am," he finally said. "This military unit…" He paused, and Melanie had no doubt that whatever he hesitated to say was of huge significance to him.

"Okay," she said quietly. "I'll guess. This unit is— well, like your wolf pack? It has others in it who are—" she swallowed "—shapeshifters. You're all here together for some mutual military purpose. Did I get that right?" She didn't pause for his answer. "Did you choose Mary Glen because you thought the silly rumors around here would keep the rest of the world laughing instead of believing?"

"Something like that." His shoulders relaxed. "It was also easier to recruit because there really are more of our kind around this area. Sometimes legends have their bases in truth."

"I see. Okay, then. You don't feel comfortable trusting an outsider with this kind of information. I get it. But if it helps, consider what life would be like for a veterinarian who publicly claimed to see little green men from outer space. Or to treat animals that suddenly turned into men, or vice versa. I mean, my background is based in science, and what's commonly believed to be reality. My colleagues', too. If I ever made such a claim, who would ever trust me to treat their pets? Or hire me to join their veterinary practices? Or even renew my license to practice?"

"You have a point. And I don't really have much choice whether to hide things from you, at least the large-scale stuff. Details are another matter. Even so…well, it won't hurt to have a pro in animal anatomy and physiology on our team. You game to jump onboard?"

"Sure." If for no other reason than she wanted to understand what was real, and what wasn't…and why she felt compelled to find reasons to remain in Drew's presence. Was that real, too? Based on some hormonal reaction to the pheromones or whatever that he gave off?

Did it matter?

"Okay, then." He paused for a moment, as if to take a deep breath before diving into the deep end of a murky pool. "Here's what's going on around here, in brief."

For the next few minutes, Melanie swallowed what was left of her astonishment as he explained that his mission was to head a special group known as Alpha Force. When fully operational, it would be sent in as a last resort in national security situations where special undercover skills were needed and more conventional methods were not successful.

The letter alpha was the first in the Greek alphabet—and Alpha Force was intended to be number one at what it did. It would in fact be the *only* military unit with the special covert ops skills its members had. Many of its operatives were werewolves. Others were shapeshifters of other sorts, such as large cats, and even a hawk was in the process of being recruited. The rest were their support, handlers who kept track of their comrades while they were in feral form and watched their backs.

"There's also a wolf-pack-psychology reason to call the unit *Alpha*," Drew continued—and his explanation was just as Melanie had guessed. "All canines vie to be the alpha—the one in control. When deployed, our unit will be undercover. It may not look like it at first, but we'll definitely take charge—be alpha to our fellow military operatives."

Drew stopped talking, as if giving Melanie an opportunity to assimilate everything. Did she believe it?

How could she not? She'd seen Drew change.

She took a deep breath, watching him. He remained alert and remote and tense. And damnably handsome.

"I understand," Melanie finally said. "And I appreciate your candor." She turned to look at the lab around them. She noticed a large window at its far side. Whatever was beyond it was entirely dark. She was all alone, in the super secret basement of a remote military base with a man who was nearly a total stranger—and who had some kind of strange body composition that turned him into an animal.

And despite all that, she was intrigued, not scared.

"If you're using your abilities to change for national security purposes, does that mean you have some control over it?" she asked.

"Yes, though not entirely. My family developed, over many centuries, a tonic that permits us to change almost anytime. We've also nearly perfected a version that allows us to maintain human consciousness while in animal form. We still change under the full moon with no control over it, but we're working on that, too, here." He gestured toward the lab.

"Then you formulate your tonic here?"

He nodded. "And study it—and us and our reactions as we modify the formulas. We intend to develop an unstoppable force of shapeshifters who can completely control the process and what we do with it." He leaned forward. "That's where you might be able to help."

She nodded slowly, even as her heart raced. While in veterinary school in California, she had participated in research projects to earn credits and tuition money. They'd involved work on inoculations against canine diseases as well as studies of genetics and aging.

She had a knowledge of lab procedures and analysis, and the use of control groups and studies. She also had a fascination with the experimental process, even though she had elected to specialize in hands-on treatment of animal patients.

"I'd like that," she said simply, then gave him a rundown of her background.

"Good stuff," he said when she was done. "I took on what research I could in medical school, too."

"How on earth could you get through that kind of

intense curriculum while not giving your…special talents away?"

"Not easy," he admitted. "I had a number of 'family crises' to tend to now and then."

"I'll bet." She grinned, and was graced with one heck of a breathtaking smile in return. She basked in it, then said, "Okay, let's discuss the nature of your current experiments and how I can help."

"Soon," he said. "We'll need to work on getting your security clearance. Because of the sensitive nature of our work, special clearance is required to be here officially."

"Okay."

He stood and approached her. "But in the meantime…."

She stood, too, wondering what was on his mind, especially with that amazingly sexy gleam in his eyes. He stopped, facing her. Close to her. She was even more aware of his height. His muscular breadth. His masculine scent—nothing but human and sensuous and appealing.

"If you happened to be romantically involved with someone here," he said in a low, throaty voice, "it wouldn't be much of a surprise if you turned up here often."

"No," she agreed, equally huskily as she studied his face. "It wouldn't."

His arms went around her, even as his mouth touched hers, softly at first, and then filled with suggestions and promises that weakened her knees.

His tongue parted her lips, parried with hers. Heat rocketed through her, from every point of contact with him, down to where they were not touching…yet. But, oh lord, she wanted him. And he clearly wanted her, too, judging by the hard pressure of him against her midsection.

"Drew," she murmured, wanting to ask where the nearest place was that they could go for privacy. Couldn't other people access this lab?

But before he answered, the silence was interrupted by the absurd sound of dogs barking to the tune of "How Much Is That Doggy In The Window?"

She pulled away, laughing regretfully. "My cell phone," she said breathlessly, then reached below the chair where she had tossed her purse.

The phone number in the caller ID screen wasn't familiar. "Sorry," she mouthed to Drew, even as she opened the phone and said, "Dr. Harding here."

"Melanie, this is Angus Ellenbogen. I'm back at your clinic. There's been a break-in."

Chapter 15

In her office, Melanie hugged Rudy, the Jack Russell terrier with the injured leg, who had been limping around loose when she reached the clinic. His recovery collar was still on, and the poor pup shivered in her arms. At least he was here, safe. So were the other couple of dogs who remained in the infirmary. Rudy had been the only one out of his enclosure. Melanie had intended to send him home tomorrow, and he fortunately still seemed well enough to leave.

Drew stood in the doorway, his angular features irate and intense, even as he appeared to hide the residual pain from his wound. Grunge, on a leash, sat obediently at his side. The military dog was much larger than the small terrier and much calmer, even as his long nose sniffed the air.

Drew and Melanie had stayed on the base only long

enough for him to get his dog from his quarters. Drew hadn't even changed from his uniform into civilian clothes. They had sped back here in separate vehicles, Melanie in the lead.

"Can you tell if anything's been taken?" Chief Angus Ellenbogen asked, his bloodhound features on alert. Someone driving along Mary Glen Boulevard had spotted Rudy running loose, and his collar had been a giveaway as to where he'd come from. The Good Samaritan had called the cops, and the patrol officers had discovered the clinic's open door. Fortunately, they had retrieved Rudy on the way.

"I-I'll check," Melanie stammered. Why would anyone break in here? This wasn't a hospital for humans. The medications she kept weren't kinds drug addicts would go after…were they?

She tucked Rudy under her arm and approached her desk. A couple of drawers were open and clearly rifled, with things hanging over the edges or on the floor below. She didn't keep anything too noteworthy there— only pens, pads of paper, some personal correspondence…

"Oh," she said as she thought of what she had stuck in the bottom of a box of doggy vitamin samples in her top drawer, for want of a better place to put it.

She gently set Rudy down on the floor and looked inside that drawer. Most of its contents had been dumped out, but the box of vitamins was still there. Alone, in the front.

Her heart sinking, she pulled it out. It no longer contained a small plastic bag at the bottom. What the bag had held was gone.

The bullet that had passed through Drew.

She had already found it. Before leaving for Ft. Lukman, she had scrubbed it, hopefully removing all blood residue that could complicate the cover story she had helped to devise for Drew.

She had intended to "discover" it and turn it over to Angus after cleansing it more carefully. She hated the idea that she'd obliterate any evidence the shooter might have left on it, like fingerprints, but it was critical that Drew not be found out.

Should she mention the missing bullet now? The chief would suspect she had tampered with evidence. If he only knew the half of it! She had intended to turn the bullet over clean and say that was how she had found it, but doubted she would be entirely believed.

If she didn't tell Angus now, the intruder was even more likely to get away with the theft.

That person just might have gotten exactly what they'd been after: proof that Drew was a shapeshifter.

"What is it?" the chief asked, obviously aware Melanie had something on her mind.

She glanced toward Drew, who watched her intently. He looked a little pale, which might be a good thing since they maintained he had been hit by that missing bullet.

He *had* been hit by it, she reminded herself. And his injuries were every bit as painful as the dog's had been—since he had been that dog. Wolf. Whatever.

She took a deep breath, then realized that, since the bullet was no longer within any semblance of a chain of custody, there would always be an argument that whoever had stolen it had been the one to "fix" it to provide evidence of whatever he or she wanted to prove.

If any slight trace of canine blood remained on it, that might not matter.

"The bullet that hit Drew," she said, shaking her head. "I found it while walking one of my patients today but I had an emergency come in and forgot about it. I'd planned to call you, hand it over, but now it's gone."

"Damn!" the chief exclaimed. He turned a suspicious scowl on her. "Why didn't you have one of your staff call me right away? I'd have sent someone to pick it up. You'll need to show my crime scene folks exactly where you found it."

"Of course," she lied. Despite her efforts, any blood residue there could be the wrong kind. Why, exactly, was she lying so much to the cops?

To save Drew's nice, firm, military—human—butt.

Besides, right now, she had no choice about lying, to save her *own* butt. She had already told so many untruths that she'd be arrested for obstructing justice if Angus ever figured it out.

"Chief, Grunge is a trained scent dog," Drew interrupted. "Let me see if he picks up anything on whoever was in here."

Melanie felt relieved that, at least for now, attention was being redirected away from her. If the chief demanded that Drew take him outside to show where he was shot, he'd be able to obfuscate the location and any evidence there, too.

She watched as Drew brought Grunge to the desk and let him smell the area. "Follow," he told the dog.

Grunge seemed to pick up a scent, then track it along the floor, out of the office, down the hall and into the infirmary. The couple of dogs still there stood in their crates and jumped around in excitement.

"Hang on, Sherman," Melanie said soothingly to the medium-sized dog being boarded for a few more days. "You, too, Wrangler," she said to the shepherd mix there for observation for a mild fever after surgery. She reached into their crates and stroked their heads. Both settled down.

Whoever had gotten in must have come through the window. Melanie usually liked that the place where she kept her charges overnight was airy and had light pouring in during the day.

Now, its large window only seemed ominous.

Drew took Grunge outside, where he again picked up the scent in the small, fenced yard. He lost it at the driveway. "Probably got into his vehicle here," Drew said. "Unless someone saw it drive in or away, we won't be able to tell who it was. Might have left prints inside, though."

Angus had already called his crime scene investigator on duty, and the lady soon arrived. She quickly determined there was no evidence she could lift from the scene.

"Dead ends," the chief said as he sat in the clinic's reception area with Drew and Melanie. "Too many of 'em. Anyway, my guys checked your house while they were here, Doc. No sign of a break-in there, at least."

No, because whoever had done this had looked in the most obvious spot for Melanie to hide what they were seeking. And of course it had been there.

Why hadn't she been more creative? Secreted the bagged bullet in the area where the animals' defecations were dumped temporarily, or someplace equally repulsive?

"You might still want to stay in a hotel tonight," the chief said, looking morosely at Melanie. "And I'd suggest you get a security system here. Hate the idea that such things are necessary in Mary Glen, but you don't want this happening again."

"No, I don't," Melanie said quietly. "But I can't go somewhere else while I still have animals here, not after this."

"Grunge and I will hang around," Drew said. "He'll let us know if anyone who doesn't belong comes back."

"But—" Melanie protested.

"Good idea," Chief Ellenbogen said. "You can call about that security system tomorrow, Doc. Meantime, having a military guy and his dog around will be a deterrent to other mischief—now that the major's on alert and unlikely to let himself get shot again. I'll also have my officers patrol this area every half hour or so. It's got to have been one of those werewolf-chasing strangers. That's what I figure. I'll go talk to them in the morning."

"Thanks, Angus," Melanie said. That was what she figured, too.

But whoever it was, the fact that they had the bullet could wind up being very damaging to Drew.

"Great job covering for me," Drew said. "I appreciate it."

They were in her house. It was nearly twenty-two hundred hours that Wednesday evening, and Melanie still looked wide awake. She sat on her bright red sofa that was covered in a fuzzy, velvety material. Her entire living room was decorated in bright reds and golds, a combination that somehow fit the dynamic, outspoken veterinarian. The aromas of the place suggested that she cooked her own meals and favored citrus-scented cleaning agents.

"Yeah, well, I'm a whiz at lying to the authorities to protect werewolves I know." Her wry smile lifted one edge of her full lips, and he laughed.

Even as he made himself sit still on the golden loveseat at the side of her oval oak coffee table. If he moved, he might grab her and kiss away both that smile and the slightly frightened look in her brilliant blue eyes.

"What do you think Chief Ellenbogen really believes?" Melanie continued. "I think he bought that I had the bullet and it was stolen, which was true. But how did he think I came across it? Or why I didn't call him immediately when I found it? Or who—or what— really was shot the night before last?"

"If he'd hinted he didn't believe it was me, I'd have shown him my wounds."

A look of concern immediately shadowed her lovely face. "You should go back to your place now," she said. "I'll be fine, and you need some rest so you can heal."

"Like I told Angus, I'm staying here tonight. Grunge, too." He looked down at the gold rug where his dog lay. Hearing his name, Grunge lifted his head and gave a couple of pants with his long tongue out, then settled down again.

Melanie closed her eyes. "Drew, I need some time alone now, to assimilate this whole situation. I've been pretending that I wasn't bothered by what I saw, but I am. You're a werewolf." She gave a short, almost hysterical laugh and covered her face with her hands. "I can't believe I just said that out loud, let alone believe that it's true."

He took a seat beside her on the couch. "Yeah, it's not part of what most people grow up believing in, is it?"

"The stuff of old horror movies. I used to like them as a kid, till I got older and realized how silly they were." She shook her head. "If I'd only known."

"Where I grew up, in a remote part of Wisconsin, there were quite a few of us," Drew told her. "A lot of us were related. My family settled there because the real gray wolf population is substantial, so a few more sightings weren't noticed much. Plus, the human population isn't large outside major urban areas. It was a good place for us to do our experiments. Our ancestors had already developed some of the basic tonics that my family worked with, and that I helped to improve as I got older. Same stuff I'm trying to refine today to let us control when we shift and what our human awareness is in feral form."

"You make it sound so normal. I grew up in California, and the biggest hereditary issue I had to deal with was whether I'd hit puberty as late as my mother told me she and her mother did. Both were around fifteen before their bodies started to develop, and that worried me when I turned twelve and my friends began growing breasts before I did."

"I'd say you caught up." Drew glanced appreciatively toward that part of her anatomy. Melanie no longer wore the suit jacket she'd had on earlier, and her white blouse, although businesslike, was soft enough to hug her lush curves.

"I guess." She sounded a little embarrassed.

Their eyes met, and she all but leaped off the couch, away from him, apparently seeing on his face how much he wanted to touch her. To kiss her. Again.

He stood, too. "There may be things, and people, around here to be nervous about, Melanie, but I'm not one of them."

"But you're—" she began.

"A man," he said, and as if to prove it he got close enough to gather her into his arms and press his body against hers.

He lowered his mouth, willing to fight for what he wanted. But despite her initial shying away, her lips met his as eagerly as if she'd been the one to initiate the encounter. He groaned, even as he moved against her.

Her body was soft, curvaceous, yet slender. He wanted to feel not just her flimsy shirt and concealing pants, but her. All of her. Her flesh against his.

Still pressed tightly to her, his mouth savoring hers, he pulled up her shirt. Her skin was soft and warm and inviting. Her floral scent was enhanced by a womanly aroma that proved she was as sensually excited as he. Even as he stroked her warm, damp flesh, she managed to run her fingertips along the bare skin of his back and beneath his shirt.

"Drew," she moaned. "We shouldn't—"

"Shouldn't what?" he murmured against her mouth. "This?" He moved to cup one breast in his hand, rubbing the nipple still beneath the silky fabric of her bra. "This?" He slipped a finger beneath that obstruction until he was able to play softly with her and she moaned again.

"No, this," she whispered. Her hands, which had

been stroking his back, moved forward, pressed against his straining erection.

His turn to moan. He could only guess where her bedroom was. Didn't want to wait. Quickly, he pulled her blouse over her head without completely unbuttoning it. Stared at her lovely, curvy body even as he managed to remove her bra.

Dipped down to take first one golden nipple, then the other into his mouth. His enhanced senses drove him wild with lust as he tasted ambrosia.

He felt her tug at his trousers and moved to help her get them off. His shorts, as well, and his erection sprang free, hard and yearning, and she grabbed it with searching hands.

"Wait," he ordered. Too fast, and he would lose control. He breathed steadily, pulling back enough to undress himself.

Her hands reached up to rub gently against his bandages, even as her eyes, hot yet unfocused with need, glanced toward his injured shoulder. "We should stop," she said softly. "Not now. Not while you're hurt. Not—"

"Not stopping on my account," he inserted gruffly, and undressed her, too.

This wasn't right, Melanie's mind insisted from somewhere far away. Too much. Too soon. With a man so different. Hurt.

Gorgeous. Hot. Muscles everywhere where it counted. Even—especially—down below, where the sight of his bare body made her nearly pant with lust, as if she were as much a wild creature as he.

She was consumed by need for him. And when he

removed the last of her clothes and touched her there, where she ached for him, she cried out.

"Melanie," he said gruffly, even as he pulled away. She groaned. Would he be the one to come to his senses?

Not now. She needed him. Now.

She heard something crinkling, realized he had grabbed for protection, appreciated it, appreciated him. She lay back on the sofa, her senses piqued by the wait. The velvety material scratched softly at her back. His breathing was loud, irregular, blending with her own. And then, there he was, between her legs, smiling. Hot. Eyes slitted but filled with need, with lust. He teased her with the tip of him against her sensitive folds until she cried out, "Please."

And then he was inside her, fiery, thrusting until she nearly sobbed with pleasure at each stroke. Harder and harder until she called, "Drew!" and climaxed.

Chapter 16

Still breathing hard, Melanie opened her eyes and saw Grunge's golden eyes staring from beside the sofa. His expression looked both quizzical and comical, and she laughed.

"Your dog's a voyeur," she told Drew, who had collapsed on top of her. He was heavy, but the weight was all welcome.

All sexy.

"Yeah." He turned his head on top of her chest to look at Grunge. His dark, silvery hair tickled her. "Forget what you saw," he commanded, then gave a brief hoot of laughter.

Slowly, he lifted himself off Melanie and looked down. Was that still lust shadowed in his eyes?

The thought of more sex with him sent a twinge

through Melanie's own body, and she took a deep breath—until her gaze lit on his bandaged shoulder.

"You sure you don't want to go home tonight?" she said, praying he'd say no.

"No way," he said. "Although a bed might be nice."

"We'll sleep better that way," Melanie agreed.

"Who said anything about sleep?" His eyes gleamed greedily once more.

Grabbing her clothing, fully aware of the bare, incredibly tempting body beside her, Melanie led him down the hall to her bedroom.

Only…

She had to be direct. How could she be otherwise? Sitting on the edge of her queen-sized bed, she drew the blue-and-white comforter around her and looked at Drew. Lord, was he gorgeous. He hadn't picked up his clothes, nor did he appear to be self-conscious at all as he stood in the doorway looking at her.

"What?" he asked. "Don't tell me you didn't enjoy that."

"You know better. It was phenomenal. And I appreciate that you thought of protection. But…well, you've already said that matings between regular humans and shapeshifters can result in babies. Shapeshifting babies. I'm just— well, curious. Concerned. How does it work? I mean, I'm interested, from a scientific and medical perspective."

Not to mention the emotional perspective.

He joined her on the bed, draping a warm and strong arm around her shoulders. His touch was reassuring, not seductive. But despite the fact that she'd been sated only a few minutes earlier, the idea of another heated bout of pleasure with him started percolating deep inside her.

But not yet. Not until she had more information about what she could be getting herself into. Not that she would ever agree on unprotected sex with him. Yet accidents did happen…

"Our gene makeup is dominant, so nearly all children of those matches are also shapeshifters. And for reasons I can't explain, I know more people like me who marry humans like you than I do unions of two shapeshifters."

"Could be my kind finds your kind irresistible," she said, only half joking. "Or maybe whatever the magic is in you, you've found a way to hypnotize poor, ordinary women like me. Or—"

"Yeah, I know your kind considers my kind unreal and woo-woo. But do you really want to argue about who's hypnotized who?"

"Well—"

"Hush now," he said softly, punctuating his words by kissing her so sensuously that the idea of further questions fled.

He'd been right about at least one thing, she thought drowsily a long time later, when, even more satisfied, she lay beside him in her bed, breathing hard, yet, even then, wanting more of him.

Who said anything about sleep?

Her clock radio woke her on time, at 6:30 a.m., as a talk radio host rambled about spring weather on the Eastern Shore. Melanie's gaze met Drew's. Was that lust she saw in his eyes…again?

She had lost count of their heated encounters last

night. Surprisingly, he'd brought enough condoms to ensure she wouldn't need further genetics lessons from him just now. He'd obviously thought ahead—or at least been hopeful. She didn't own any condoms, since she'd thought she had sworn off men. Maybe she should feel irritated about Drew's arrogance…but instead she was happy for his foresight.

Her insides stirred when she realized she remained bare beneath her sheets. "Hold that thought," she whispered. "I have a day full of patients about to descend."

"Yeah, and I've got lab work to complete this morning or I'll need to start over." His deep voice was a low, sexy rumble.

"I might be able to squeeze out another ten minutes if I hurry later," she said hopefully and was gratified when Drew's bare arm reached out, pulling her close. When his fingers started exploring again, she tingled everywhere. Rushing—later—to get ready would be a good thing.

It was a half hour later that Melanie finally sprang from her bed. "I really have to get started," she said regretfully. "But I'm glad you stayed here last night to…to take care of me."

"Yeah, me, too. Good thing no one tried to break in. I was a little distracted."

"Grunge would have warned us." Melanie patted the dog, who'd stood and started wagging his tail. "Want to go outside, boy?" she asked. She threw on a robe and showed Grunge out the back door.

Drew was right beside her, his camouflage pants on, gorgeous chest bare in the cool April morning air. His bandages looked askew. "I'll change those for you if you'd like," she told him.

"If you touch me again, it'll be even longer before I can get out of here," he said with a slow, sexy grin.

"You're right." Melanie turned to watch Grunge, who romped playfully in the small backyard where a few flowers had begun to bloom. Suddenly, he stopped, nose in the air.

"What is it, boy?" Drew stepped into the yard. He, too, raised his head as if smelling something.

Which reminded Melanie not only of all the wonderful stuff they had done last night. This man had talents she couldn't begin to imagine.

Both man and dog returned to the back door shortly. "Anything wrong?" Melanie asked.

"Someone was around last night using a lighter version of whatever was used to disguise the odor in my lab the other day." Drew looked angry. "You should be fine in daylight, with your staff and patients around, but I'll be back this evening."

"Good excuse," Melanie said, running her fingers up the warm, smooth skin of his back, even as she trembled inside. What really was going on around here?

And Drew—were his senses enhanced even while he was in human form? She'd smelled nothing out of the ordinary from the usual aroma of her backyard in spring.

"Do I need an excuse to come back?" Drew looked down at her once more.

"Nope," she said, and stretched up to kiss his sexy but grim mouth. "But I think one of us had better make a run to a drug store today."

"Melanie, thanks for taking this call." Drew sounded as upset as Melanie had ever heard him.

"What's wrong?" she asked. She sat at her desk making notes. It was late afternoon, and her last scheduled patient for the day had left.

She had thought of Drew a lot today. No big surprise, after the night they'd spent together. Sex with him had been awesome. More wonderful than she had ever imagined a joining of two bodies—especially two such disparate bodies—could ever be.

Of course she had been tired, but she had not allowed her exhaustion to affect her treatment of patients that day. Fortunately, her schedule hadn't been heavy.

"Can you come here, to the base? An issue's come up that requires a vet's attention."

Melanie read between the lines. He didn't want to explain over the phone, but it probably had something to do with one of the shapeshifters.

"I can get there in—" she looked at her watch "—half an hour. Will that be all right?"

"It'll have to be."

Melanie quickly checked the bag she always kept ready for non-clinical emergencies, then informed Carla she was leaving for the rest of the day.

"Where are you going?" her assistant asked.

"One of the dogs at Ft. Lukman had an accident." Melanie wasn't sure it was a lie, and she needed a story Carla would buy.

This time, the guard at the entry kiosk waved Melanie in as soon as she identified herself. Drew met her. "Thanks for coming." He slipped into the passenger seat of her SUV. She parked where he told her to, but before she got out he grabbed her, gave her a hot but brief kiss.

"Can you tell me what's wrong?" Melanie asked breathlessly.

"I've got to show you." He led her into the K-9 building and down the stairs. "Ever treated a lynx?" he asked.

"No," she said, taken slightly aback.

"But you've worked with other cats."

She nodded. "This one is a shapeshifter, too?"

"That's right. It's Lt. Nella Reyes. Her apartment's near mine in the officers' quarters. We've been working with a new formulation of the tonic that allows shifting at times other than during the full moon, or even at night. I've taken it, and so has Patrick Worley. And Nella—but something's wrong."

"I—I'm not sure how this works. When she—you— are in animal form, I thought you said you maintain your human awareness. Can you shift back at will?"

"Yes, and no. That's one thing we're working on, but right now there appears to be a minimum of an hour or two before electing a change back."

Drew led her down the hall. Inside the lab stood Jonas Truro, Patrick Worley, and a couple of guys Melanie hadn't met. Facing them on the floor near the door to the clean room, hissing angrily, was a moderate-sized feline. The area where she stood shone wetly. And even Melanie, with her normal, human senses, could tell something smelled awful.

"What—?" she began, but Drew lifted his hand.

"Watch her for a minute."

The lynx spit, then began coughing uncontrollably. She threw up, and whatever came out was a grayish-green liquid that suggested bile. The animal collapsed and moaned.

But when Patrick approached her, she stood again, issuing angry, defensive sounds while arching her back. Jonas mopped up her mess.

"Any idea what caused this?" Melanie reached for her medical bag that Drew had insisted on carrying.

"It started soon after she changed. She'd tried some of the newest generation of shapeshifting tonic under the same old catalyst light. The stuff worked fine on me, and we planned a trial run in the field. But then this happened."

"Has Lt. Reyes ever used your tonic before?"

"The last generation, but not since we've made the latest changes. We increased the kick and enhanced the stuff's qualities big-time. The additives were fairly innocuous. Or so I thought." He gave her a rundown of the mostly natural ingredients.

"Nothing sounds bad, but…well, let's see what we can do." Melanie gingerly approached the lynx, talking quietly and soothingly. "Nella, I understand that shapeshifters around here retain their human awareness. I'm here to treat your symptoms so you can feel well enough to change back, okay?"

That seemed to calm her. Melanie was able to get close enough to check her over, then gave an injection to calm her stomach.

A while afterward, she was rewarded by the lynx's slow, apparently painful change back into human form. Melanie felt her heart rate accelerate but tried not to freak out watching this latest proof of the truth of the Mary Glen legends.

Soon, a young, slender woman with sandy hair lay writhing on the laboratory floor. Drew covered her with a blanket. "Can you tell us what happened, Nella?" he asked.

"I think so," she gasped. She explained her theory, that it was a female thing, her two forms' reproductive organs reacting to the tonic and, maybe, against each other. "Lynxes generally breed early in the year, so this was a little late for my cycle, but I also happened to have my human period, and somehow, the reaction combined with the tonic... Well, it wasn't fun." She drew herself into a sitting position. "Looks like you'll be helpful to have around the base, Dr. Harding, since our changing experiments are really increasing these days. Thanks."

"Why?" Melanie asked a while later.

Before Drew allowed Nella to return to her quarters, he'd conducted a medical exam. Then, he had Jonas walk her back to her apartment.

Now, he sat with Melanie in the cafeteria, where they both nursed soft drinks. He appreciated the deep concern that caused her soft brown brows to knit together.

"Why what?" he asked softly, wanting to smooth away her frown.

"Why are your changing experiments increasing?" she whispered, leaning toward him while looking at others in the room. They'd chosen as secluded a table as possible, but there were still people nearby, and Drew appreciated her discretion.

"We're preparing for our first multi-unit field exercises," he said.

She scooted her chair closer. "You mean, you guys are shapeshifting and going undercover somewhere? Where?"

"That's still classified," he said after a brief nod of acknowledgment. "It'll only be those like Patrick and me." Meaning werewolves. Nella's situation that afternoon suggested that those who shapeshifted into other forms might not be able to fully use the latest, greatest form of elixir. Or maybe just female members of their unit needed further experimentation and observation.

Otherwise, they were nearly good to go. Or at least to do some field testing. Their unit had been formed nearly two years earlier. Time to show positive results.

Not near Mary Glen, though. Certainly nowhere that the lunatic fringe of wannabe shapeshifter groupies would know what was going on.

"Then you're leaving soon?" Melanie sounded sad. Which did odd things to him inside. He wanted to reassure her that he would return.

Only…that would imply some kind of commitment. Not a good thing. He couldn't get enough of her luscious body. But commitment meant trusting. Completely.

"What?" she demanded, as if seeing his doubt on his face. "You're not going to answer? Then you are leaving, without explanation. Without trusting me." Her voice hardened, then grew more sarcastic. "Anything else I can do for you first? Any more animals to treat? Secrets to keep?" She stood, her hands on her hips. "Never mind. I asked if I could help, and I meant it. But right now, I need to go home."

"I'll go with you." It was one thing to have his doubts about her. But he needed to assure himself that she was safe.

"Don't bother. Surely whoever's getting kicks out of

shooting animals around my clinic has had enough by now, especially since the world is now apparently accepting that you were shot, and not a werewolf." The last word came out as a taunt. She grabbed her medical bag from the chair and started to storm from the cafeteria.

Outside, where a soft spring rain had started to fall, Drew grabbed her. "I'll come to your place now, Melanie," he said. "Grunge and I will. And if you don't object too strongly, I intend to make a detour. To a drugstore, to pick up some supplies." He placed a gentle finger over her mouth when she started to protest. "Just in case I can convince you that, whenever I go, even if I can't say more about it, I'll come back here. And what happens between us? Well, we'll just have to see. But, in any case, the other place I'm hitting tonight is an electronics store. It's time to listen to that cop. You need a good security system in your clinic and home, but I want to install something in the interim, to ensure your safety and your patients'. Okay?"

"Okay." She sounded as if all the air had been let out of the balloon of her ire.

To make sure it had, Drew bent down and, despite the rain and their public location, gave her one hell of a kiss.

Chapter 17

Crack!

The sound was followed by a loud slap that sounded as if someone had struck the house. Grunge leapt against the bedroom door, alternating ferocious growls with his barks, and the alarm Drew had just installed late the night before started to wail.

Melanie sat up in bed. So, beside her, did Drew.

Crack...crack!

"Wait here," he commanded. He stood and reached for the jeans he had shed along with the rest of his clothing early that morning, when their passion had brought them hurtling into the bedroom in a torrent of kisses and caresses.

"Forget it." Melanie blocked his path. "Those damned lunatic werewolf groupies! You're unarmed, Drew. No sense getting shot...again. Who's to say they'll stop shooting just because you don't look like an animal? Remember the Worleys? I assume none of your group was changing last night."

He shook his head curtly. "Not without clearing it with me."

"Then some poor, ordinary dog may be the target." She grabbed the phone off the bedside table. "I'm calling the cops."

She was nearly frantic by the time Angus Ellenbogen arrived in a convoy of cop cars with sirens blaring. Drew had called his own troops, who were also on the way, and hadn't stopped swearing at himself for not bringing a battery of armaments. He made it clear how badly he wanted to go outside, do a recon of the area, see what evidence—tangible and sensory—he could find, but when Melanie played poor scared woman in need of protection, he stayed with her.

And she *was* scared. Especially about the idea of him getting hurt again.

When the authorities arrived, the next hours were a jumble of questions and accusations and people who interacted but failed to mix well. Thank heavens Melanie's infirmary was empty, since caring for patients was impossible. With Carla's assistance she rescheduled the patients she was to see that morning.

"Come with me, Melanie," Angus told her. His crime scene team had already interrogated Drew and her. A different group had gone outside to figure out what had happened.

She had apparently been wrong. No animal had, fortunately, been shot. But one silver bullet was embedded in the rear wall of her house, another couple at the clinic.

"Looks like a warning this time, from whoever doesn't like that you treated supposed werewolves." The sad-faced police chief rolled his eyes.

"But Grunge was shot last week," Melanie protested. "So was Drew. The moon isn't full, and there weren't any stray dogs around that I'm aware of. Why do this?"

Angus turned toward Drew. "Don't suppose you remember seeing anything when you were shot besides what you told me, do you?"

Drew shook his head. "Wish I did. Maybe we could put an end to this once and for all."

"You didn't run outside this time when you heard a noise?" Angus asked. A logical question, Melanie figured, recalling the story they had devised to explain why Drew, and not a dog, had been shot. He'd stayed here night last night, which bolstered the story. But it also let people believe she was sleeping with him.

Okay, she was—but she wasn't comfortable with the world knowing about her personal life.

"Didn't hear anything this time till shots were fired and hit the building," Drew explained. "Besides, I learned my lesson." Sure, he had—as long as Melanie reminded him.

"Figured that," the chief said.

Melanie accompanied the men toward the front of the clinic, only to find that the media horde had descended, as they had on the morning after Grunge was shot. But why? This time, not even a dog was hurt.

She learned the reason quickly. Mike Ripkey, head of the SSTs, had apparently called a press conference, damn him. Right by her clinic. Again.

He stood at the front door, facing the reporters, clad

in jeans and an SSTs T-shirt. And he wasn't alone. A woman, maybe mid-thirties, stood beside him. Almost as tall as he, she wore a gauzy top over a short skirt, with black leather boots climbing her calves.

They faced a large group of tourists Melanie recognized from the City Hall meeting, some townsfolk including the mayor, Angie Fishbach and her waitress Crystal, and a lot of reporters.

Go away, she wanted to shout. But that would be useless.

Standing on the periphery of the group were some of the guys from Ft. Lukman, dressed inconspicuously in casual civilian garb. Jonas Truro, Seth Ambers, Patrick Worley were there, along with an older man Melanie didn't recognize.

"That's General Yarrow," Drew whispered at her question. "He's been stuck in D.C., so I'm a little surprised to see him here. He wants to meet you—and I figure he also wanted to see this nonsense for himself."

Standing by themselves were Melanie's technicians Astrid and Brendan. They seemed scared and upset, and Melanie hoped they wouldn't quit on her.

"Glad you're all here," Mike shouted, drawing Melanie's attention. "I wanted you to see Sheila Graves. She was attacked by a werewolf last week and lived to tell about it."

It was Melanie's turn to roll her eyes. She listened to the reporters shout questions. The two people were soon joined by Nolan Smith, who also leapt in to talk about the werewolf legends and how lucky Sheila was. Carla exited the clinic and, after an obvious glance at Patrick, stood near Nolan.

"I want to say one thing," Nolan finally shouted. "We're here because someone shot silver bullets at the Mary Glen Veterinary Clinic early this morning. Of course all of us who understand the truth of the legends know how dangerous these creatures can be, but shooting property won't help. We need to be certain that silver bullets are used correctly, aimed at the shapeshifters while in animal form. Aimed at their hearts, of course, to be sure to kill them."

As the reporters hollered questions involving hunting laws and licenses, as well as the legends, Melanie carefully kept her gaze expressionless, centering it on the three people on her doorstep. She would learn the reactions of the military guys later, but didn't want any attention shifted toward them, not even hers.

The most vocal reporter was, unsurprisingly, June Jenkins. The tall woman from the *Maryland Reality Gazette,* in a fuchsia suit that day, towered over most men and women. Her microphone was clasped in her hand, and she seemed eager to goad the interviewees into guessing who had fired the shots—suggesting it could even be one of them.

"We don't discourage the disposal of werewolves," Mike Ripkey said solemnly. "And it's not the same as shooting real game, so licensing laws don't apply." *Yeah, sure,* Melanie thought. "But if you're accusing us, you'd better back up your story with proof unless your paper is interested in defending a lawsuit for defamation, Ms. Jenkins."

That only deterred June Jenkins for a moment, and then her bombardment of questions and innuendoes started again.

Eventually, Angus and his cops apparently thought they'd allowed enough freedom of speech, and began dispersing the crowd. Most reporters left first, excluding the persistent June Jenkins, who hung out with the SST group when they stayed where they were.

Drew introduced her to General Yarrow. The dark-haired officer shook her hand firmly and stared into her eyes, as if assessing whether she could be trusted. She stared right back and said, "Good to finally meet you, sir. And I'm glad to be of assistance at Fort Lukman—in all ways."

His brief smile suggested that he got her underlying message. "I'll see you around, Dr. Harding."

Next, Melanie assumed a cordial attitude as she met Sheila Graves and expressed pleasure that the woman had survived the mauling…or whatever. Melanie wasn't about to get into a debate.

Carla clung to Nolan's arm as the man shook his head. "It's not your fault, Dr. Harding, that there are werewolves around here. No one should take it out on you."

"I agree," Melanie said. "With the last part, at least. The legends? Well…"

"We hope we got our point across," Mike Ripkey said. "Sheila's doing as well as possible, but the creature that hurt her is still loose. We don't want you harmed, Dr. Harding, or anyone else unless they're helping these evil beasts. But if you did, you didn't know any better…before."

"Is that a threat, Mr. Ripkey?" Drew demanded, stepping closer to Melanie, fists clenched at his sides.

"Of course not," Melanie said, wanting to defuse the situation. "But I'd rather you tell your group, Mike, that no one's person or property should be shot at, for any reason. Not animals, either. I didn't like having to extract a bullet from a poor dog who might, in the darkness, vaguely resemble a wolf. And I absolutely hated that Drew was shot for no reason at all. Besides, even if the legends were true, which I doubt, and there are werewolves around here, no one has the right to take the law into his or her own hands—hunting licenses or not. Right, Chief Ellenbogen?"

"Sure thing, Dr. Harding. Add that to your story, Ms. Jenkins," he ordered the reporter. "Got it?"

"I heard you, Angus," June Jenkins said. "And I'll keep it in mind." She grinned and left.

Melanie watched TV news and read local newspapers over the next days. The stories resulting from that pseudo press conference were, unsurprisingly, all over the map as far as reality was concerned.

June Jenkins's article that Friday afternoon quoted Chief Ellenbogen as saying that his department should be contacted if anyone believed they saw anything unusual around their homes or businesses—such as a shapeshifter.

Other stories that day and over the weekend made fun of the legends, often in what appeared to be an unbiased report. The fact that most well-respected media took that position soothed Melanie's fractured nerves just a little. Maybe some of the loonies would now stay away from Mary Glen.

Maybe not.

Melanie decided not to make an issue out of Carla's relationship with a ringleader of the furor, Nolan Smith.

If she fired Carla, Nolan could claim on his Web site that believers in the legends were martyrs as well as the only clear thinkers.

If he only knew.

Over the weekend, Melanie didn't see many patients, so it was a good time to visit Ft. Lukman, ostensibly, as usual, to check on the health of the K-9s. Melanie was, in fact, getting to know and adore them.

And the shapeshifters?

Well, first and foremost, there was Drew. She didn't need to go to the base to see him. He spent each night at her house to bolster their cover story. And their extraordinary lovemaking? An added benefit.

To Melanie's pleasure, she was becoming good friends with Lt. Nella Reyes. Nella couldn't thank Melanie enough for helping her stop vomiting and allowing her to change back to human form after her disastrous bout with the latest formula.

Nella changed once more, on Sunday afternoon, in a controlled experiment with Melanie present. Her lynx form's estrus cycle had ended, which undoubtedly helped. And Nella was determined not to let the testosterone-governed shapeshifters do better than those who had estrogen instead.

Melanie sucked in her continued amazement and incredulity, and watched the woman change into a beautiful lynx who proceeded to prowl the lab area.

Then there were the werewolves, including Patrick Worley and, of course, Drew.

She was present during several weeknight evenings, as they discussed the latest version of the drink that caused them to change. She learned about its contents that allowed them to choose when to morph into animal form, then back again. About the light that simulated moonlight when turned on to the optimum intensity, the needed catalyst for the tonic to work.

She stayed near them, even communicated on some level with the large, highly intelligent dogs they became. Yes, they actually retained their human awareness, as Drew had told her. They howled now and then, whether out of pure joy or just to freak her out she didn't know. But they didn't attack anyone or anything.

When she checked them over, using her veterinary skills, they obeyed her. Even teased by anticipating which paw she wanted them to lift.

Weird. Unreal. And very unsettling, Melanie told herself over and over, even as she observed canines' fur recede into lengthening skin as they turned back into nude men before her eyes. Good-looking, muscular men—Drew the most gorgeous of the bunch. Those she didn't know as well seemed self-conscious at first, but she was careful to remain clinical and professional, and to ensure that there were sufficient sheets and other coverings to protect their modesty.

Not so with Drew. His eyes invariably caught hers as he changed, and she went hot all over as his sexy human body returned.

She was now part of the group. Her official top-secret clearance was still in process, but it was almost superfluous.

She felt as if she lived a dual existence—a regular veterinarian most days, a mad doctor participating in incredible experiments during evenings and on weekends.

And nights? Well, they were of course incredible in a different way. Drew always came to her home, bringing Grunge. She'd had an enhanced security system installed at both the clinic and her home. Her medical practice was such that most nights her infirmary was occupied. She had to ensure the safety of any pets entrusted to her care whether overnight or otherwise.

Her employees didn't seem to recognize her semi-schizophrenia. Carla had her pert little head in the clouds, since apparently Nolan and she were growing closer. Talking marriage someday, if Carla's happy hints had validity.

Which gave Melanie an opportunity to discuss Nolan's beliefs with him on Thursday afternoon.

The tall man had come to take Carla to lunch. As always, he wore his belt with the silver wolf buckle to hold up his frayed blue jeans. He had a peculiar gleam in his eyes, behind his glasses, every time he got on the subject of werewolves—the first thing he brought up when he spied Melanie in the clinic's reception room.

"How are you today, Doc?" he asked. "Saved any shapeshifters lately?"

"Of course not," she said with a straight face. Seen any, yes. Saved any, no. "Nolan, I'd really like to understand what got you so interested in the legends. Are you just trying to make money from sponsors who buy ads on your Web sites, or do you genuinely believe in them? And if so, what makes you think they're evil?"

His long features darkened into an angry scowl. "You saw Sheila Graves, Doc. Do you think some nice, kindly animal with a waggly tail leapt on her and nearly killed her?"

"And she wasn't the first person harmed around here," Carla chimed in, nodding until her curls bobbed. "You're new to the area, Melanie. You know the old saying, 'Where there's smoke, there's fire.' Around here, it's more like, 'Where there are sightings and attacks, there are shapeshifters.'"

Obviously nothing would change their minds. And in some ways, Melanie admitted to herself, they were right. Perhaps there had been sightings. There certainly were shapeshifters. And there were attacks—*on* those shapeshifters, not, as far as she knew, by them.

She told Drew about the encounter when he came to spend the night. "No big surprise," he told her, sitting close beside her on her sofa as late news played on her TV. "No matter what those kinds see or don't see, it's all signs of what they want to believe. Far as I know, no one has ever seen any of our group changing, or even in changed form, except for the night I was shot. That was a fluke, and it won't be repeated."

"I hope not." Melanie reached down to pat Grunge's head. "The idea of any of you getting hurt again—" She shuddered, then burrowed her face under Drew's strong chin. She was getting much too used to having him around at night. She didn't care about his ostensible reason for being there: to protect her, and her clinic. Oh, that part was good.

But later, when they went to bed—that was when he really showed his abilities. Not supernatural, maybe, but really hot.

It wasn't only the sex, though, that kept her wanting him around.

She had, despite all rationality, fallen in love with him.

"I need to ask you something," he whispered into her ear that night.

"What?" He smelled good, all masculine, human enough to project a soft tang of shaving cream mixed with shampoo, but there was also a hint of something wild and canine—an aroma now familiar and endearing.

"Things are going well enough that, this weekend, we're going to conduct exercises at another military facility. We'll be undercover, in essence playing out a scenario that could actually occur—an Alpha situation, where troops with our special abilities are used as a last resort."

"Interesting." Melanie tried to sound excited. Instead, she was worried. Would the other military personnel know not to harm what appeared to be stray animals on their base?

"Right. If this works, we'll expand our operations, deploying to other locations as needed. But you've become an integral part of our work. I'd like your help. Come onto the base while we're gone this weekend, check out the K-9s and spend some time in the lab to add to our cover. Pretend we're there."

But Drew would be gone. And if this succeeded, maybe he'd leave permanently.

While her services were still being used. Oh, he had worked things out so she was receiving monetary compensation. But she couldn't help thinking of the situation that had resulted in her coming to Mary Glen.

"Mmm-hmm," she said brightly. "So I'd be here, running the veterinary operations, while you're off doing…whatever."

"I'll be back, Melanie, if that's what you're worried about." His tone was curt. "You sound like you're equating this with the guy who let you run his clinic while he ran around with other women." She should never have told him about that. "This isn't the same. It's why our unit exists. We're finally close enough to conduct test covert ops, and you've even helped."

"Right. And I know this is different. I hope things go great for you, Drew. I really do. But right now, I'm tired. I think I'll go to bed." *Alone,* she thought, but that wasn't how things had been on the many nights Drew had stayed over.

"Fine," he said. "I'll just sleep out here on the couch."

"Fine," Melanie echoed, and she hurried down the hall to her room.

Chapter 18

*L*ast chance. Alpha Force had been called in. Only really *Special Forces could pull this one out for the good old U. S. of A.*

Or so the manufactured scenario went.

He put his nose in the air, inhaling the odors of the thick woodlands inland from the Potomac, at Quantico Marine Base. The forest creatures, who stayed far out of their way. The humid aroma of the river nearby, and the intrusion of the smells of the gasoline-powered craft upon it.

Also inhaling the scents of his fellow Alphas. And, drawing closer, the other soldiers participating in the exercise, where the abilities of Alpha as a military unit were being challenged for the first time.

The opposition forces played the roles of tangos—terrorists, in military terms. They had broken through the last bastions protecting unwary civilians from weapons of mass destruction. Only the Alphas could save the world.

Beside him were the others. Also changed. Also charged up to attack.

And win.

At any cost.

Or so it would be, should this scenario ever become real.

It was one night shy of the full moon. Perhaps too close for comfort, but problems had arisen that delayed this test. Problems that were resolved. The latest formulation, with its new ingredients in different strengths, had been tested and retested. The artificial moonlight's portability had been confirmed. Tonight, it all worked well.

The attackers came ever closer. All they knew was that this exercise would be no-holds-barred. Different. Dangerous.

This was it. Alpha's first test. They had to succeed. To win. Or their exposure here would be for nothing.

His work that he had focused on, a major purpose of his life, would be for nothing.

He looked toward his comrades. His pack. Bared his teeth. Held back the howl that formed in his gut.

Together, they charged.

The phone beside Melanie's bed shrilled. Her eyes popped open and she glanced at the clock even as she rolled in her black silk pajamas and reached for the receiver. 2:00 a.m.

Instantly awake, as she had trained herself for a veterinary crisis, she answered. "Dr. Harding here."

"Melanie? Patrick Worley. Can you come to the base right away? We'll meet you there. It's an emergency."

Last time, it had been Nella, throwing up. But Melanie knew of the Alpha group's exercises that day. And Patrick's distant, clipped voice also told her this was worse. Much worse.

Her heart hammering, she said, "Is Drew—?" But Melanie heard the click of the phone before she could finish.

It wasn't Drew who was hurt, but Seth Ambers. Melanie found that out nearly as soon as she reached Ft. Lukman. Relief surged through her, followed by guilt at her reaction, but she had no time to dwell on either of them.

After Patrick's call, she had dashed to the clinic for her medical bag. She ran through the infirmary, scanning the animals in overnight care—two dogs and a cat. Fortunately, none required her attention. She turned the security system on again. Then she drove fast, breaking speed limits on the tree-shrouded, twisting roads. Roads she had been reminded, now and then, that had been the scene of more than one fatal accident.

Reaching the base, she was immediately ushered in by one of the guards. She hurried to the K-9 building, where a grim-face Drew, wearing a dirty uniform over an exaggeratedly stiff body, met her and brought her down into the lab.

A corner had been set up as a makeshift infirmary for the wolflike animal. He lay panting on a cot covered in white sheets stained with blood. Patrick was there, with General Yarrow and Jonas Truro. All were silent. All were clearly devastated about the injured animal.

And the injured man who was somewhere inside him.

Melanie worked far into the night, using the base's resources and her own, as well as her skills and veterinary knowledge, determining the extent of the head trauma, stabilizing him, treating him. She was determined to save not only Seth's life, but his mind. His animal mind. His human mind? Well, they would have to see, once he was stabilized and healing.

He seemed to improve. But he did not change back into human form.

She enlisted a few of the guys to move him to the nearby human infirmary to use its diagnostic equipment, then back again. They all joined her in her vigil for a while, watching hopefully, silently, anxiously. Eventually, they thanked her and left.

Except Drew.

"Okay," she whispered as they sat in the lab watching over the unconscious canine. "Time for you to explain."

"The experimental Alpha exercise was a success." Drew's voice was edgy, ironic. "The Marines acting the role of tangos were well chosen. They were instructed this was an exercise, not to be surprised by anything, and not to harm the attacking force, just try to stop it with the usual exercise weapons and, if they couldn't, to come up with ideas that an enemy in their position might use. One apparently panicked when confronted by a pack of dogs as intelligent as they were, who anticipated every defensive move. He lashed out with a rock. Seth was injured. End of story. Unless, of course, you can't save him."

Melanie glanced down. The canine remained unconscious, but who knew what he could hear? "He'll be fine," she said. "Concussions hurt, but give him time. I'll need to leave soon. I have a full day scheduled, and there's nothing more I can do for now. Keep close watch over him, and call me immediately if there's any change."

Drew nodded. "Sure thing. But…"

"But?" Melanie prompted.

"Tonight's a full moon. We'll be…preoccupied tonight." Drew's tone sounded bleak. "Same goes for our respective observers."

"What about the guy assigned to Seth? Won't he be able to stay and keep an eye on him?"

"He's in the hospital," Drew said ruefully. "Like all our observers, he watched the exercise, and when the guy slammed Seth, he leapt on him and was slammed, too. He'll be okay—he wasn't hurt as badly as Seth, since he was clearly a person, but he's out of commission right now."

"Got it," Melanie said. "So I'll watch over Seth tonight." What choice did she have?

Besides, this would be her first opportunity to watch Alpha Force morph into animal forms under a full moon, when they had no control. Would it look different from times they initiated the change?

Much to her own surprise—and, to some extent, chagrin—Melanie's fascination with shapeshifting kept increasing. That could have something to do with her feelings for Drew. Feelings she would be a whole lot better off without.

Okay, so he was sexy. What woman wouldn't fall for a man like him—especially after the no-holds-barred sex they'd shared?

But so what if she thought she loved him? She was too smart to think there was a future for them. And too aware of the fact he was using her. He headed this special forces unit that required a dedicated, closed-mouthed veterinarian's services. She was a damned good vet who could keep a secret. He used her services. Maybe even seduced her to get her to help.

She recognized it. Went into it with her eyes more or less open.

"Okay, then. I'll count on you to watch Seth, right?"

"That's what I said," she answered irritably. Hadn't she already agreed? "I've other patients waiting at the clinic, but I should be able to get my employees to check on them now and then overnight. That's not possible with Seth, and he needs the most care right now. So, yes, you can count on me."

She didn't see it coming. She was suddenly engulfed in Drew's arms so tightly they almost suffocated her. His anxiety was translated into his embrace. "Drew, it's okay. I—"

His mouth covered hers, and the kiss took her breath away. No, it reminded her just how alive she was. Lust exploded inside her as his lips tasted hers, his tongue playing sensual havoc with hers. They were somehow standing, pressed tightly together. All of her nerve endings were at attention, especially where her breasts were crushed against him. His erection pushed against her, reminding her of how it had been to lie down beside him, beneath him, and make love so passionate it had awakened her to new needs, new desires. New dreams.

His hand slid up her back beneath the cotton shirt she'd hastily thrown on before leaving home. His touch was hot and searching, and his fingers roved quickly around to her breasts.

But her senses were not tuned only to her own body and its needs. She heard a small, pained sound and pulled back.

The injured dog that was Seth Ambers was whimpering. Was he waking at last?

"What's the matter, boy?" Melanie crooned, kneeling beside her patient. Her breathing was still heavy, but she was suddenly back in reality.

"Is he waking up?" Drew sounded out of breath, as well, but he made no move to touch Melanie.

But Seth settled down again. Melanie checked his vital signs. He seemed no better, but no worse, either. "I don't think so," she said. "But I'd better keep an eye on him." She checked her watch. It was nearly four a.m.

"Just stay another fifteen minutes in case there's another reaction from him." Drew also made no reference to that heated kiss. "Then I'll have someone accompany you back to your place. Maybe you can nap before your patients start arriving."

"You okay, Melanie?" Carla asked as the last patient of the day exited the clinic. "You look pooped."

"Didn't get much sleep last night," Melanie admitted, though she couldn't explain the truth. Instead, she made up something close enough, piggybacking on her earlier lie to Carla. "That Ft. Lukman K-9 who'd been in an accident the other day? He was hit by a car, and though he was doing better, he had a setback, so I went there to take care of him. In fact, I need to stay with him again tonight. Can you get Brendan and Astrid to come?"

Melanie's cat patient went home that day, but another had been brought in who needed to be boarded for a week. Plus, the two dogs there the night before both needed another overnight for observation. Carla and the two technicians promised to each visit the clinic once in the middle of the night. Carla would come at eleven, Brendan at two, and Astrid at four.

"That should cover it. I'll be home by six tomorrow morning." She hoped. Dawn would break around then, so surely someone else who knew the truth about Alpha would be able to watch over Seth after that.

Melanie thanked her staff, then hurried through her evening obligations, including one more check on her patients. "Okay, guys," she told them. "Looking good. I'll see you in the morning."

She headed to Ft. Lukman. Dusk was just falling, and she hurried to the lab area. Seth still hadn't recovered consciousness but was breathing more easily.

Even if he had improved that evening, he would remain in animal form. Hopefully, the fact that he didn't have to change would increase the odds of his survival.

And then it was time. Melanie accompanied members of the unit to a secluded, woodsy area at a corner of the fenced-in base. There, Drew, Patrick, Nella and the other shapeshifters went through their metamorphoses, humans one moment, writhing in pain and transformation the next, and in animal form shortly thereafter.

Astounding, Melanie thought, not for the first time.

All loped into the woods to participate in the exercises planned for them this night, in which their change was preordained, not elective.

Melanie had been informed that, to enhance their cover, all non-Alpha troops stationed at Ft. Lukman were sent to other bases for exercises around the time of full moons, as well as other, irregular times so those exercises weren't too obviously the result of the lunar cycle. During those times, Alpha was in charge of base security, which meant locking all gates but those they were using.

Shaking her head in both awe and the residue of her disbelief, Melanie returned to the lab. "Okay, Seth." She took a seat beside the sleeping wolf-dog. "Maybe in daylight, when everyone else changes, you will, too."

No response, but she didn't expect any. She settled into the chair, pulling a blanket over her. She didn't need to stay awake, since she had been primed, by her veterinary training, to awaken to the slightest sound that might bode an emergency.

"I'll wake up now and then, I'm sure," she told Seth. "But if you need anything, just holler."

It wasn't Seth Ambers that awakened Melanie around three o'clock in the morning. It was her cell phone.

Instantly awake, afraid of hearing of another mishap with the shapeshifters, Melanie answered uneasily, "Dr. Harding here."

"Melanie, this is Astrid." She sounded hysterical.

"What's wrong?" Melanie demanded.

"You have to come back to the clinic right now. It— it's terrible. Those poor animals? Blood everywhere. Please, Dr. Harding, come home."

Chapter 19

The infirmary was as horrible as Astrid had implied. The animals who were supposed to be safe had obviously been attacked by some other creature, viciously and brutally.

Melanie had raced back to the veterinary hospital faster than she had driven yesterday to Ft. Lukman. Faster, even, than she drove to her clinic the last time it was violated, by the break-in.

When she arrived, Astrid sat on a chair in the middle of the bloodbath that was the infirmary, cradling Kewpie, the yellow cat. The two dogs, Jake, a large mixed breed, and Dixie, a Golden Retriever, lay on the floor beside her. All were covered in blood.

Astrid turned her watery brown eyes toward Melanie. "I can't believe this." Blood stained her white "Animals Rock" T-shirt and jeans.

"They're all still alive," Melanie asserted, willing it to be so. The two dogs were watching her, but Kewpie hadn't moved.

"Y-yes, but they're hurt. Every one of them."

"Okay, then I'll need you to be strong and help me treat them. Can you do that?"

"Yes. Yes, I can." The young woman seemed to gather her strength, even as she hugged the cat even tighter.

"I called the police as I drove here," Melanie said. "They may treat this as a crime scene, so we'll take the animals to the surgery room. You carry Kewpie. I'll deal with Jake and Dixie."

As Melanie worked to save the three wounded animals, she mentally swore at whatever, or whoever, had done this. They had all been savaged by another animal, one with large teeth.

Werewolf sized.

Melanie shaved fur off Dixie's torn neck. The dog was asleep now, under the anesthetic Melanie had administered. Before, Dixie had been so brave, her fuzzy, bloody tail thumping the floor as she regarded Melanie with adoring, pleading eyes…

Which broke Melanie's heart even more. What if she couldn't save her?

"Melanie?" demanded a sharp voice.

"In here, Angus," she called.

The police chief appeared in the doorway. The expression on his paunchy face was thunderous. "What the hell happened here this time? I saw Astrid crying in the room with all the cages. I've sent for my crime scene folks—again. Is that all animal blood in there?"

"Yes. Three patients were apparently attacked by

another creature. There's no sign of how it got in despite my security measures, or how it got out, either. But it's not here now."

"I'll have my guys check it. You okay, Melanie?"

"Not really, but I've got injured patients to treat."

Dixie's wounds were ugly. Deep. But survivable… Melanie prayed.

"I'll leave you to it."

Hours later Melanie was finally done cleaning and suturing wounds and treating the animals with antibiotics.

Kewpie, the cat—the smallest and most severely hurt—was touch and go. Dixie and Jake were going to make it.

Carla had come in, and so had Brendan. With Astrid, they had all worked at Melanie's side to help the injured pets.

Carla had called their owners, told them what happened. She had also called the owners of the day's first patients to reschedule them.

Angus Ellenbogen's group had come and gone, blocking off the infirmary with crime scene tape—although he had muttered that something about investigating crimes by animals against other animals weren't in his job description.

And now, Melanie and her crew sat in the waiting room, catching their breaths.

"Thank you all," Melanie said. "You did a phenomenal job of jumping in. I'm giving you all bonuses."

"Not necessary, Doc," Brendan said. Although in his early twenties, he appeared to have aged overnight, his usually merry blue eyes sunken into his skull.

"Did Angus or his guys find evidence of what animal did this?" Carla asked. Her usual perkiness had disappeared, replaced by a look of exhaustion and fear.

"Nothing certain," Melanie said. "And, yes, I know what you're going to say. It could have been a canine. Even a wolf. But don't start spouting a werewolf legend again. I don't want to hear it." Even though she had been thinking it.

There was a full moon last night. Those people carrying werewolf genes had been forced to change into animal form.

Ft. Lukman had been overrun with them.

But why would any come here, to attack defenseless pets recuperating from other problems, who couldn't defend themselves?

But if not one of them, who? Drew had said that at least some of the local werewolf legends were true. There could be other, non-Alpha shapeshifters in the area. But why would they do something like this?

Or was someone trying to set this up to appear as if Alpha Force operatives were involved?

Which led back to the first question—why?

"When's our next patient scheduled, Carla?" Melanie asked, knowing she sounded as dispirited as she felt.

"Not till two this afternoon."

"Good. It's ten o'clock. Why don't *you* all leave for now?"

"I'm staying, Doc," Brendan said forcefully. "Why don't you leave, get some rest? I'll keep an eye on the patients."

"I'll do that, Brendan, if you're sure. Thanks."

* * *

But as exhausted as Melanie felt, she knew she wouldn't sleep. She needed to talk to someone who might have answers—at least about the Alpha team members. But Drew and the others who'd have been awake all night were probably sound asleep.

She decided to go to the Mary Glen Diner—even though it was the place Drew and his group had been drugged. Hopefully, a cup of coffee would be okay. She might even take a chance on something to eat. She hadn't heard of anyone else being affected by the diner's food.

But mostly, she wanted to listen. She had no doubt that rumors would be flying about what happened here last night. Maybe someone would even say something insightful that she could eavesdrop on.

First, she went home, took a quick shower and changed out of the clothes she'd worn last night—fortunately old enough that if the bloodstains that leeched through her lab jacket did not come out, she wouldn't think twice about tossing the stuff. She put on a button-down shirt and slacks.

She looked in on Brendan and the patients and found they were doing as well as could be expected.

As she got ready to walk toward town, her cell phone rang. "Melanie? Drew. What the hell's going on?"

"Do you mean why didn't I stay with Seth all night?" Melanie's heart leapt into her throat. On top of the guilt she felt about the attacks on her patients, what if something had happened to Seth after she'd left? In all the excitement, she had nearly forgotten about him. "He seemed to be doing okay, and I had an emergency call—"

"That's what I meant. I got a phone message from Chief Ellenbogen demanding that I call him back to talk about the attacks at your clinic. What happened?"

She gave a summary.

"Damn. I'll be right there."

"What about Seth?"

"Doing well. Patrick came back to see how he was when we all…around dawn. Seth was awake, looked like his old self."

Melanie did a mental translation. The cell phone transmissions might not be secure. But Patrick had gone to check on their fellow werewolf as they were all changing back, when daylight lessened the intensity of the full moon.

Seth had changed back to human form, too.

"Great!" Melanie said, relieved. "If you'd like, meet me at the diner. I'm on my way. Right now I need some coffee."

She was certain Drew could read between *those* lines, too.

Drew called Melanie on his cell again as he arrived in Mary Glen. The sky was dark. A spring storm might be brewing. "I'm parking on your street," he told her. "You at the diner yet?"

"Nearly."

"Wait for me." He paused long enough to pull up to the almost empty curb on Choptank Lane, nearest the antique shops. Too early for them to be open. The whole street looked peaceful. No indication that just a block away someone had violated Melanie's security, hurt her patients. He didn't like it.

It smacked of a setup.

"Let's strategize," he continued, "about what we'll say and how we'll say it. What do you want to bet word's out everywhere about the attacks on your patients last night?"

"No doubt about it." She didn't sound happy. "I don't know who did it or why, but…"

Her sudden hesitation bothered him. "But what?" He turned off the sedan's motor and opened the door. He had put on a blue windbreaker over his long-sleeved shirt as he'd rushed out of his base apartment. No need to pull up the hood. The rain hadn't started.

"Were all your…operatives accounted for last night?" Melanie finally asked.

He stopped, suddenly angry. She thought it could be one of them who caused the mayhem at her clinic?

Presumably she meant while they were in animal form. When they'd shapeshifted because they had to. And perhaps lost control in other areas, too.

Only, it didn't work that way. Hadn't she learned that yet?

Too angry to answer, especially since he wasn't sure no one monitored this unsecure call, he strode fast onto Mary Glen Avenue toward the diner.

Too bad he'd left Grunge in their quarters. The dog would have enjoyed this brisk walk. But sitting outside wasn't an option this chilly, menacing morning. And scenting out the source of what had gotten into Melanie's clinic? Drew could give it a once-over, but figured this intruder would have masked the odor the same as had been done before. He'd no doubt that all these incidents were related.

But why? And who?

"Drew? Are you still there?"

"Yeah." He spoke curtly.

"You don't like that question? Well, sorry, but I had to ask."

The diner was only a block away now, and he spied Melanie standing on the sidewalk near it. Not surprisingly, no one sat at the outside tables. Even from this distance, he could tell she looked lovely and professional in her crisp white shirt and dark slacks. She wore no jacket, carried no umbrella.

As he got closer, he saw that her posture was tense, as if she anticipated additional attacks on her, even here. Her blue eyes looked shadowed by lack of sleep and anxiety.

Drew fought an urge to take her into his arms. He understood why she'd all but accused his guys of attacking her patients, but he didn't have to like it.

"Hi, Drew," she said, so softly and sadly that the urge won. He clasped her tightly and kissed her.

She started to respond but pulled away. "Let's go in. I'm glad—what's the phrase?—you'll have my back."

"Yeah," he said. But would she blame him for not having her back last night? Or her patients'?

The diner was crowded, perhaps more than usual for early morning. Being pretty much an outsider himself, Drew wasn't sure how many patrons were locals and how many from out of town, but the familiar faces outnumbered the unfamiliar. Many of those he recognized he'd seen during the town meeting and here, afterward. That meant at least some were werewolf chasers.

Not surprisingly, he and Melanie were approached nearly immediately by Angie Fishbach. "What happened at your place last night?" she asked Melanie. "People are saying everything from one of the animals there attacked the others, to a break-in by a whole pack of werewolves."

"Neither," Melanie said. "All I can tell you is that the patients I held overnight were attacked by some kind of creature, maybe a dog."

"Then it was a werewolf." Drew wanted to erase the smug smile from the woman's round face. "That's what I thought."

"That would certainly support the Mary Glen legend, wouldn't it?" Melanie's tone was clipped. "Not to mention your story about how your husband was killed. Me? I'm keeping an open mind, but it'd be a good thing if someone could prove it was a werewolf. Whatever it was got past my new security system, and it sure would make me feel better to think that only something supernatural could do that. Now, is there a table available?"

Drew was initially surprised by her outpouring. Then impressed. Kind of. But while daring Angie or the shapeshifter chasers might get them to toss her some information, it could also be hazardous to her health, and he wasn't about to let her go on. Before he decided how to react, she grabbed his hand and squeezed.

Which felt good. And did what she had undoubtedly intended: got him to keep his mouth shut. For now.

There was a table available near the row of booths, a good spot for hearing any surrounding conversations. He ordered a cheese omelet, like any regular guy instead of one with a need to eat meat. Which he especially did on the day after a night of the full moon. He remembered the last time he'd been here. He figured whoever

had drugged him and his team members was unlikely
to try it again—but he still determined to stay alert.

Melanie, too, ordered an omelet. And then she gazed
into his eyes, softly, moodily, as if she were madly in love
with him and couldn't look anywhere else. It made his
body react. He had an urge to run his fingers through her
softly flowing sable hair. To touch her skin, anywhere.
But they were separated by a table, and the lack of
privacy. "When we're done here—" he finally said.

"Shh," she whispered. "Just look at me. Pretend we
really care for each another. No one will pay attention to
two people mooning over one another, and then we can
both listen to who's saying what. *You* can, especially."

Sure he could, but that deflated him. Irritated him
even more. She was obviously mad at him. As he was
with her. She had a point, though. And so, frustrated,
he looked but did not touch. And listened.

As anticipated, the restaurant hummed with the story
of the attack at the veterinary clinic. Glances, curious
and covert, were tossed their way.

The rumors? Well, werewolves were, not unexpect-
edly, the main suspects in what had happened. Who were
they, in human form? That varied, from some of the
SSTs—that suggestion accompanied by huge laughs—
to the mayor to Melanie herself. And renegade politicians
from nearby Washington, D.C. And soldiers from Ft.
Lukman like Drew—mentioned with a furtive glance his
way—since wasn't he the one Melanie had saved in the
first place? Did he really have a dog named Grunge?

Many discussions involved Nolan Smith's Web site.
He had apparently gotten wind of the attacks early this
morning and started his own speculations. He also ref-

erenced the news media and other Web sites all over the country that were rumored to be paying him for his nearly exclusive insight and information.

Too soon, breakfast was over. "I need to get back to my patients," Melanie said, her formerly adoring look turning cool enough to stab him. "I gather that my…K-9 patient at the base is doing well enough that I don't need to check on him this morning, right?"

"Right," Drew agreed. Since Seth had changed back into a person, he was under regular medical care, so a vet would now be superfluous. Even so… "It would be a good idea for you to stop by later today for any follow-up that might be needed."

She looked at him searchingly, as if trying to assess if this was real or part of the act. Well, hell. Why was she acting this way? He wasn't responsible for the attack, and neither were his guys—whether she believed it or not.

"We'll talk later," she finally said, not sounding too enthused about it.

"Yeah," he responded. "I'll let you know when I'm coming by this evening, to stay the night."

"No need," she said in a low voice. "After last night, Angus will undoubtedly send additional patrols along my street. I'll stay at the clinic, ready to protect my patients, if necessary."

"But who'll protect you?" Drew growled.

"Forget the macho human thing," she whispered through gritted teeth. "If I'm not distracted by injured shapeshifters, I can take care of my patients and myself."

Chapter 20

When they finished breakfast, they kept up the facade of being a caring couple as Drew walked Melanie back to the clinic—at least while anyone in town might be looking.

So why, when no one could see them, did he look down at her just inside her reception room with a gaze that could convince her he wanted something from her—and not just veterinary services? Something hot and wild and sexy.

Well, she was angry with him. With the whole situation. He had used her. Used her services. She had walked right into it, knowingly. Her patients had been the ones to suffer.

But was she turned on? Yeah. When he kissed her, her insides lit like a match.

"See you later," he said.

"No need." She had intended the words to come out firmly, not breathlessly.

And then he was gone.

Fortunately Brendan waited till then to come out to find her. "How are our patients?" she asked.

"Not bad." She went with him to check and was relieved that he was right. She insisted that he go home at last and rest.

The owners of the three injured pets insisted on coming to see them. Each time, Melanie both apologized and attempted to explain the security breach, the assault by...whatever had hurt their babies so awfully, even though she had no answers.

At least she could tell them that Jake, Dixie and Kewpie would all be okay. She wanted to keep them another day to watch over them. And she was greatly relieved when each owner appeared to trust her enough not to let anything else happen to them.

She would not break that trust. She called a security company out of Annapolis to beef up her system, and amazingly they were able to come at once. Or maybe not so amazingly, at the price they charged. She even had cameras installed.

The patients still scheduled for that afternoon all arrived. No one, it seemed, blamed her for what had happened. No one, except herself.

At least her veterinary skills remained in demand. Or maybe everyone just wanted to see the scene of last night's sad, scary crime.

Carla and Astrid returned in the early afternoon to pitch in and do their jobs as if nothing had happened. She appreciated them—especially Astrid, who seemed as livid as Melanie herself about how someone had apparently decided to lend some truth to the Mary Glen werewolf legends at the poor animals' expense.

Carla, though, seemed even more convinced that what had happened was further verification of the legends. Seated at her small desk in the waiting room, she almost beamed at Melanie during a lull between patients. "You should see what Nolan thinks," she said almost ecstatically. "He's got so much posted on his Web site now, and the entire world is commenting on his bulletin boards. As much advertising as he was selling before—well, if this keeps up, he'll be really famous."

And rich, Melanie figured, thanks to his lucrative advertising. Which made her wonder about the guy even more.

She had, of course, wondered before about Nolan and his apparent fascination with werewolf lore. Absurd but harmless, had been her earliest surmises. Less absurd, and less harmless, she had decided when she learned the truth about Drew and Alpha Force and the secrets they needed to keep. They may have selected the location near Mary Glen for the good it could do the group, but the legends were probably proving more harmful than helpful now.

But could Nolan, with his fixation on shapeshifting, be willing to harm animals to make his point? Shoot them, then steal back the silver bullets? Find a way to maul defenseless pets to make it seem that a legendary creature did it?

Maybe so, if it brought in advertising revenue to his Web site, and fame to him and his cause.

If only she hadn't become involved…

When she had seen her last patient of the day and sent her assistants home, Melanie decided it was time to do as Carla had said and check out the latest updates to Nolan's Web site.

And was stunned—and frightened—by what she saw.

She immediately picked up the phone. "Drew," she said when he answered. "There's something you need to see."

The bastard had to be the one who had engineered the attack on the animals at Melanie's clinic. Drew was sure of it, staring at the lab's computer screen at the gruesome, bloody photos on Nolan Smith's Web site.

How else could Smith have gotten those pictures?

Sure, he said on the Web page that they had been sent to him anonymously, obviously by the shapeshifter who had done this, to taunt him and all his wonderful friends who wanted to stop the "evil monsters" before they hurt any more people or animals.

But he himself had to be the evil monster who'd done this. And Drew was just the one to make him admit it.

He checked out one more thing before putting his computer into sleep mode: Smith's address. And then he stood.

Just as Patrick Worley, dressed in civvies, entered the lab. "Drew, you okay?"

Apparently his fury was as obvious outside as he felt it in every inch of his body. "Yeah, you?"

"Sure, but Seth's wound appears to be getting

infected. The guys and I are taking him to Walter Reed to get him looked at."

"Yeah, that's the best human military medical center around." It was in D.C., not next door, but not too far, either. "Go for it. Jonas, Nella and you are all going?"

"Unless you need us here."

Would he need backup handling a twerp like Nolan Smith? The guy might expect retaliation, whether or not he genuinely believed in shapeshifters. He might figure someone would guess he committed the atrocities on Melanie's patients and come after him.

Well, Drew would be careful. And he would be armed. "No, you go ahead. I'll stick around and keep an eye on things. But keep me informed."

"Will do." Patrick shot him a half-hearted salute and left.

Melanie would want to know this latest development, so Drew called her. He told her about Seth, and his impending hospital run to Washington, accompanied by other team members. And then he told her about Nolan Smith. She sounded upset, but thanked him for the information. "Did you check out that Web site?" she asked.

"Yeah. Strange, but okay. Don't worry about it." He needed her to stay out of this. Figured she would stay out of it, since she was clearly so angry about what had happened.

But him? He *would* worry.

And do something about it.

Melanie paced her office, wanting to act but unsure what to do. Damn Drew! Not worry about it? Hah!

She could call Chief Ellenbogen, but then what? He

would contact Nolan, who would again spout his flimsy story that some unknown source had e-mailed him the photos.

If this were a terrorist act against humans, the authorities would follow through, do whatever was necessary to trace the origin of the correspondence, arrest the perpetrator, whatever. But her patients, though dear to their owners and her, were not human. Not entitled, under the law, to the same protections.

Edgy and irritated, she strode down the hall and into the makeshift infirmary set up now in the room where she normally performed surgery. All of them—Kewpie, Jake and Dixie, sat in their crates and regarded her expectantly. Happily. As though they appreciated what she had done for them.

"But no one should have hurt you in the first place, guys," she said softly. "Not on my watch." She laughed ruefully to herself. Wasn't that something said in the military? She was a civilian, notwithstanding the fact that she had gotten herself involved with one hellish military project.

She patted each of the animals gently through the bars, then hurried out of the room once more.

Well, she might not know what to do, but maybe Drew did. Maybe he was already doing it. She returned to her office and called him again, but she got his voice-mail recording immediately. She didn't leave a message. What would she say?

Maybe she should just go home. But she wouldn't sleep, not feeling like this.

Bury herself in more paperwork here? Sure. That's what she always did.

She went to the restroom first and washed her face. She heard the clinic's phone ring but was too far from an extension to answer.

The light on her extension wasn't blinking when she got to her office, so she went to the reception area to check Carla's line. Sure enough, it was flashing. If someone had just tried to make an appointment, Carla could call back tomorrow. But in case it was an owner of one of the injured animals wanting to check on them and say goodnight, she decided to listen.

She pressed in the password for Carla's extension and heard the excited voice that had left a message.

Was that Nolan Smith? Melanie had mostly forgiven herself for all the eavesdropping she had been doing lately. She let the message play.

"Carla? You didn't answer your cell or your home number. Are you there? Guess not. But I had to tell you. I got a message—another of those anonymous things over the Internet. It told me how to get into Ft. Lukman, near where there's supposedly a secret laboratory—and if I go there right now, I'll get to see a werewolf. I wanted you to come, but I can't wait. I'm on my way. I'll take pictures, I promise. Bye."

Melanie's breathing was fast and loud. He'd gotten an anonymous message inviting him onto the base to see a werewolf?

No way. Unless—could one of the Alpha team members be perpetrating this? Or did Nolan want to get Carla there for a nefarious reason of his own?

One way or another, he might be heading to Ft. Lukman right now. To an area near the lab? To the lab itself? Melanie had to find out. She grabbed her cell phone and tried once more to call Drew. And got his answering machine again.

Picking up her purse and heading for the door, she searched her cell phone number list for the base's main number. When she tried it, she got only a crazy, pulsating tone. Weren't the phone lines working?

What about one of the other Alpha team members? But if one was doing all this, whom could she trust?

Damn. She wasn't in the military. But something was definitely wrong. Maybe she could just find Drew when she got to the base. Or enlist one of those civilian guards at the gate to get involved. Or…something.

But she couldn't stay here. She turned on her security system, checked to make sure it, at least, was working, and headed for her car.

Where the hell was the guy?

"Can you find him, boy?" Drew asked Grunge, who, on his leash, sniffed the ground. "Is he here?" But Drew was pretty certain what the answer was. Especially since his own senses had found no trail.

He had driven like a maniac to the address he'd found for Smith—not the P.O. box on his Web site, but a home outside Mary Glen, near one of the creeks that ran into Miles River. It was more of a shack, but, peering through the windows, Drew could see a whole lot of high-tech computer equipment. Which probably meant the place was wired with a security system.

There was no garage, but the place had a roofed carport. It was empty. Out here, that had to mean the guy wasn't home.

"Still no scent to follow?" Drew asked Grunge.

His furry, silvery buddy whined and looked up in confusion, obviously sensing Drew's anger and frustration.

"It's okay," he lied to Grunge. "Forget it." But he wasn't forgetting anything. Okay, so he couldn't get into the house easily, but that wouldn't necessarily keep him out. First, though, he'd check out anything that was more easily accessible.

Like the cabinet at the far side of the carport. Not that anything important was likely to be there, but it was locked. Which piqued Drew's curiosity. And his determination to break in. Was it wired for security, too? He kicked it in anyway and heard no alarm. Saw no camera. But he figured right away that it should have been secured as tightly as anything else. Even more so, since inside, Drew found exactly what he had been looking for: a couple of .45 caliber Glocks.

And with them were packages of bullets.

Silver bullets.

Was that Nolan Smith's car? Melanie recognized the gray vintage Chrysler parked along the road, far from Ft. Lukman's entry gate. Beyond the vehicle was the base's fence, obscured by the thick trees.

He'd suggested to Carla that he had a secret way in. Had he also done something to cause the phone system to act so oddly?

Melanie had slowed to peer at the car. And then she saw a movement beyond the vehicle, in the woods—a flash of white.

She grabbed her cell phone and pushed the base's main number in again. Still just noise. Same went for Drew's number. And even Patrick's.

She could go to the front gate, alert the guard, have whatever military guys were around rousted, assuming any were back after their full moon deployment off the base. But that would give Nolan time to work whatever mischief he was up to.

Seeing werewolves. Harming them, maybe.

Okay, then. She'd park, too, and hopefully follow him just long enough to figure out what he was doing. *Then* she'd go for reinforcements.

She pulled her minivan onto a dirt pad beside the road and got out. Did she still see him? No, not even any movement.

Yet again she tried calling Drew, but now her phone didn't work at all. Not even when she tried 911, hoping to get Angus Ellenbogen's attention. What was happening here?

Well, she wasn't a kick-ass military type, but she did have a good set of eyes. And a cell phone that, even if it couldn't make calls, took pictures. She would be careful, watch Nolan and photograph what he was doing, then get out of there.

As quietly as she could, she sneaked past the car and into the woods. The aroma here was mossy and wild. She even heard birds chirping.

She didn't see Nolan at first. But what she did see made her nearly gasp aloud: the gate in the chain-link fence nearest the lab building was ajar. Just a little, but enough for a person, or a K-9, to crawl through, with brush beside it that had obviously been put there to obscure the small gap. How long had it been open?

Was someone at the base aware of it?

Melanie got down on her knees and parted the brush.

Nolan stood at the edge of the forest within the fence. He wasn't looking in Melanie's direction but into the wooded area near the lab.

He paced anxiously, holding a backpack in one hand. What was in it? Explosives? Or just some of his high-tech wizardry? If so, what was he planning?

To do something here on the base, to harm the Alpha members?

To harm Drew?

This part of the base was so isolated, so far from any help.

She was a veterinarian, not an expert in national security. Even if it took time, she needed to find someone who could—

What was that?

A movement in the trees.

Was Nolan meeting someone?

And then something huge appeared. Furry. As large as a man, on two legs, with a long snout.

It approached Nolan.

It wasn't one of the shapeshifters—not one Melanie had ever seen. She tried to focus her cell phone's camera, but she was too far away.

Whatever it was drew closer to Nolan.

He seemed to stare at the…thing. Quickly Melanie slid through the opening in the fence, slipping behind one of the nearest, largest trees.

She snapped a picture.

She could hear Nolan speaking now, his tone high-pitched and excited. "Oh, this is so great. I've wanted to meet you. Can you talk? You aren't exactly what I expected, but—"

The thing suddenly dashed beyond Nolan. Oh, lord, it had spotted her! Melanie ducked and tried to run, but the creature was fast. Running by Nolan, it came toward her. Moved so it blocked any possibility of her exiting again through the fence.

A feral growl issued from its throat.

And Melanie knew how really bad her judgment had been. She shouldn't be here. And now she couldn't leave. Her heart thumped erratically inside her chest. Was this a real shapeshifter, one she hadn't yet met? Or something a lot more menacing?

Undoubtedly the latter.

"Melanie?" Nolan called. "Is Carla with you? I hoped she would come to meet the werewolf, at last. Isn't he wonderful?"

"Nolan, run!" Melanie shouted, her eyes warily on the thing looming near her. "Go find a guard. Anyone. This isn't—"

"Don't be frightened," Nolan said in a soft and soothing voice. Melanie realized he wasn't talking to her, but to the—whatever it was. He reached slowly into his backpack and brought out a gun. "See, here's one of them. I've done all you've asked of me so far. Shot the other shapeshifters. You know you can trust me. And of course I won't hurt you unless—"

Without warning, the thing attacked Nolan. Nolan dropped his gun and yelled. The creature didn't bite, but used some kind of mechanical thing in its hand to slash Nolan's throat. Quickly.

So quickly that Melanie hardly had time to react. "Nolan! No!" she shrieked, then started to run.

But as she tried to get back through the gate, the thing grabbed her leg.

Chapter 21

On her knees, inside the fence once more, Melanie demanded, "W-who are you?"

The thing—person? It had to be a person. It wasn't like any shapeshifter Melanie had met. In their nonhuman forms, they all appeared to be genuine animals.

This resembled something from a horror movie—tall, on two legs, covered in fur and with a huge head that resembled a wolf's.

A costume? Probably. But she saw no zippers, no fasteners of any kind. The pelt looked realistic, even if the head didn't. She saw muscles ripple beneath the fur. If it was a costume, it was a damned good one.

The thing had let her go but closed the gate so she was trapped here, at this remote end of the base. It had returned to Nolan's side, only a few feet away. It bent for a moment, then rose, making an eerie, growling sound. Trembling, Melanie tried to back away—but it rose and leapt toward her, grabbing her arm.

She started to scream, but the wind was knocked from her by a quick, hard slap that threw her to the ground.

"Shut up," said a muffled but very human voice. The mouth moved, but it didn't form the words. They came from somewhere beneath the surface.

No doubt. It was a person. That frightened Melanie more than if it had been a real animal, even one that had shapeshifted from human form. She understood wild creatures. Knew how to handle them. How to soothe them.

But a crazed man dressed like a large pseudo-wolf—she hadn't a clue what to do.

She had to figure it out. Fast.

He held what looked like a cell phone in one large paw, and he pushed a button with a curved nail. And then he said to her, "Come with me, Melanie, and you won't get hurt."

Sure she wouldn't. She started to edge sideways, hoping to rise again, to run—but he dropped the cell phone.

And turned a gun on her—the one Nolan Smith had been carrying. Filled with silver bullets, no doubt, but they killed people as easily as the lead kind.

She froze. But in a moment she was being dragged along the ground, still beneath the cover of the trees. She had watched Drew and the others work out in military exercises, both in animal and human form. As people, they performed self-defense maneuvers, even knocking weapons out of their opponents' grip. But she had never tried it.

Bad decision, Dr. Harding.

Maybe it didn't really matter. She clearly wasn't as strong as…whoever he was. He was definitely not a werewolf. But he had wanted Nolan to think so.

Nolan. Was he still alive?

They approached the back door of the K-9 building, Melanie dragging her feet, as much as she dared. Could she get to the dogs, signal them to attack?

"Keep moving," the man said. "To the stairway. We're going downstairs, to the lab."

He knew about the lab. Was he one of the military guys? A base civilian? But why pull this?

"Who the hell are you?" Melanie demanded, trying again to pull away.

"Does it matter?" Her captor laughed. "You're going to listen to me anyway. And you make such delicious bait."

Bait? What was he talking about?

Realization dawned. Drew. The guy believed that Drew would show up here to rescue her.

But he wouldn't know she was here. She wasn't on the best of terms with him now, and according to Drew she wasn't supposed to be worrying about whatever was going on.

None of the other shapeshifters was here, either—not if they'd all gone to Washington with Seth.

That cell phone call—had it been made to Drew? But his phone wasn't working. No phone around here was, so this creep hadn't gotten a call out—had he?

If the freak had reached Drew, he'd mentioned the base. And her. If only Melanie had a way to talk to Drew, to tell him it was a trap of some sort. But why?

"I'm really confused here," she said. "Why don't

you tell me what's going on? Maybe I can help you get what you want."

Or not, if it meant blowing the shapeshifters' cover. Hurting Drew…

They were inside the building now. It was nearly dark in the hallway on the main floor, with only the faint recessed security lighting emanating from ceiling fixtures. The K-9s had heard them come in, and a cacophony of barks erupted from behind closed doors.

If Melanie could only open one, maybe she could slip inside and let the dogs out. She knew the attack command: "Kill."

But the man still had her in a firm grip. She tried again to pull back, but he yanked her forward. "Come on."

He apparently knew exactly where he was going, since he towed Melanie to the stairway door. He all but shoved her down the stairs, and when they arrived at the lower floor he yanked Melanie with him into the hallway. He used a key card.

And then they were in the lab.

"Hell!" Drew shouted toward the driver in front of him. Normally Drew would have understood someone driving slowly and carefully on the winding road. But not now.

Beside him, on the passenger seat, Grunge whined. "Yeah, tell me about it," Drew said. "We've got to pass."

They had been in downtown Mary Glen on the way toward the diner to hunt for Nolan when his cell phone had rung. Caller ID had shown an unfamiliar number with a local area code.

And then he had heard a woman's voice. Melanie?

It had been followed by a muffled voice that mentioned the base and Melanie's name, then nothing more.

The base was where they were heading. Nolan was probably there with his gun and silver bullets. Ready to kill werewolves. Luring them to him by cryptic phone calls.

A trap? Probably. But one Drew walked into with his eyes open. And his heart? If that was Melanie, yeah, his heart was pretty vulnerable here, too.

He made a couple of calls on his cell. Seth was improving, and the other members of Drew's team remained near him. At his command, they were heading back. Fast.

But they wouldn't be fast enough.

He called Greg Yarrow, too. Gave the general a heads-up. But he was at his Pentagon office this week. Greg promised to send out the troops— although this was a week of a full moon so not much help was available on base. "Don't do anything stupid, Drew. Stay back, find out what's going on and wait for backup."

Yeah, sure, that's just what he would do.

Too much coincidence here, that whatever was going on just happened to be occurring this particular week. Someone knew something.

Was he being set up? Was it really Melanie he'd heard? And if so, could he trust that she wasn't involved in whatever it was?

He'd made mistakes by trusting the wrong people before.

Yeah, Greg, I'll be careful, he thought. Just in case.

There. Finally. An open area straight enough to see

ahead. He passed the car, narrowly missing another vehicle that approached in his lane, then flooring it. Weaving on the narrow road, he neared the base.

And went beyond it to where he saw Melanie's van and an unfamiliar car outside the gate near the lab building. He pulled into the woods, parked, and threw open his door, grabbing for Grunge's leash.

As silently as he could in human form, he approached the secluded gate—and paused as Grunge pulled him under some trees.

There. On the ground, a body—not moving. Smith's. Covered in blood.

Drew knelt, touched the side of his slashed throat. A pulse. Slight, yeah, but he was alive.

Was Melanie?

No time to think about what could have happened to her. "Come on," he whispered, pulling Grunge's leash.

As if understanding the urgency, the dog lunged toward the gate.

Melanie sat behind the desk in the corner of the lab. The chair felt hard against her back. She gripped the arms, willing herself to stop shaking and to figure out how to save herself. Her captor had insisted she sit there. He still aimed the gun at her as he paced the room, glancing often at the gleaming metallic counters.

"What are you looking for?" she asked conversationally.

"If I considered it your business, I'd tell you." His tone wasn't menacing now. In fact, he sounded pleased, as if he was exactly where he wanted to be.

Melanie figured that was true. "You're keeping me

captive," she said. "I think you've made your identity and why you're here my business."

"You expect me to rip off my mask and confess all?" She could sense the smile hidden beneath his costume. "Know what? I think I'll do just that. Since I intend to kill you."

The pleasure in his tone made her shudder all the more. But if she could get him to talk, that might delay the potentially inevitable. Although at least she was probably safe until he achieved whatever had brought him here.

To harm Drew, too? How was she going to warn him?

The figure stopped walking. "This is damned uncomfortable. And it's served its purpose." Slowly, maintaining his aim at her, he removed the mask.

Mike Ripkey. A surprise? Not really. He looked older now as he grinned malevolently, continuing to remove his costume. Beneath it, he was dressed in a white muscle shirt that emphasized his scrawniness, and a pair of tight sweat pants that hugged his legs. His long hair looked damp and stringy.

She'd considered him one of many suspects in the break-ins and attack on the animals in her clinic, but hadn't focused on him. He'd seemed too nerdy, too involved with leading his gang of woo-woo aficionados up silly pathways to be doing such nasty things.

"Mike?" Melanie shook her head. "I don't understand. Do you really believe in werewolves, or is your group a front for—what? What are you really up to?"

"Don't play games with me, Melanie. You know that shapeshifters exist. That's what's really going on here at Ft. Lukman, despite all the games about training for covert K-9 activities. I know about the formulas and stuff they're working on. It's all going to make me a wealthy man—all the potions, plus the real werewolf I'll hand over to the buyers."

"I don't understand," Melanie said quietly.

"Simple. As quiet as everyone keeps it, lots of officials of foreign countries know about shapeshifters, want to use them in their own national defense if they could get them to turn at will. And now that ability will be in the hands of the highest bidder—along with your dear Drew, to show them how it works."

He'd drawn closer as he spoke and now glared down at her. She refused to show her fear. But the look in his eyes told her that his threats weren't idle.

As with Nolan, he intended to kill her.

"Do you know where they keep the stuff that's already mixed?" he demanded.

"What stuff?" She attempted to sound bewildered.

He slapped her. "Don't bother playing dumb with me. It won't help you. In fact, it's likely to hurt."

She glared at him, ignoring the stinging heat in her cheek. "Slapping me around won't get you what you want. I've come here as a veterinarian, to help with the K-9s." She drew in her breath. Lying wouldn't help her, either. Would telling the truth—at least part of it? "And the shapeshifters while in animal form. Not only during the full moon. I don't know nearly as much as I figure you do about the legends, but I'd always heard werewolves only changed form then."

"Unless they have what this Alpha Force has," Mike said. "And that's what I'm after."

"Interesting. But you're barking up the wrong tree to ask me." She tried to smile at her puny attempt at a joke.

"Maybe." He'd begun pacing again and reached the clean room. He peered into the darkness inside the windows. "In there?"

"Could be, but all anyone ever said was that I shouldn't go in, since even just stepping inside would contaminate everything. I know they mix their formulas in there. If the room contains what you're after, you'd better not just stroll in and grab it."

"Your buddy Drew can take care of that when he gets here." Mike leaned a shoulder against the wall, still aiming the gun at her.

"He's gone to help with Seth," she said hurriedly. "You know, one of the other shapeshifters? He was hurt on the night of the full moon, and now that he's in human form again they had to get him to a hospital." Drew hadn't gone along, but Mike might not know that. "If he decides to come, it'll take a while."

"Where'd they go, damn it?" Mike's posture was rigid again.

"D.C." Melanie leaned earnestly over the desk. "Look, Mike, I found all this stuff really crazy. Why did you believe in any of it?"

"Because I knew the truth. And used it, right from the time I came here. These shapeshifting jerks killed my uncle, but not before he told me what was going on. He was a nice guy. A local. Me? I was a scientist, and I didn't believe him—not until they killed him." Mike's fury radiated from his eyes. Would asking him to continue only make him angrier?

But he had opened a door that Melanie intended to step through. "How did your uncle die?" she asked quietly.

"Those damn Worleys! Uncle Charley lived around here. Charley Drake, my mother's brother." The name sounded vaguely familiar to Melanie. Hadn't he been one of the supposed werewolf hunters Carla had mentioned—one who'd died, like Angie Fishbach's husband? "He knew the werewolves were real. He caught Patrick's mother changing, so he killed her. He told me, like it was proof that what he claimed about the Mary Glen werewolves was true—but then he died in a car wreck, supposedly. Well, I came here the first time last year as the head of the SSTs—that was my cover, just like this damned military base is their cover. I visited old Dr. Worley, and he denied everything, even when I threatened him. The guy had to be a werewolf, too—I don't know which Worley bit the other."

"But changing by biting—" Melanie stopped. Contradicting him with the truth she'd been told, that shapeshifting was only hereditary and could not be caused by being bitten by another shapeshifter, wouldn't convince him. And it might shut him up. "Was your uncle bitten, too?"

"No. But way I figured it, he was seen by Doc Worley, who ran him off the road. But not before he'd written notes I wound up inheriting, all about the shapeshifters. When I came here, I didn't let people know I was related to him, but planned to check things out while doing all I could to make life difficult for the Ft. Lukman shapeshifters. Putting 'em on the defensive and making sure they couldn't do anything in full secrecy—even as I studied them. Figured out how I could use them. For one thing, I encouraged Nolan Smith to let the whole world know, with his Web site, what was going on around here. Even sell advertising. Of course I didn't want real info getting out, so I encouraged all the stupid stuff Nolan publicized. Fed it to the idiots who joined the ShapeShifter Tracers, even as I started doing stuff to undermine what went on around here. The military guys suspected Nolan of sneaking into their lab here, didn't they? And you probably thought it was him who made it look like a werewolf hurt the poor, defenseless little animals at your clinic." He'd changed his voice into a mocking tone.

Melanie stifled an urge to lunge at him. "You did it? You bastard! You could have killed them."

"Sure." He sounded smug. "But I didn't. It had the effect I wanted. Convinced more people around here that the werewolf stories are true. And that the creatures are vicious. Should be shot by silver bullets on sight. Which made it easy to get guys out on the night of the full moon to shoot anything that moved. I encouraged my club members to do that, too. And Nolan Smith, especially gullible Nolan who wanted in the worst way to meet a real werewolf. I got him to shoot that dog, Grunge, and Drew Connell while he was in wolf form. I e-mailed him the pictures I took after I used the super gadget I invented—the one I used on him, too, by the way, and on that tourist Sheila Graves—on your patients. And tonight I told Nolan when and where to go. I'd already promised he'd get to meet a genuine, friendly shapeshifter who needed help with the bad guys if he shot, but didn't kill, those nasty creatures. He got his wish—kind of. He met me. And now, assuming he survives, he'll have even more to say about the Mary Glen werewolves—the fool!"

Through her fear, Melanie kept trying to get her mind around what he was saying. What he had done. "But didn't calling attention to the shapeshifters make it harder for you to achieve what you wanted? It kept them alert."

"It kept them defensive, sure. Added to my challenge, but I loved it! I outsmarted them, didn't I?"

Maybe he had—unless Melanie could figure out how to stop him. Drew might arrive at some point, and he'd be in even more danger than she. She might wind up dead. He might wind up—what? Abducted? Dragged off, handed over to some foreign government, and used as an example of a controlled shapeshifter?

"Oh, Mike," she said sadly. "So much bizarre stuff around here. I'm just an ordinary veterinarian. All I want to do is help animals. I don't care about supernatural idiocy. Look, what if I just help you get what you want and leave Mary Glen? I'll go back to L.A., get a job at a veterinary clinic there. Put all this behind me. I couldn't talk about what happened to me here anyway. Who'd believe me? I'd end up in a loony bin."

"Yeah? I'm supposed to trust you?"

She smiled conspiratorially. "I lied. I can tell you where they keep the premixed tonic. And I know what computer files contain the formula, too."

"You do? Hot damn! With all my tech skills—and I have a lot of 'em, believe me—I couldn't get past their damned passwords when I broke in here before. Even drugged all of them at the diner—what a waste. But now, if you get me into the system, I'll think about letting you go." Mike was grinning now. The gun in his hand drooped, just a little.

If she lunged now—

Out of the corner of her eye she saw a movement near the lab door.

Mike must have seen it, too. "What the hell?" His gun hand rose, even as he dashed not toward the door, but toward her.

In an instant he had her around the neck, even as Drew appeared in the doorway.

"Let her go, Ripkey," he ordered.

"Only if you do exactly what I tell you to." And Mike tightened his grip until Melanie could no longer breathe.

Chapter 22

Drew watched in fury as Melanie's eyes rolled. "Let her go, Ripkey," he repeated. "I'll do whatever you want."

"I figured." The tall, ugly jerk let her fall to the floor. She was halfway behind the desk and didn't move, apparently unconscious.

Even so, Ripkey kept his gun pointed down, right where Drew assumed her head was. He wanted to rush forward. Grab the guy by his slimy hair and shove his face through the wall.

"Tell you what you do, Major. See that pile of stuff?" He pointed toward what looked like a dead animal on the floor. "Find the inside pockets and pull out the string that's there."

Cursing silently, Drew approached the thing. Judging by the big mask resembling a caricature of a wolf head, this had to be a werewolf costume Ripkey had worn. He groped around the furry mess that smelled of man-made materials as if searching for the pocket. He pulled out a large contraption with wicked-looking, nearly realistic enamel fangs and pushed a button on its side. It immediately spewed a viscous yet cloudy liquid that resembled…saliva. This was what he'd used to maul Nolan outside. And probably the injured tourist.

"Clever," Drew said. "The injuries you inflicted with this thing looked damned real."

"Of course they did. Everything I've done here worked perfectly, since I studied you. All of you. And so did my uncle, before that bastard Dr. Worley killed him."

What was that about, Drew wondered. But he didn't stop the man from talking.

"But with his notes and all I learned, I was able to get you going, wasn't I? Keep you on the defensive with all the break-ins and attacks, around here and at the doc's veterinary clinic—those I didn't instruct Nolan to do. Even stole back the silver bullet he shot you with, so no one besides me would find out what you were— wasn't that kind of me? And if you're really nice to me, I won't force you to inhale that putrid stuff I used to mask odors and put you and the real K-9s off my scent—only the good stuff that got you to follow where I wanted you to go. Now, get that damned string."

The bastard was bragging about all he'd done. Maybe Drew could keep him talking a little longer. Reinforcements were on their way.

He just hoped they weren't too late.

"And the doc," Ripkey continued. "She just didn't get it, did she? I shot up her house and clinic when you were there with her. But did she back off? No. Well, now it's too late—but if you don't cooperate, I just might use my clever little toothed invention on her, to make it look like she was killed by a werewolf. Poetic justice, after the vet before her, Worley, was killed by a silver bullet." Ripkey laughed, and Drew fought the nearly irresistible urge to lunge at him—which would only earn *him* death by one of those damned bullets.

Instead he said calmly, "One more question. You've been on the base before, got into this lab. I admit our security measures here are more lax than a lot of military facilities—purposely, since we need the ability to do our shapeshifting ops without a lot of interference from other soldiers. But how'd you get onto the base? How'd you know about this facility? And—"

"You ask too damned many questions, Connell. Easy answer? You're right. Your security's pathetic. And I'm a techie genius. I duplicated ID cards, fixed the metal chips in 'em so I looked legit, got onto good old Ft. Lukman and followed you and the others till I saw where you went. Even played games with the base's gates on nights of the full moon so you had canine chaos with your dogs and shapeshifters getting out. Loved it! And tonight I had a lot of fun jamming the communications systems." But his boastful grin suddenly shifted to a scowl. "Now. Get. The. Damned. String." He aimed the gun straight at Drew this time.

He pretended to rummage through the costume yet again, then shook his head. "Sorry, can't find it."

"Don't give me that." Ripkey knelt and dragged Melanie toward him. "Find it and tie your own ankles, or she dies now."

Drew saw a slight motion of Melanie's eyelids, the

tiniest glance toward him. She was faking unconsciousness. He didn't react.

He again rifled the pile of fur and shook his head. "I'd be glad to cooperate, but I can't find it. You get it, and I'll tie myself."

"Move over there." Ripkey motioned the gun toward the left, at one of the long metallic counters. Drew slowly obeyed.

He watched as Ripkey stalked toward the costume and, using his left hand, reached in and extracted some nastily strong-looking nylon twine. "Here." He tossed it toward Drew as he again aimed the gun in Melanie's direction.

Drew did as ordered, binding his own ankles. Not as tightly as he made it appear. He didn't intend to make himself more vulnerable than he had to. But even so, this would hamper his ability to run toward Ripkey and grab the weapon.

"I'll assume you didn't do an excellent job, but it's better than nothing," Ripkey said. "Here's what we'll do." Before Drew could react, Ripkey aimed the gun toward him and fired.

Pain ripped through his shoulder. And then Ripkey lunged at him with the weapon raised. As it came down on Drew's head, there was more pain. Then darkness.

Melanie saw it all. *Drew!* Was he dead?

Surely not. From what Ripkey had described, he needed Drew alive—to sell to the highest bidder.

It was all she could do not to run to him. But she had to stay where she was. Pretend she was still unconscious.

It was the only chance they had.

She had an idea. But would it work with Drew out cold? Injured? She didn't know.

But she had to try—if she got the opportunity. And that would only come if Ripkey thought both his victims were rendered defenseless.

She kept her eyes slitted open. Watched Ripkey approach Drew, rifle through his pockets and beneath his windbreaker. Extract a nasty-looking weapon that Drew had apparently been saving for the right opportunity—which hadn't come.

Didn't let herself flinch as Ripkey kicked Drew, who didn't move. He, at least, was actually unconscious. And Ripkey used the opportunity to take that damned string and tie his hands.

Which jeopardized Melanie's plan even more.

"Okay, time to wake up, wolfman," Ripkey said. He pushed Drew again with his foot. This time, Drew moaned. "Wake up," Ripkey repeated.

Drew's eyes popped open. His glare suggested he would have killed his assailant right then, if he could. But he was still on the floor. Bound. Bleeding from the shoulder.

"Okay, here's what we'll do, if you don't want me to kill your lady." He waved in Melanie's direction.

"What, you bastard?"

Ripkey gave him detailed instructions. He wanted the information about where to find all the formulas on the lab computer, which he gleefully said he would both print and e-mail to himself—after, of course, Drew gave him all the passwords. Then he wanted to know how to get into the clean room and extract the vials of premixed formula. "You do that, and once we're gone

I'll even unjam the base's flimsy communication system."

Slowly, groaning, Drew spewed information. Melanie wasn't certain but figured he had a way to give legitimate-sounding but incorrect computer info.

Ripkey figured that, too. He extracted a thumb drive from his pocket—a small gadget onto which one could download a lot of computer data. "I'll copy it all, but it'll be easier to find the right info if you give me the location and passwords in advance. If not, I'll have some time to figure them out while they're in my possession—and you are, too. And the already mixed samples?"

Drew's fury appeared even greater, but his eyes were narrowed. He was obviously in pain. And Melanie couldn't help.

But she knew that at least some of what he revealed was only partial information. Even so...

Ripkey took a few minutes to work with the computer, and then he removed the thumb drive. "I'll play with this later. And now, the clean room." He didn't bother suiting up, but he wasn't concocting anything, just stealing it.

He turned his back as he headed into the room and closed the door behind him.

It was Melanie's chance! Carefully she crawled toward the refrigeration unit beneath the metallic counter near Drew. She extracted some of the tonic.

She didn't dare talk. Drew, too, remained silent. But when she turned toward him, he was smiling grimly—and approvingly.

Carefully she reached for the light switch that changed the glow within the lab room.

She opened the container and slipped the rim of the glass into Drew's mouth. He drank it.

"Hey!" Ripkey shouted. He stood in the cleanroom door, his gun waving wildly in his hand.

Drew was starting to change. Could he live through it, injured as he was? Had Melanie, by trying to save them, killed him? She shook, even as she shielded him with her own body. Glancing down, she saw his face elongate as fur erupted from his skin. She hadn't been able to untie him. But he would emerge from the change with a different size, different dimensions.

Different strength.

"No, you son of a bitch," Ripkey yelled. "Not now. I didn't want to kill you. You're my model, my paradigm. You have to live, under my control."

Drew's limbs contorted, contracted, his clothing shrinking. The blood from his shoulder gleamed. Could he move? Could he help?

"You bitch!" Ripkey shouted at Melanie. "I should have killed you before. I need him to change back, now. Tell me how to stop this and get him back!"

"Damned if I know." Melanie sat on the floor beside the writhing, moaning man as he transformed into wolf form, wanting to hold him, to keep away his pain. Hating herself, for putting him through this, especially now. He was hurt. The change could kill him. What had she done?

"You do know," Ripkey insisted. "Tell me. Tell me now, or I'll shoot you."

"Shoot me or don't. It won't make a difference. I can't stop it now."

She flinched as Ripkey brought up his gun, aimed it at her face. She didn't want to die. She didn't want

Drew to die. She continued to shield him, even as she waited for the bullet that would end her life.

"Do it!" Ripkey yelled. He seemed to squeeze the trigger.

A ferocious growl sounded from behind Melanie. She was thrust aside by a lithe, fur-covered, leaping body. She felt something hot tearing at the side of her head—and watched as the wolf tore Mike Ripkey's throat.

Chapter 23

"Of course a werewolf killed Mike Ripkey," said Angie Fishbach, shaking her head sadly. Dressed in her usual shirtwaist uniform—blue this time—and comfortable shoes, she had the podium at the latest Mary Glen town meeting, where the most recent occurrences were being discussed.

Sitting beside Carla, who had come with—who else?—Nolan Smith, Melanie started to rise, slowly and still somewhat painfully. Was the cover story that the Alpha Force guys had created to explain all that had gone on at Ft. Lukman two days earlier about to be torn to shreds?

"Come on, Angie," Nolan said, his voice raspy. Looking pale but resolute, he, too, stood on the stage by the microphone, one of the evening's scheduled presenters. White bandages covered his throat, contrasting with his black shirt, but fortunately his wounds had been severe but not life-threatening.

"No, really. A werewolf did kill Mike," Angie said, elbowing her way back to the microphone. "Maybe a little like the one that killed my poor Bill. I can't swear now about what I saw that night, but I've been willing enough to blame my own actions on the Mary Glen werewolves. They've caused so much havoc. So what if the werewolves don't exist? The legend is so ingrained here that it's part of the area. Part of us."

"So you're saying—" Nolan began.

But Angie didn't stop talking. "The legend made Mike Ripkey go crazy trying to prove it—crazy enough to hurt the animals in Dr. Harding's clinic and then attack you, Nolan, and then the doc, and Major Connell, who came to help her, and—"

"Then you *are* saying," Nolan said even more loudly, "that the fact that Mike drove off too fast and hit that tree and burned up in his car…that in a way it was the werewolf that did it? The imaginary one in his mind?"

"Exactly," Angie said. "Like the one I imagined I saw that awful night. I was just tired. And upset from fighting with Bill. And didn't want to accept responsibility, so I unconsciously latched onto the legend. It's all just a convenient excuse we use around here." Her plump shoulders sagging, she moved away from the podium at last.

Applause followed her, along with sympathetic calls from the audience. Melanie relaxed enough to look around. Most townsfolk seemed to nod in understanding and agreement.

The few SST shapeshifter-chasers who were left

didn't seem too happy. But Sheila Graves, who'd allegedly been attacked by a werewolf, had admitted that what attacked her looked a whole lot like the costume Mike Ripkey had created. And her wounds had been a lot like Nolan's—probably caused by the metal gadget with realistically damaging fangs and the ability to drip saliva taken from real dogs that had been found with Mike's costume.

"Thank you, Angie," said Mayor Ed Sherwin, taking the podium. "And Nolan."

"Mayor!" An abrasive female voice resounded from the back of the meeting room. Melanie didn't have to turn around to realize it was June Jenkins, that miserable reporter from the *Maryland Reality Gazette.* "Are you, on behalf of the town, willing to make a statement repudiating the entire notion of the Mary Glen werewolves?" She strode down the aisle in black stiletto heels. She was, as always, dressed in a suit for her on-camera work—lime green this time. A technician with camera and microphone hurried behind her.

"Oh, I don't think so, Ms. Jenkins," the mayor said in a loud drawl. "You want a statement? Here you go. The City of Mary Glen deeply regrets the terrible death of Mike Ripkey, President of the ShapeShifter Tracers. However, evidence suggests—" He looked behind him toward Chief Angus Ellenbogen, who sat, looking uncomfortable, on the stage behind him along with members of the Town Council. Angus nodded as if approving how the mayor was phrasing his comment, and Mayor Sherwin continued, "Evidence suggests that Mr. Ripkey was possibly overzealous in his attempt to show that the werewolf legend was true, possibly taking it on himself to stage attacks on a fellow SST member, Nolan Smith, and our town veterinarian, Dr. Melanie Harding, as well as on some of Dr. Harding's animal patients. He even went so far as to break into our local military base to stage his costumed attack on Nolan Smith before driving off so erratically. But such evidence did not need to be manufactured. We stand behind our legends. We hope that Nolan, our local expert and webmaster, will continue to look for evidence and post photos that prove the possibility that such creatures do exist."

Nolan, who'd taken a seat, nodded vehemently. "Of course I will, Mayor."

June Jenkins asked a few more questions. Everyone seemed to support the mayor's position, which was probably a good thing, Melanie thought. The Alpha guys' cover had been jeopardized, but not completely compromised.

And why should that matter to her now? She was still their chief veterinarian. But with the recent mysteries solved, and their perpetrator dealt with for good, there wouldn't be much need for her to visit Ft. Lukman often.

The meeting continued for only a short while longer. After the mayor said his final words and hurried from June Jenkins, Melanie rose, wanting to get out of there. She moved into the aisle, which was already filled with people exiting the room.

"Wait a minute, Melanie," Carla said. Her assistant had also gotten to her feet. "Nolan said he wanted to ask you to write your story, in your own words, to put on the Web site."

"That's right." Nolan slid into the row behind Carla.

"Will you?" As always, he wore his belt with the silver wolf buckle. His eyes looked tired but hopeful behind his small-framed glasses.

"Give me time to figure out what I can say that won't blast away at the whole legend idea after this fiasco," Melanie said, considering both her need to maintain friendly relations with the townsfolk and protect the Alpha cover story. "Then, sure, I'll give you my take on it."

"Great! Thanks." His broad grin showed his large teeth, nearly as white as the bandages at his throat.

As Carla turned and went into Nolan's arms, Melanie saw her opportunity to slip away. She walked up the aisle as quickly as possible in the crowd, careful to stay far from June Jenkins and her microphone, as well as the other reporters who'd shown up.

She stopped when she saw Major Drew Connell near the exit door at the top. He wore a denim workshirt tucked into jeans, and he looked like one really hot guy. It didn't hurt that he gazed straight into her eyes and smiled.

She didn't want to smile back, but she did. Reaching him, she asked, "How are you, Major?" There were too many people around for her to ask the other questions on her mind. Was everything now all right at the lab? Had they learned anything more about Mike's motives and plans for stealing the formula and tonic—and Drew?

"I'm fine, Doc." She heard some undefined emotion in his deep voice and blinked. "And you?"

"Couldn't be better," she lied cheerily. Being in his presence again had reminded her of all they had shared—and not just the danger. His tall, broad body shouted to her of the steamy sex that had turned her into a mass of lust.

But that was in the past. He'd obviously come here tonight to listen to the town meeting.

"How's Grunge?"

"Just fine. I left him back at the base. I had some things to take care of that didn't call for canine company."

"Oh." They walked outside and down the City Hall steps.

"You going back to your place now?" Drew asked.

"Yes. And you?"

"Going back to your place?" She started to explain that what she'd meant was whether he was heading back to the base, but he laughed. "I thought you'd never ask."

She laughed, too—a little.

The crowd had nearly dispersed. It was late enough on this Saturday evening for the sun to be setting and the streetlights along Mary Glen Road to start to glimmer on.

"Seriously," Drew said, "may I walk you to your clinic?"

"I thought you'd never ask." Melanie had attempted to sound flippant, but the tone came out much too seriously. To hide her gaffe, she said, too softly for anyone else to hear, "Is there anything you can tell me that explains…well, you know."

"Yeah," he said. "Quite a bit."

But they chatted about the warming spring temperatures and the latest unclassified training planned for the base's K-9s, even as Melanie's mind churned about what they weren't saying. About all she had been thinking about over the last days since Mike Ripkey's attack at Ft. Lukman.

She already knew a lot about that night, after Drew, in wolf form, had saved her life by killing Mike Ripkey.

The Alpha Force guys, who had sped back from D.C., had gone off with Mike's body and staged a terrible, fiery car accident that appeared to have taken Mike's life—and obliterated any sign his throat had been savaged by a wolf. They had also planted Ripkey's werewolf costume near Nolan, complete with the false fang gadget, before calling for Chief Ellenbogen and the EMTs.

She had joined their assertions, based on what had happened, that Mike must have gotten carried away with wanting to prove werewolves were real, so he created his own werewolf costume and went nuts in the manner discussed at the town meeting. That fateful night, he had attacked Nolan to provide ostensible proof of the local legend, then went after Melanie to get her to admit to the "real" proof she had—that she had treated animals that turned into people in the morning. When he got nothing helpful from her, and Drew showed up to help her, he got desperate and shot them. That's when others from the base finally arrived. He panicked, drove off fast and erratically, and hit a tree so hard his car burst into flames.

Some of it was, of course, true. The rest—well, weaving partial truths into outright lies made them more believable.

Drew and she turned onto Choptank Lane—alone. Melanie asked urgently, "What have you found out about Mike?"

She looked up to find Drew shaking his head. "You'd

think that guys involved with covert military operations would know to dig deeply enough into back-
grounds of all potential subversives to look for
problems, but we didn't. Turns out Ripkey's real name
was Michael Ripkey Prager. His maternal uncle was
Charley Drake, like he told you…that night. The family
wasn't close, so Ripkey hadn't spent much time here
before. Drake died in—not entirely coincidentally—a
car crash, last year. We believe he murdered Eva
Worley—Patrick's mom and Martin's wife—by
shooting her with silver bullets."

"Oh, no." Melanie stopped walking and looked up
at Drew. "Do you think Martin knew and killed Drake?"

"That's what we surmise. Drake had apparently
saved data on his computer that suggested Eva was a
shapeshifter. He'd called Prager—Ripkey—that night
before he died, babbling into his cell phone, according
to notes on Ripkey's computer. And from what Ripkey
said, he inherited Drake's data—handwritten notes,
computer drives, and all. Ripkey believed Martin was
also a shapeshifter who'd been turned because his wife
bit him. Which of course—"

"Isn't possible despite legends to the contrary."
Melanie nodded and started walking again. "See, I'm
smart when it comes to shapeshifters now. I've
learned a lot."

"Yeah, you have." Melanie heard what sounded like
amusement in Drew's voice and looked up at him. He
was striding beside her—and he took her hand.

She liked the feel of it. She gripped his hand firmly, too.

"But here's some stuff you don't know." Drew explained how the Alpha guys had unearthed Ripkey's real

identity—and then had done a thorough search of his travels and contacts.

Several years ago, Ripkey had been in the U.S. Marines, stationed at several foreign embassies for security. Those embassies were located in countries not particularly friendly to the U.S. "That's where he met some of the officials he intended to sell me and my shapeshifter tonics to," Drew said grimly. "He visited those countries again this winter, between the SST visits to Mary Glen, and even got audiences with some of those leaders—presumably those who had some indication of shapeshifters in their countries, too. Maybe even recruited some of them for their military forces. I'd guess not many, if any, had something like my formulas."

They had reached Melanie's clinic, and she turned off the security system, unlocked the door and went inside.

There, Drew helped her check on her patients—only one of which, Jake, the friendly mutt, remained after the savage attack a few days ago, and he was doing well. Then they sat in Melanie's reception area, where Drew told her the rest.

When Ripkey got out of the military, he went to college, studied technology and biology, and worked his way through with jobs in medical research labs. And then his uncle died. Mike apparently intended to avenge his death, which was why, when he came to Mary Glen last year as an SST, he killed Martin Worley. But that wasn't all. He had scoped things out, confirmed at least some of his uncle's allegations about local shapeshifters and what was going on at Ft. Lukman, and returned this spring to use it for his own enrichment. They still weren't certain how he got a working key card to enter the base, but he had bragged about his high-tech skills, and the assumption was he had used them somehow to bypass all security systems.

"That's the best we could figure." Drew scowled. "And we were too involved with our own activities to search deeply enough to find all this…before."

"Well, you know now. And that part is finally over. From what went on at the town meeting tonight, you should still have the cloak of some shapeshifting legends to hide behind if anything going on at the base gets out. And now you'll also be able to get people to laugh nervously at the idea, since a loony werewolf aficionado really went nuts."

"Yeah, that part might actually be to our benefit. People will pretend to believe in shapeshifters to keep tourist bucks flowing around here."

"Exactly." Melanie made herself smile. He'd told her what she'd asked. There wasn't much left to say. Now he could thank her for her help, ask for it to continue, shake her hand and go.

She closed her eyes. That wasn't how she wanted things to end. It wasn't as simple as not wanting to feel used. Being with him despite everything, including who he was, felt right.

She loved him.

"Drew," she began, opening her eyes once more.

"Melanie," he said at the same time. Standing in front of her chair now, he reached down and drew her to her feet.

And then they were kissing. Melanie wasn't sure who initiated it. No matter. Fire melted her entire body. She tasted his lips, his tongue, the hot, rough skin of his face, as her hands tugged his shirt from his jeans. Her fingers ran up his hard, smooth skin, along his chest, then down, where she tugged at the fastening of his pants. Her body almost made her quest to bare him impossible as she rubbed against his hardness.

His laugh rumbled deep in his throat. "Let's take this a little slower, okay?"

"No," she protested. Soon, very soon, they were both naked. "We should have gone next door to my house," she said. "The rug here isn't—"

"Shh," he said softly, then followed up the order by silencing her with his mouth as he drew her down to that less-than-comfortable rug. He kissed her lips. Then her sensitive, straining breasts. Then even lower, until she moaned.

She stroked him, held him, reveled and writhed under his touch and the sensations he caused.

And when he entered her, she gasped…and smiled.

A long time later, she lay panting beside him, feeling the rough fabric of the rug against her back. She held his hand, watching the rise and fall of the expanse of his chest. At least they had sex. Great sex. Maybe that could be enough. Only—

He turned suddenly onto his side. "Melanie, I'm sorry. We didn't use—"

"Protection? I just thought about that." She tried to frown as if angry, but at his worried expression she smiled. "So shapeshifting is passed on genetically. And if I happen to get pregnant from tonight, that means *what* chance that the baby would have the werewolf gene?"

"Probably ninety percent if it's a boy. A little less if

it's a girl. We're still researching why, but— You don't look particularly upset."

Somehow not bothered by her nakedness, even here in her clinic—with the doors locked and, fortunately, the blinds closed for evening security—she sat up. "Turns out I happen to know a number of shapeshifters. I like them all." She studied his expression. He looked hopeful. And lustful all over again as he looked at her body. And…loving? Well, now was the time to find out. "And I happen to love one of them."

"Yeah?" She was suddenly engulfed in a tight hug against that amazingly muscular and hard body of his. "And I happen to love a veterinarian who seems to know just how to treat not only regular animals, but shapeshifted ones, too."

They kissed again. It led to more. Much more.

"You know," she said when she could no longer move except to snuggle against Drew on the floor, "Good thing I'm an animal lover."

"I'll say."

"A lucky one, too. I'd imagine most women who fall for shapeshifters have to deal with them having no control over when it happens or even maintaining their human consciousness. But me—well, if we wind up having kids and they happen to be shapeshifters, too, imagine all we can do for them. We can help them not only control what they do, but use it for good, too, like their dad."

"Any kids like that ought to have parents who are happily married. So, Doctor Harding, will you?"

"Are you proposing, Major Connell?"

"Guess so. I love you, Melanie." He sounded so serious that she smiled.

"I love you, too." She burrowed into his waiting arms. "You sure Grunge won't mind if we get married?" she asked against his mouth. "Or your wolf form?"

"How could they resist having a vet in the family?

"Smart canines," Melanie said, and kissed him.

* * * * *

*Look for more gripping Silhouette Nocturne books
from Linda O. Johnston later in 2009.*

*Celebrate 60 years of pure reading pleasure with
Harlequin® Books!*

*Harlequin Romance® is celebrating by showering
you with DIAMOND BRIDES in February 2009.
Six stories that promise to bring a touch of sparkle to
your life, with diamond proposals and dazzling
weddings, sparkling brides and gorgeous grooms!*

*Enjoy a sneak peek at Caroline Anderson's
TWO LITTLE MIRACLES,
available February 2009 from Harlequin Romance®.*

'I've found her.'

Max froze.

It was what he'd been waiting for since June, but now—now he was almost afraid to voice the question. His heart stalling, he leaned slowly back in his chair and scoured the investigator's face for clues. 'Where?' he asked, and his voice sounded rough and unused, like a rusty hinge.

'In Suffolk. She's living in a cottage.'

Living. His heart crashed back to life, and he sucked in a long, slow breath. All these months he'd feared—

'Is she well?'

'Yes, she's well.'

He had to force himself to ask the next question. 'Alone?'

The man paused. 'No. The cottage belongs to a man called John Blake. He's working away at the moment, but he comes and goes.'

God. He felt sick. So sick he hardly registered the

next few words, but then gradually they sank in. 'She's got *what?*'

'Babies. Twin girls. They're eight months old.'

'Eight—?' he echoed under his breath. 'They must be his.'

He was thinking out loud, but the P.I. heard and corrected him.

'Apparently not. I gather they're hers. She's been there since mid-January last year, and they were born during the summer—June, the woman in the post office thought. She was more than helpful. I think there's been a certain amount of speculation about their relationship.'

He'd just bet there had. God, he was going to kill her. Or Blake. Maybe both of them.

'Of course, looking at the dates, she was presumably pregnant when she left you, so they could be yours, or she could have been having an affair with this Blake character before...'

He glared at the unfortunate P.I. 'Just stick to your job. I can do the math,' he snapped, swallowing the unpalatable possibility that she'd been unfaithful to him before she'd left. 'Where is she? I want the address.'

'It's all in here,' the man said, sliding a large envelope across the desk to him. 'With my invoice.'

'I'll get it seen to. Thank you.'

'If there's anything else you need, Mr Gallagher, any further information—'

'I'll be in touch.'

'The woman in the post office told me Blake was away at the moment, if that helps,' he added quietly, and opened the door.

Max stared down at the envelope, hardly daring to open it, but when the door clicked softly shut behind the P.I., he eased up the flap, tipped it and felt his breath jam in his throat as the photos spilled out over the desk.

Oh, lord, she looked gorgeous. Different, though. It took him a moment to recognise her, because she'd grown her hair, and it was tied back in a ponytail, making her look younger and somehow freer. The blond highlights were gone, and it was back to its natural soft golden-brown, with a little curl in the end of the ponytail that he wanted to thread his finger through and tug, just gently, to draw her back to him.

Crazy. She'd put on a little weight, but it suited her. She looked well and happy and beautiful, but oddly, considering how desperate he'd been for news of her for the past year—one year, three weeks and two days, to be exact—it wasn't only Julia who held his attention after the initial shock. It was the babies sitting side by side in a supermarket trolley. Two identical and absolutely beautiful little girls.

* * * * *

When Max Gallagher hires a P.I. to find his estranged wife, Julia, he discovers she's not alone— she has twin baby girls, and they might be his. Now workaholic Max has just two weeks to prove that he can be a wonderful husband and father to the family he wants to treasure.

Look for TWO LITTLE MIRACLES by
Caroline Anderson,
available February 2009 from Harlequin Romance®.

From *New York Times* bestselling author

Gena Showalter

Enter a mythical world
of dragons, demons and nymphs...
Enter a world of dark seduction
and powerful magic...
Enter Atlantis...

Catch these thrilling tales in a bookstore near you!

THE NYMPH KING • Available now!

HEART OF THE DRAGON • Available January 2009

JEWEL OF ATLANTIS • Available February 2009

THE VAMPIRE'S BRIDE • Available March 2009

"Lots of danger and sexy passion give lucky readers a
spicy taste of adventure and romance."
—*Romantic Times BOOKreviews*
on *Heart of the Dragon*

HQN™

We *are* romance™

www.HQNBooks.com   PHGSAT2009

Silhouette®

nocturne™

USA TODAY bestselling author

MAUREEN CHILD

VANISHED

Guardians

Immortal Guardian Rogan Butler
had no use for love, especially after his
Destined Mate abandoned him. So when beautiful
mortal Allison Blair sought his help against a
rising evil force, Rogan was bewildered by the
undeniable electric connection between them.
Besides, his true love had died years ago,
and it was impossible that he could even
have another Destined Mate—wasn't it?

Available February 2009 wherever books are sold.

www.eHarlequin.com
www.paranormalromanceblog.wordpress.com

SN61804

Silhouette

nocturne™

COMING NEXT MONTH

#57 VANISHED • Maureen Child
Guardians

Immortal Guardian Rogan Butler had no use for love, especially after his destined mate abandoned him, terrified of his life as a chosen demon slayer. So when beautiful mortal Allison Blair sought his help against a rising evil force, Rogan was bewildered—and annoyed—by the undeniable electric connection between them. Besides, his true love had died years ago, and it was impossible that he could even *have* another destined mate—wasn't it?

#58 DRAGON'S LAIR • Denise Lynn

It started mere centuries ago when the Dragonierre's Manual, the single written form of Druidic elders' spells, was created. Someone was out to find the manual and use its powers for evil—and only Braeden Drake and his estranged wife, Alexia, could prevent it. Together, the two had to prevent the family nemesis from taking a supreme reign of terror. But when working as a team proved to be a challenge neither was ready for, the stakes got even higher....